WILDER RUMORS

 This Large Print Book carries the
Seal of Approval of N.A.V.H.

A LEWIS WILDER MYSTERY

WILDER RUMORS

MOLLY MACRAE

THORNDIKE PRESS

An imprint of Thomson Gale, a part of The Thomson Corporation

THOMSON

GALE

Detroit • New York • San Francisco • New Haven, Conn. • Waterville, Maine • London

THOMSON

GALE

™

LIBRARY OF CONGRESS CATALOGING-IN-PUBLICATION DATA

MacRae, Molly.
  Wilder rumors / Molly MacRae.
    p. cm. — (Wheeler Publishing large print cozy mystery)
  ISBN-13: 978-1-59722-573-1 (pbk. : alk. paper)
  ISBN-10: 1-59722-573-8 (pbk. : alk. paper)
  1. Museum curators—Fiction. 2. Burglary—Fiction. 3. Murder—Fiction.
4. Tennessee—Fiction. 5. Large Type books. I. Title.
PS3613.A2833W55 2007 b
813'.6—dc22
                                              2007015565

Published in 2007 in arrangement with Tekno Books and Ed Gorman.

Printed in the United States of America on permanent paper
10 9 8 7 6 5 4 3 2 1

For the Jonesborough-Washington
County History Museum and the
stories it tells,
with my love and gratitude.

ACKNOWLEDGMENTS

Thanks to my writing friends across the years and the country: Teresa Thomas Bohannon, Jean Flanagan, Michal Strutin, Joan Coogan, Carol Jackson, and Sarah Wisseman. And thanks, always, to Mike, Gordon, and Ross Thompson.

CHAPTER 1

Lewis Wilder looked up from his bowl of chili and swore into his napkin as he wiped his mouth. Here came the third reason he wasn't going to be enjoying his meal. At least three was a number that gave the whole evening a sense of balance. It rounded out the general tone of disaster. Presented with a fourth reason, though, he might need to call it quits. He crumpled his napkin and dropped it on the table. He watched Paul Glaser get out of the sheriff's car he'd parked at the curb and head for the café door.

"Evening, Lewis."

"Paul."

Wilder didn't ask Glaser to join him. Glaser smiled and slipped into the booth opposite him anyway. Wilder pushed the bowl of chili aside and waited.

"Aren't you going to ask me what I'm doing here?" Glaser asked.

Wilder didn't answer, instead picked up his glass of iced tea and drank.

"Well, it ain't museum business," Glaser said, still smiling. "Or is it? Of course, you maybe already know this, but that fool who's calling himself the Fox hit a house out near Sycamore last night. Took the portable silver. Heirloom quality, according to the receipt he left. The guy's got a hell of an eye for good old stuff. Hell of a nerve, too. Real professional, every way you look at it. But, I gotta tell you, Lewis, he's got us running in circles. I'm about beat."

Wilder thought about suggesting Glaser spend more time on his treadmill or at the gym. He let his eyes linger too long on Glaser's paunch. When he met Glaser's eyes again the smile was gone.

"What, Paul?"

"He's been lucky so far."

"Not getting caught? Maybe he's smart."

"Smarter than me? Pshaw. More like full of himself. No, what I'm waiting for is the unexpected, which is something I always expect. Someone's going to walk in on him one of these times. And someone is going to get hurt. Or dead."

Wilder crushed a packet of crackers into the chili. He brushed the crumbs off his

10

hands then met Glaser's eyes. "What do you want me to say, Paul?"

"Where were you last night?"

"Home."

"Alone?"

"As usual. What have you heard this time?"

"Same old."

Wilder ignored his stare and looked out the window onto Main Street. What a pleasant, sleepy little town this had seemed when he arrived six months ago. Virtually snoring. He glanced back at Glaser who looked close to snarling. He bowed his head and studied the oilcloth on the table, pushed cracker crumbs around with a finger. Then he shrugged, looked Glaser in the eye again, spread his hands, and gave his best insincere smile.

"I don't know anything about it, Paul."

"You say that every time."

"It's uncomplicated. I like that. I'm going to finish my supper now. I'll see you later."

Glaser slid back out of the booth, his stomach pulling the cloth cockeyed. He stifled a belch and left.

Wilder heard muffled giggles on the other side of the café. Swell, the second reason for this evening's indigestion reappearing for an encore. Two teen-aged girls popped

11

out of their booth and blushed their way over.

"Hi, Mr. Wilder," one of them breathed.

"Was that the sheriff talking to you?" the other asked. Her eyes were alarmingly large and moony.

"Mmhmm."

"My mom doesn't think he should always be bothering you."

"Do I know you?" Wilder asked.

"Yeah. Well, no, but you gave our class a tour of the museum."

"Oh." Wilder decided not to eat out anymore except during school hours.

"Well, bye, Mr. Wilder. Bye."

They crowded through the door. He watched as they walked down the street, nudging each other in fits of giggles, heads together comparing notes and looking back to see if he was looking after them.

Being blushed over was one thing. Being admired because the sheriff considered him suspicious was something else entirely. And that made reason number four and time to head for the door himself. He passed his hand over his face and gave the back of his neck a hard rub.

"Hey, Lewis." A young woman touched his shoulder and slid into the booth. Wilder relaxed and gave her a genuine smile.

"Hey, Pam. I didn't see you in here."

"I was in the kitchen talking to my sister."

"Willie's your sister?"

"Has been all my life. Say, weren't those girls a little young for you?"

"I'm not sure, I think they might've been trying to set me up with their mothers."

She grinned and pushed a Styrofoam container across the table to him. "Here, Willie says yours is cold by now and you've hardly touched a bite. Take this home for later; have it after the board meeting."

"Oh hell, what time is it?"

"Better run."

"Thanks, Pam. See you in the morning." Wilder grabbed the container and a stack of folders from the seat next to him. "Tell Willie thanks." He fumbled with the door then jogged down the street wondering again why he'd thought this town and this job were such a good idea. As he passed a trash barrel he tossed the Styrofoam container into it. The number one reason for his indigestion was Willie's godawful chili.

"And what do you make of our mysterious good fortune, Lewis?" Dr. Edward Ramsey asked fifteen minutes later, as the "new business" portion of the monthly meeting of the Nolichucky Jack History Museum's board of directors got underway. He leaned across the broad boardroom table and raised one hairy gray eyebrow at Wilder.

Wilder considered scanning the faces of the other board members. It might be interesting to see how many of them showed more than casual interest in his answer. But Ed Ramsey was big on eye contact so he returned the look with his own serious gaze.

"As much use as I possibly can, Ed. There's an itemized list of recent expenditures in the monthly report you have in front of you."

"Thank you, Lewis," Ramsey said with a tight smile. "Next item . . ."

"Wait a minute, I'd like to catch up here." This from a usually absent businesswoman, Elaine Pagels. "Sorry, but what exactly is this good fortune you're referring to?"

"How can you not know that by now, Elaine?" This from Lillian Bowman, an always present and accounted for retired schoolteacher.

Wilder ducked his head and bit his cheek to keep from smiling too obviously. Elaine and several other board members, including Ed Ramsey, had survived fourth grade in Lillian's classroom. She still had the tyrant's moves down pat.

"It was in the minutes. If you read them,

or at least paid attention, you would know."

"Elaine?" Ramsey asked.

"Oh, now, what'll it hurt to fill her in?" drawled Paul Glaser, sitting across from Wilder. "How about it, Lewis?"

"A waste of time," Lillian Bowman muttered.

"Go ahead, Lewis," Ramsey said.

"We've been receiving anonymous donations for the past several months," Wilder said.

"Money?"

"Yes."

"That's wonderful. No idea where it's coming from? How much, by the way?"

"Two hundred dollars," Glaser said, smiling like a shark. "Each and every month for the past four months. And, no, we don't know where it's coming from. Do we, Lewis? In fact I'd say the donor's a real sly fella."

"Even if Lewis knows who the donor is, Elaine," Ramsey said, addressing both his glare and his words to Glaser instead of Elaine, "he wouldn't tell us. The donor wishes to remain anonymous and I think Lewis has demonstrated that he can keep his mouth shut."

"Exactly my point, Ed, the boy's nothing if not good at keeping secrets."

15

Wilder groaned.

"Lay off, Paul," George Palmer murmured. He was sitting next to Glaser, running a finger around his clerical collar. It was a gesture Wilder had seen him make from time to time. Whether it was an unconscious habit or calculated he wasn't sure. It tended to have a quelling effect, though, even if accompanied, as now, by Glaser's snort. "The donations are a boon for the museum, Elaine. We're grateful and hope they continue. Shall we get back to current business?"

"Please," Lillian snapped.

"Report from the Acquisitions Committee," Ramsey said, and Lillian adjusted her glasses preparatory to summing up her committee's progress.

Wilder let Lillian's precise words march past him. She'd cornered him earlier in his office and given him the gist, including a rapturous description of a fern stand she'd located for the museum's Victorian parlor. He glanced around at the other board members who were variously paying attention to Lillian or, in the case of Ramsey, Palmer, and Glaser, paying attention to him. Heckle, Jeckle, and Hyde. Not quite right for Ramsey and Palmer, but Glaser definitely had a streak of something running through him. Something Wilder didn't want to see closer up. As he caught Palmer's eye, Palmer winked at him. Wilder quirked the corner of his mouth in return. Nice to have a friend.

The rest of the meeting traveled the typed agenda without detour until the last item. This was a request Wilder had fielded from a CEO in California for information on the original Grindstaff Pepper Packing Plant. He'd found a photograph in the archives but hadn't been able to pinpoint the building's location out in the county.

"My father traded with Mr. Grindstaff. I know exactly where that plant stood," Lillian said, emphasizing each word with a peck of her pencil on the papers in front of her.

"Jake or Lloyd?" demanded Charlotte Reed, one of two board members older than Lillian, and so, immune to the remnants of her imperious classroom demeanor.

"What?"

"I said Jake or Lloyd. Because Jake was kin to the Grindstaffs of Watauga but never had anything to do with peppers. Tobacco. That was Jake. And he ran a dairy herd. You just don't see dairy the way you used to anymore, do you? Except for Morris Ledford. He has a pretty little herd out there on the Holston. Holsteins on the Holston. That sounds like a title for a bovine romance novel, doesn't it? Now if you mean Lloyd, he was kin to the Grindstaffs of Little Limestone over there past the rock house and . . ."

And so the begetting of Grindstaffs and their farming particulars exhausted the remaining minutes of the meeting.

"Excuse me, Charlotte." At nine P.M. Ramsey stood up, his gathered papers already tucked under his arm. "Folks, I'll be out of town this Thursday through next. Back in time for the Pickers' Picnic. Lewis, any problems that come up that you can't handle probably aren't worth bothering any of these folks with, but if you must, let it be on your own head. Meeting adjourned."

Ramsey was a stickler for starting and ending meetings promptly and Wilder felt like kissing his hem every time he called a timely dismissal. He'd quickly learned how memories, both long and short, derailed any given meeting in Nolichucky. Before Ramsey became chairman, museum board meetings had been the worst by far. They'd often degenerated into contests of reminiscence with Wilder wondering when he'd get to see Lillian slug it out with some lesser mortal.

Chairs scraped the floor and those members speaking to each other started in on the first round of good nights. A simple good night was practically unheard of in Nolichucky. A gauntlet of good nights developed in most cases and Wilder was always on the lookout for shortcuts. He gathered his papers now, and tried to look both relaxed and on his way somewhere else.

"You look pained, Lewis," Elaine Pagels said as he pushed his chair in. "Don't those donations make you happy? Lighten the load just a bit?"

"They're great, Elaine." He looked past her. Only Ed Ramsey between him and the door and Ramsey was building steam for his own escape. "Thanks for making it tonight," Wilder said, edging around her. "Will we see you next month?" Ramsey had cleared the door. Wilder looked back over his shoulder to catch Elaine's answer.

"Do my best. Good night."

"Night." Wilder turned and slammed into Paul Glaser.

"Good way to get whiplash, Lewis. Here, let me." Glaser stooped to help Wilder collect the file folders and papers that had ejected on impact.

"Lewis, are you all right?" Lillian tottered over.

Wilder took the papers Glaser was shuffling, jammed them into the folders, and stood up.

"Just clumsy, Lillian. I'm looking forward to seeing that fern stand. Good night." Wilder brushed past Glaser without meeting his eye and started for the door where Palmer intercepted him.

"Liar," Palmer whispered out of the side of his mouth as he waved goodbye to Lillian and Glaser. "You'll hate her fern stand."

"Damn right."

They made it through the door and clattered down the stairs of the county office building where the board meetings were held.

"Don't take Paul seriously, Lewis. I'm sure he doesn't take these rumors seriously. He's got an unfortunate sense of humor."

"Like stopping by the café to ask me for an alibi."

"He likes to needle you."

Wilder held the outside door for Palmer. Under the streetlight, he stopped and looked at him.

"What?" Palmer asked.

"Nothing. Good night, George." Wilder watched as Palmer headed toward his rectory at the east end of Main Street, then he turned and walked in the opposite direction.

Nighttime Nolichucky was washed in the soft glow of new reproduction Victorian gas streetlights, the latest effort in reinforcing the myth of a town lost in time and the foothills of the Blue Ridge Mountains. Wilder thought it would be nice if certain of Nolichucky's residents got lost. Starting with Paul Glaser.

He walked past the mixture of mostly Federal- and Victorian-era buildings and around a corner into a narrow drive between the Doak building and the old mercantile. He turned another corner into the unlit alley running behind Main Street. A network of these alleyways threaded between some and behind most of the buildings in town. Wilder liked the sepia tones of the gaslit streets at night, but he liked even better these shadow lanes behind the scenes. Here his footsteps echoed in the dark, a sound that hadn't changed over the last hundred years. He could pretend for the space of a few blocks that he'd been transported, maybe not to a simpler day, but at least away from some of the complications of this one. Tonight, home and a beer sounded good.

■ ■ ■ ■

Wilder held the long-rifle loose, but ready across his knees. Twenty-five open-mouthed children, transfixed by his sinuous whisper, were rooted to the floor in front of him, the only movement in the room his mesmeric rocking.

"And just at sunrise, the Widow Brown sees movement at the edge of the woods. There," he pointed and twenty-five heads turned to see the men he'd conjured out the window. "She sees them coming. The early light glints on the bridles of their horses, on the stirrups, on the rifles they carry. Tipton and his men are here to arrest John Sevier and take him to prison, over the mountains in North Carolina. The men approach the house, bridles jingling, leather creaking, horses snorting. The men are tired. They've been riding half the night searching for Sevier. You can see the weariness in their faces. All except Tipton's. Tipton's face is hard and he's looking for a fight.

"But Mrs. Brown sits in the doorway, rocking, just as she has all night. She is as solid in her chair as she is solid in her conviction. No one will take Nolichucky

Jack without first getting past her.

"She watches them now, as they draw closer. She rocks slowly, back and forth, back and forth."

The hypnotized children swayed in time to Wilder's rocking.

"Tipton and his men, still mounted, are in a semicircle now, in front of the cabin. Everything is quiet. No birds sing, no crickets chirp. Even the horses have stopped whickering to each other. The only sound is the slow creak of the Widow Brown rocking in the doorway with the long-rifle across her knees.

"Then Tipton bellows, 'Sevier!' "

The children jumped at Wilder's unexpected roar.

" 'Sevier, you'll hang!' But there's no answer from the house," Wilder continued, reverting to his near-whisper. "So Tipton raises his rifle. The Widow Brown's eyes follow his every move; they don't waver for even one second. Just as Tipton brings his rifle level, she jumps up." Wilder leapt out of the chair, sending it flying backward, long-rifle to his shoulder, aiming at the front window.

The children screamed and laughed and scrambled around to see what Tipton thought of that.

A startled George Palmer stood framed in the window. The children screamed again. Wilder rolled his eyes and lowered the gun.

"Tipton!" Wilder shouted, as much to regain the children's attention as to continue his story. They swung back to him and Wilder saw Palmer slide from view.

" 'Tipton!' And here's John Sevier, Nolichucky Jack, governor of the state of Franklin. He's standing tall in the doorway next to Mrs. Brown. 'Tipton,' he says, 'I'll surrender, but not to you. I'll give myself up to Colonel Love who rides with you. But only on the condition that no harm come to Mrs. Brown.' He steps down off the porch and he's surrounded and tied up. Mrs. Brown watches Tipton's men ride away with him, heartsick, but knowing she's held her ground, she's done her part, and now it's up to others to rescue Nolichucky Jack and bring him home."

"Yippee!" a child squealed and the rest started clapping.

Wilder fielded their excited questions and let admiring eyes but no hands roam the length of the rifle. Then he turned the students over to their teacher and excused himself. He found Palmer sitting in one of the rockers on the porch.

"The Widow Brown didn't hold off Tipton's men half as well as you do, Lewis. Though don't you think the museum might be sued someday over someone's heart attack?"

"We're a non-profit organization and can't be held responsible."

"Is that true?"

"I don't know. What can I do for you?"

"I just came to get a look at Lillian's fern stand. You don't do that bit with the rifle for the senior citizens, do you?" Palmer eyed the long-rifle Wilder still cradled.

"No. Hard facts and Victorian interiors for them. I'd hate to find out I was wrong about being sued."

"Oh, I don't know, it might do one or two of them some good. Did I ever tell you about the first time I looked through that window?"

"No, was I doing something rude with one of the mannequins?"

"Not you, no, this was oh, say fifty years ago."

"Ah, before respectability slapped the place around. What were you doing looking through these windows at such an impressionable age? What were you, six, seven? I'm shocked. What was your mother thinking?"

"She had nothing to do with it and never would have known except I let it slip."

25

Palmer gave his backside a reminiscent rub. "It was a dare. Very popular place, this was, for dares."

"I'll bet. So did you get an eyeful or were the ladies and their festivities confined to the upper rooms?"

"There was a chink in the curtains."

"Don't be racist, George."

"I've never called a gap a Chinese, but if you insist. It was just large enough for an inquiring eye. Quite an education for a seven-year-old. Hmm, well. Anyway, Lillian swears that fern stand was the perfect piece at the perfect price so I'd better take a look and then I'll be on my way."

"Whoa, stand back and let the sea of budding humanity out." Wilder held the door as twenty-five aspiring historians, or at least future vigilante riflemen, rushed through and down off the porch. The teacher and several parents were swept along with the tide. "Come, Father Palmer, into the calmer interior." Wilder ushered him into the smells of age and preservation, overlaced with a hint of more recent pink bubblegum.

"So, tell me, Lewis, do you think it was worth the money?"

The two men stepped into a room so thoroughly Victorian it made the faint of heart fear suffocation amidst all the bedraping and bedecking. They stopped in front of the fern stand.

"Well, I've said before, I'm no expert on Victorian furniture."

"Yes, but you have some idea, don't you?"

"It looks awful enough to be the real thing. My aunt had one something like it in the attic, I think. She loathed it and I'm sure she would loathe this, too. Those are good credentials for it right there. But I wish Lillian would listen when I say we need more than just some old geezer's word for where this stuff comes from. That coffee grinder she bought might have been made in the county a hundred and fifty years ago but who knows? There's a man over in Chester . . ."

"You've been to Chester recently?"

"Yeah, why?"

"Didn't the Fox break into a house . . ."

Wilder's glare shriveled anything further along those lines Palmer might have said.

"As I was saying, there is a man in Chester who can turn out a hutch table next week that anyone would swear was made a century ago. The pieces Lillian brings in just don't mean much unless we've got some sort of documentation."

"I know it, I know it. They have no 'historical significance,' as you say. But Lillian and

some of the other members of the committee don't . . ."

"Then they shouldn't be on the Acquisitions Committee."

"Sorry, Lewis. We're all sinners and we're
not the Smithsonian."

"Oh for God's sake."

"It's frustrating for you, I know, but we
have to work with what we've got. Speaking
of which, I'd still like you to teach that
junior high Sunday school class."

"Sorry, George, it's frustrating for you, I
know."

"That's all right," Palmer said, patting
Wilder on the arm, "we can but try. I think
you're probably right about this stand,
though. If you can vouch for your aunt
loathing it, then it passes muster." Palmer's
eyes widened as though he'd had a revela-
tion. He snapped his fingers. "I have a
wonderful idea. Why don't you call your
aunt and ask her to come look at it?"

Wilder looked sideways at Palmer. "Sorry,
George, it's frustrating for you, I know."

"Someday, Lewis," Palmer said, shaking
his head, "you're going to realize that taking
the curator's position here in our lovely out-
of-the-way town was not a successful attempt to get away from anything, but was
instead a first step towards returning to

something. Seventy-five miles is no distance at all and . . ."

". . . And you've said it all before, thank you. Now, goodbye. I hear your flock bleating for you. See you Sunday." Wilder more or less pushed Palmer back out onto the porch and closed the door.

He went into the front room where the tour had finished up and glanced around to see that everything was in order. He'd left the rocking chair tipped in the corner. That was careless. He righted it and crossed over to the window to watch Palmer walking down the sidewalk back toward Main Street. He would probably stop in at Lillian's to report his pleasure with the fern stand. Yes, there he turned in at the gate. And he turned and waved back at Wilder, framed in the window. Clever bastard. Wilder liked him.

One more tour was scheduled for the afternoon but there was time before that to get something else done. He locked the rifle away. Then he walked back past the Victorian parlor, turning his head in time so he didn't have to see the fern stand again, and climbed the graceful stairway to the second floor. He paused at the door to his office thinking he ought to check on the growth rate of his mound of paperwork, but with a mental raspberry in the paperwork's direction, he opened the opposite door and climbed another set of stairs to the attic.

His first project after taking this job had been to evict the uninvited feathered guests from the attic. Then he pigeon-proofed it and vacuumed up what they'd been contributing over the years. Then he'd started in on the fun.

Inventory in one hand, hands correctly, though resentfully, clad in cotton gloves to protect whatever he touched from the insidious oils of his skin, he'd started opening boxes and pulling out drawers, shifting trunks and uncovering "forgotten" acquisitions: a tiny pair of red leather shoes not quite worn out by a child in the 1870s; several dozen pairs of mule shoes someone had carefully cleaned and oiled and donated to the museum; clay marbles; ancient rusty black wedding suits; quilts; firearms; a fire-hose stiff with age; brittle photographs; newspapers; diaries; embroidery projects half-finished a century ago; a stereopticon; projectile points; broken and intact pottery, both delft and Cherokee; glass slides of a long-ago trip to Egypt.

The inventory had been kept up-to-date only haphazardly before his arrival. That meant minor chaos for the collections but bliss for Wilder. It became his personal, protracted treasure hunt. Much protracted because he couldn't spend all his time working on it.

He flipped on the attic lights now, filled his lungs with the still air, and smiled. He wondered if someday someone would catch him up here rubbing his hands and licking his chops.

Being the sole professional employed at the museum, Wilder kept busy juggling his various duties and spent a lot of his time working alone. But that suited him. He preferred the long stretches of solitude to the social parts of the job, though even they had a certain charm. And he'd inherited a capable staff.

Pam Sluder and Marcie Hicks spelled each other as part-time receptionists at a desk in the foyer. They welcomed visitors, answered the phone, and set up tours for groups not wanting to do the self-guided bit.

Jim Honeycutt kept the lawn mowed, the leaves raked, and the floors swept. Hc also lent a hand on whatever exhibit construction project might be going. He liked power tools. He loved the Skil saw.

A small cadre of volunteers gave tours to students and other groups. But often Wilder had to drop his other duties and guide tours, too.

"Lewis?" Susan Peters called from the bottom of the attic stairs. Susan Peters was that godsend all museums pray for, someone trained, experienced, and reliable who could afford to volunteer her time. She came in twice a week and worked at cataloguing old photographs. "Lewis? Your tour is coming up the walk."

"They're early. Tell them to go away."

"Lewis." Susan climbed the stairs. "Stop fondling those corsets and get down there. I swear, every time I look up here you're doing something with old underwear."

"Research. This is research I'm doing for an exhibit on unmentionables."

"So long as you don't start wearing them." She disappeared again.

Wilder laid the corsets in a box lined with protective acid-free tissue. He peeled off the cotton gloves he hated. They made good museum sense but any magic in the artifacts was lost in the translation through the thin fabric. He dropped the gloves into a drawer with several other pairs and went to meet his tour.

"Are you really planning an exhibit of antique underwear?" Susan spoke to Wilder's back from the doorway of the Victorian parlor. "How long have you been standing there and what are you staring at?"

"Hm," Wilder murmured to all three questions. He remained immobile, his hands jammed in his pockets.

Susan walked around in front of Wilder and snapped her fingers under his nose. She'd told him once about her pet theory concerning the necessity of involving more than one of his senses before he could come to grips with the intricacies of logical conversation.

"What's wrong with the fern stand?"

"Nothing. It's exactly right. It's awful." He continued to be absorbed by it.

"Ah." Susan pondered the answer and the person who'd uttered it. "Well, if you do want to do an exhibit of naughty things, I've come across some photographs you might be able to use. I will tell you all this again, next time I see you, as you seem not to be here right now. I'm leaving now. Don't bother to see me out. By the way, I'm developing a new theory, Lewis, about the psychological profile of people attracted to working in museums full-time. Goodbye."

Wilder flapped a hand, and remained staring at the fern stand.

"Are you locking up, Lewis?" Pam looked

in as she passed on her way to the door.

Wilder made an effort and roused himself.

"Yeah." He took his hands out of his pockets and with one fingertip traced the carved edge of the stand. With his other hand he rubbed the tightened muscles at the back of his neck.

The front door slammed behind Pam and Wilder went to lock it. He walked through each of the rooms downstairs, performing the evening security check, repeating the procedure upstairs, finally coming to the attic door. Something about the attic stirred in his mind. He stood there for a minute thinking. But it wasn't this attic. It was the attic of his Aunt Katherine's house.

He'd been staring at Lillian's miserable fern stand too long. A noise between a snort and a sigh stirred him. After checking to see the door was locked, he retraced his steps through the darkened museum, set the alarm, and let himself out the back way into the chilly autumn evening.

The museum made its home in a solid, square house built in the 1850s of red bricks, fired on-site, mostly by black hands. It was a typical piece of antebellum architecture, with symmetrical rows of windows up and down. Upper and lower porches with plenty of gingerbread had been added across the front in the 1880s when a traveling millwright passed through Nolichucky. By the end of World War I, though, with no one in the family left to care, the house sat empty and neglected on the hill at the northern edge of town.

In the thirties it experienced a revival of spirits when it was refurbished with several dozen rolls of flocked wallpaper and turned into a roadhouse. Most of the patrons were men from the surrounding mountains down in town for trade, gossip, and entertainment. Overnight lodging didn't cost much, and if they wanted something less wholesome and a little quicker, that was available, too.

That enterprise folded sometime in the sixties, either because the Law or the Church got the better of it, or maybe just because the roof leaked.

It took a strong-willed committee of citizens and a concerted effort at fundraising to rescue and resurrect the house as the Nolichucky Jack History Museum, dedicated to the history of the town and the area comprising the "Lost State of Franklin." Nolichucky Jack, formally known as John Sevier, was the governor of the lost state and subsequently the first governor of Tennessee. His colorful memory lived on at the

Nolichucky Jack History Museum, and especially in the minds of those children who went through the museum on one of Lewis Wilder's livelier tours.

Wilder shivered as he walked down the brick path that ran across the lawn between the museum and the former slave quarters. The quarters, a low clapboard building, had survived as a structure through the various transitions of the big house, enjoying a few of its own along the way. In its latest incarnation, it was a perk for the museum's curator — free housing.

Wilder pulled his few pieces of mail from the box on the porch railing. More fodder for the recycling bin. It wasn't so dark yet that he stumbled up the steps or fumbled his key in the lock. He tossed the mail toward the sofa on his way past, grabbed his jacket from a peg in the kitchen, and went out the back door. He shrugged into the jacket and sat down on the steps.

"Evening, Lewis." A hat and the long handle of a garden tool were visible over a fence smothered in blackberry brambles.

"Evening, Grady," Wilder said to the hat.

"You all right?"

"Can't complain, Grady."

"Or you could, but you won't."

Wilder smiled.

Grady had introduced himself over the fence to Wilder as a compost-pit philosopher. "I'm interested in all kinds of ideas," he'd told Wilder one evening soon after Wilder moved in. "I don't care where they come from. I just toss them into the compost pit of my mind and sooner or later something good grows out of it." Grady was a retired funeral home director and ex-marine. He was seventy-eight.

Wilder had listened to Grady's story in installments on fine evenings throughout the summer and fall, rarely seeing his face; sometimes surprised by the hats he wore.

"Is it broccoli or turnips tonight, Grady?"

"Cabbage."

"Cabbage."

A breeze pulled a few early red leaves off the maple in the corner of Wilder's small yard. The crickets tuned up. Grady's disembodied voice came over the fence.

"Yeah, I come out here in the evening, Lewis, and I yank up a few of the cussed weeds and I stir up my compost heap a bit. Then I plant something or I pick something."

"Are you talking about your head or your garden?"

"Garden, wise guy. I'll be picking these cabbages in February. They'll taste better than any you've ever had because they got some frost. Nothing wrong with a little nip of frost for members of the cabbage family."

Nothing wrong with a little nip of something else for the Wilder family, Wilder thought.

"I enjoy my evenings in the garden, Lewis," Grady continued. "Soothing. That's what it is. And I truly believe that if more people gardened in this world things would be different."

Wilder sat listening to the sounds of the end of the day and of the old man working in his garden. Soothing.

Grady said good night and Wilder went in.

The darkest part of Wilder's dreamless sleep was shattered by voices and pounding on his door.

CHAPTER 2

Or a voice. Wilder waked instantly but muddled, the pounding of his heart almost enough to drown out the beating on his door. His first coherent thought was that the museum must be on fire. The fist on the door sounded frantic enough. But the voice was indistinct and didn't match the fist for urgency. He peered out the window. No rosy glow or smoke. It went through his mind that now might be a good time to call 911. And say what? Besides, the phone was in the kitchen. He had to pass the front door to get to it so he might as well find out what was going on first.

He slipped out of bed and put on his shoes, congratulating himself for that bit of good sense. Shod feet would be better for any occasion, be it retreat or defense. Maybe Paul Glaser could dig up statistics in some law enforcement journal backing up the advisability of wearing shoes when opening one's door to strangers in the night.

He went to the front door and flipped on the porch light. Then, his prickling scalp whispering caution, he put his eye to the edge of one of the front window curtains.

What he saw was the most wizened old man still able to stand up and yell he could have imagined. The man looked more bewildered than Wilder felt and so Wilder opened the door. At the same moment, the old man hurled himself at what had been the closed door. He fell into Wilder's arms and the momentum carried both of them into the living room, Wilder leading unconvincingly in an odd sort of two-step and glad it wasn't his bare feet being tromped on. He dropped his whiskery partner when they reached the sofa.

Rheumy eyes stared out of a shriveled walnut of a face, darting glances around at the walls lined with bookcases, the aquarium on the coffee table, and the general lack of sensuous purples, reds, or hot pinks. Wilder watched as the light of disappointment dawned.

"Thishain't the place I thought it was."

Wilder knew from personal experience that rumors ran fast in eastern Tennessee. But he hadn't thought useful information would lag so far behind.

"No."

"Reckon I oughter be goin'. You don't happen ta know of anyplace a feller could . . ."

"Sorry, I'm pretty new around these parts, myself."

"New feller, eh? Tellya what. I find something good, why, I'll giveya a holler." The old man listed out the door and off the porch. "Goo' night."

"Good night. Watch out for the hedge . . . Oops."

Wilder shut the door and turned out the light. He swore as he headed back to bed. Nothing like a dose of noise and cold night air, not to mention an unexpected waltz, to ruin any chance of getting back to sleep. But he crawled back under his warm quilt and discovered that the lingering fumes of cheap alcohol were wonderfully soporific.

He woke to his radio alarm the next morning refreshed and hungry. A glance out the bedroom window assured him his visitor had at least cleared the hedge at the edge of the yard. He did a soft-shoe into the bathroom and found himself whistling as he dressed and dragged a brush through his hair. After looking in the refrigerator he decided it was a good morning to eat

41

breakfast somewhere else.

He walked the five blocks to Willie's Café, glad to be out in the brisk, bright morning. A flock of robins was fattening up on the red dogwood berries in Lillian Bowman's yard. They startled and flew off into the brilliant sky as he passed. In the spring they'd be back in her yard, the earliest returning migrators bent on getting their worms.

Wilder turned the corner into Main Street and crossed over to the café, threading his way between the pickup trucks parked out front. The café was a favorite place for after-morning-chore coffee. Wilder nodded at the men in faded overalls already sitting over steaming cups. They nodded in return.

"What'll it be, Lewis?" called the waitress from the counter as he hung his jacket on a tree by the door.

"Scrambled eggs and biscuits, Dawn."

"Coffee?"

"Please."

He looked around for an unoccupied table but even the booth that took the brunt of the swinging kitchen door was taken. A couple of farmers he knew on a weather exchange basis smiled and indicated the empty chair at their table and Wilder made his way over.

"Sure you don't mind?" he asked.

"No," said one.

"Hell, no," said the other. His eyes twinkled as he watched Wilder tuck into his breakfast.

"I heard Vernon Buckles was in town yesterday evening trying to sell tobacco." The twinkling eyes took on a brighter glint. "Seems he brought down more than just the tobacco, though, if you catch my meaning. He was pretty nigh gone when the sheriff picked him and his jug up along about four o'clock this morning. Mumbling something about finding a pussy cat or some such for a feller new to town."

Wilder looked up from his plate and met two pairs of eyes barely containing their mirth. He took a sip of coffee.

"Yeah, I think maybe we ran into each other last night."

The farmers slapped their thighs.

"I've been thinking of taking out an ad in the paper saying the place is under new management," Wilder continued. "What do you think?"

"Won't do you no good," said one.

"Vernon can't read."

They roared at that and finished their coffee and offered to buy Wilder another cup. He accepted and told them in more detail about Vernon Buckles' midnight visit.

"How long has it been since he last came to town?" Wilder asked.

"He comes down every year. But to him every year is about 1960. Vernon's backward. He don't mean no harm, though. Just the way things is."

Words to live by, Wilder thought.

The three sat contemplating that for awhile, staring into their coffee cups. Wilder finished his breakfast.

"You do keep your door locked, don't you, Lewis?"

"He does now."

They left together, chuckling, the farmers getting into their trucks, Wilder heading back up the hill. He saw the robins were back on the job in Lillian's yard. He wondered if their work ethic was their own or if Lillian's vast powers extended even to the wildlife in her domain. He saluted them and continued on to the museum and his own job.

He unlocked the back door and used five of the sixty seconds he had in which to turn off the alarm to stare down the hall in the direction of the fern stand in the Victorian parlor. But, he thought, enough of that. It was too early on a beautiful morning to be getting morose. He switched off the alarm and took the stairs to his office two at a

44

time. Marcie would be there in another hour to unlock the front door and put out the open sign. Wilder used the extra time to get a head start on the day.

His office was in an old dressing room. It was a small space made more cramped by everything his predecessor had managed to jam into it. The board had apologized for the lack of space but Wilder liked being hemmed in by the shelves of reference books and the artifacts casually waiting around to be examined and minutely noted. He could feel the weight of the filing cabinets full of records and the permanence all that collected information gave to the lives of people he'd never known.

He hung his jacket on the hook behind the door. Then he tackled the accumulation of paperwork reproaching him from the middle of his desk. He slit envelopes, he typed, he filed, he made paper airplanes and sailed them into the cardboard box that was his recycling bin. When he heard Marcie downstairs he escaped before the last of the pile sucked him under.

"You sleep up there again last night?" Marcie had a series of running jokes. She was Wilder's age and had twin daughters in high school.

"Like a baby, Marcie," Wilder said.

"I hear you found a new dance partner last night."

"My life is not my own, is it?"

"Not since you moved to Nolichucky, hon. So, do you ballroom?"

"Hm?"

"Do you ballroom dance? You know, rumba, samba, tango?" She put a pencil in her teeth and struck a pose. "You're getting quite the reputation as a hoofer."

"How?" he asked. "Who makes up these things?"

"Oh, well after that street dance back in August . . . The girls told me you were showing some real style."

"The street dance. God. I don't know who that woman was. 'Call me Barb,' I think she said, then practically smothered me. She sure knew how to lead, though."

"Big Bad Barb?"

"Big, blousy, blond woman? That's what you call her?"

"Big Bad Barb, bold as brass, watch out boy, she'll pinch your ass."

"As a matter of fact she did that, too."

"Well, I wish I'd been there." Marcie tapped the pencil on the counter, a wistful look in her eye. Then she sighed and sat down behind the desk. "Did you remember that Bebe can't do the tour today?"

"How's her foot?"

"Not broken but she says it feels like it anyway. You doing the tour?"

"Yeah, then I'll get them to string leather britches."

"So that's how come all the green beans in the fridge. You sure have a knack."

"For what?"

"Getting people to do things for you."

"It's a patented method. Give me a holler, will you, when they get here?" He went to make sure there were plenty of needles and heavy thread to string the beans.

Wilder believed in what he called the Tom Sawyer Method of Museum Management. Not that he enticed suckers into doing his job and then sat back and watched. But visitors weren't likely to see most of what went on in the museum and neither was the paycheck-bearing board of directors. Wilder recognized the danger inherent in invisible work. The first time Paul Glaser asked if he didn't get bored sitting around all day waiting for visitors to walk through the door, Wilder set him to wiping nose- and fingerprints off the glass cases.

"And what'll you be doing in the meantime?" Glaser asked.

"Bringing the next tour of first graders and their little noses and fingers through right behind you."

Wilder regularly invited board members to help with general maintenance and dusting. He got some of them up into the attic to help with the inventory from time to time and he taught one or two how to put numbers on artifacts. He worked hard at making the invisible visible and comprehensible.

At eleven-thirty Wilder was sitting on the porch with a class of third graders and a half-bushel of green beans.

"What will you eat for supper today?" he asked the children sitting cross-legged on the porch in front of him.

"Idunno."

"Probly meatloaf 'cause it's Tuesday."

"Today is Wednesday."

"Oh."

"What would you say if I told you that you could toss a string of these leather britches and a ham bone into a kettle of boiling water and end up with something really tasty?" Wilder held up a long string of what looked like shriveled brown twigs.

"What? Is that how these beans are gonna look? Yuck."

"They aren't pretty, are they? But that was life before refrigerators and grocery stores. Now, I'll tell you what. I need some leather britches . . ."

48

"Are you gonna eat 'em?"

"Well, now, I just might. But what I really need them for is the pioneer life exhibit. So, if you'll each make two strings, we'll hang half of them up in the museum exhibit and you'll each still have one to take home for your mothers to cook up for you later on this winter. Isn't that nice?"

The children seemed to think so and set about stringing beans with a will. Wilder helped tie knots and thread needles.

"Do they get a cut of your salary, that's what I want to know."

Wilder looked up to see Paul Glaser staring at them.

"I said I'd do their homework for them."

"I wouldn't have thought you'd have the time."

Wilder stifled a groan and tried to ignore what he knew was coming by breaking up a fight over whose string was the longest.

"I mean, it can't be easy working full-time days and part-time nights . . ."

"You know, it would help a lot if you would at least smile when you say things like that, Paul."

"God, I love to get your goat. But don't let me interrupt your project here."

Wilder sighed. Glaser lumbered up the steps and scrutinized the work in progress.

He appeared to be fascinated, watching the children stringing the beans, but he managed at the same time to give the impression he thought the entire setup suspicious.

"Oh, I've got a message for you." Glaser picked up one of the finished products and inspected its entire length before letting it fall back onto the porch. "I stopped by the bookstore earlier and as I was heading in this direction anyway Marilyn asked me to tell you that she will be eating lunch at twelve-thirty. She must suppose you know what that means."

"Thanks, Paul."

Wilder brushed a few children off his knees and stood up. Glaser had already turned his back. He walked the few steps to the front door, peered in through the glass, turned back towards Wilder, and smiling with supreme self-assurance, left.

"Who was that fat guy?"

"Who's Marilyn?"

Wilder looked at the children's overcurious faces.

"Who wants to be the first one to hang their museum piece?"

They surged through the door, shedding beans and tangling strings. Wilder looked at his watch. Just past noon.

"If we hurry, I'll have time to tell you

about the Widow Brown saving John Sevier from Tipton's men before you leave."

"You mean before your date with Marilyn."

"Yeah," he smiled, "I do."

CHAPTER 3

Marilyn Wooten was a potential bright spot in Wilder's life. He'd met her soon after moving to Nolichucky, but it was only in the past few weeks that they'd detected a mutual spark of interest in each other's eyes. They'd sat next to each other at the last meeting of the town's board of mayor and aldermen and discovered they shared more in common than a mild disrespect for the town administrator.

"What a Neanderthal," Marilyn had muttered.

"Someone oughta let him know he's extinct," Wilder had answered.

They'd gone for coffee at Willie's afterwards and Marilyn had given him an entertaining oral history of the town board.

Wilder wished, now, that the invitation to lunch hadn't been relayed through Paul Glaser, but that didn't keep him from looking forward to twelve-thirty. So, after regaling the school group with his rendition of the brave Widow Brown holding Tipton's men at gunpoint, he shooed them back to the arms of their teacher, and for the second time that day he walked the five blocks down to Main Street.

He turned the corner, narrowly missing a collision with Miss Eleanor Bean, another of the endless supply he'd discovered of elderly Nolichuckians.

"Pardon me, Miss Eleanor." Wilder side-stepped the octogenarian, who smiled and fluttered her hand at him.

"Oh, that's quite all right, Henry," she called.

Wilder wondered who Henry was and continued on, passing the savings and loan, the hardware store, and the library. He was passing an antiques shop when something in the window caught his eye. Then he saw that he'd caught the owner's eye and he stepped inside.

"Hey, Boyd."

"Lewis, good to see you. To what do I owe the pleasure?"

"Just passing. That's a nice-looking corner cupboard." Wilder walked over to the piece in the window to get a better look. He ran his hand down its cherrywood side. It was smooth and felt warm.

"A real beauty, isn't it?"

"Sure is." He realized he was stroking it and stopped. He wondered how often Boyd Warren saw people petting his furniture. He pulled out a drawer to see the dovetailing.

"Interested?"

Wilder flicked a glance at him then looked at the tag.

"I guess I'll just covet it. Thanks, anyway."

"I might could come down some but not much. It's a hundred-and-seventy-five years old, Lewis. You know it's not like that modern crap you find everywhere these days. This one's got real heart. But look at me preaching to the choir. You know a good piece when you see it. You give it some thought, Lewis."

"Sure, Boyd. See you." It might not be crap, he thought, as he passed it basking in the window, but it sure as hell was modern. He'd seen it before, not quite finished, in that workshop in Chester. Talented guy. So much for the honesty of the salt of the earth. He wondered if Boyd Warren was in on the scam. Then he wondered if Warren was bent enough to sell fake antiques, was he also into stolen antiques? Maybe he should start a rumor or two of his own. They might act like a firebreak. No, he dismissed the thought as soon as it came.

Why make someone else's life miserable?

At the corner of Main and Market Wilder ducked into the small grocery owned and operated by Mrs. Edith Daniels, a fourth-generation descendant of the original merchant. He picked up two of Mrs. Daniels' ready-made sandwiches, which looked to be tuna but might not be. From there he cut across the grass in front of the First Baptist Church and ran up the steps of a blue-painted Victorian cottage.

"Hey, you made it, great." Marilyn Wooten greeted him from behind the desk she used as a sales counter. "Give me a few minutes to finish up here."

"Sure."

She turned back to the woman in front of her and Wilder took the opportunity to wander around.

"Oh, by the way," she called as he disappeared, "my mother got back last night. She might join us for lunch."

Wilder stuck his head back around the corner and raised his eyebrows.

"Oh."

"You'll like her."

Wilder ducked back around the corner cursing his luck under his breath.

Marilyn and her mother co-owned Blue Iris Books & Crafts. Marilyn worked at it full-time and her mother spent five months of each year painting in Maine. Which arrangement, Wilder figured, would account for why he and Marilyn caught sight of each other so rarely over the summer. They both had shops to run, so to speak.

Wilder headed for the Overmountain Room. This was the original front parlor of the house and Wilder knew it must be the heart of the business. The Wootens had left it looking comfortable with reading lamps and overstuffed chairs and lined it from floor to ceiling with shelves. Business sense dictated they stock the latest fiction, nonfiction, and magazines, but they'd built up a reputation for the depth and breadth of their selection of regional books. The Overmountain Room attracted scholars and local history buffs from all over. A sign invited people to sit and read awhile, which is what Wilder planned to do as soon as he could make up his mind which book to choose.

He browsed past the Smoky Mountains geology and hiking and camping guides. He skipped the cookbooks, pausing only to wonder if Vernon Buckles' recipe for corn whisky was in one of them. He ignored the genealogy section and the books on Scots-Irish and German settlement patterns. He dithered between a book on trout streams and one on snake-handling believers and compromised by picking up a slim volume on Appalachian medical folklore. He dropped into a chair next to the books on birds, mammals, and wildflowers of the southern highlands. Maps and Cherokee Indians would have to wait their turn and so would the regional fiction.

"I thought you were looking forward to meeting my mother when she got back." Marilyn came into the room after putting the "back soon" sign on the front door.

"I am. But I was also looking forward to lunch alone with you." Wilder enjoyed the rosy color creeping up her cheeks. Then, to make amends for his initial lack of enthusiasm, he asked after her mother. "How did the painting go?"

"She showed me some of it last night. I think it's some of the best stuff she's done, ever. She gets nervous, though, letting people see new pictures. It's funny, you know, because she's so good, and you'd think she'd have all the confidence in the world by now."

She said this over her shoulder as she walked around straightening books. She didn't look to Wilder as though she expected him to comment on this report of her mother's neurosis and he didn't want to anyway so he changed the subject.

"Is she glad to be home?"

"Yeah, she is. She spent her summers up there when she was growing up and some of her happiest times have been up there. But you know how it is, after you've been away for awhile it's good to get home again. Anyway, five months is an awfully long time to be away from the latest in Nolichucky news."

"You mean gossip?"

"Of course. But we prefer calling it 'popular report.' "

"So long as she doesn't believe everything she hears."

"Well, Lewis," she said, patting one last book back into place, "you know if you don't tell people anything about yourself they're bound to start making things up."

"Oh, is that what they're doing?"

"Come on, let's eat. Is that your lunch?" She nodded at the plastic-shrouded packages he held.

"Mrs. Daniels' best mystery sandwiches." He brandished the two questionable packets and followed her to the kitchen at the back of the house.

"Do you cook much for yourself?"

"Sure, I'd have gone home today and fixed my own mystery sandwiches if I hadn't gotten your beguiling message."

A charmingly cockeyed window in the south wall of the kitchen attracted Wilder. He looked out into a yard enclosed by tall bushes, a mix of lilacs, forsythia, and spyria. In the center of the yard was an old gatepost with a platform of weathered wood perched on top. Wilder stared at it, wondering, until he saw a mourning dove land on it and start in on its own lunch. A pair of binoculars hung from a nail in the window frame. Wilder picked them up.

"Nifty bird feeder."

"Mom's. She takes pictures and then sketches them. And she keeps track of the numbers for the Ornithological Society."

While Marilyn fixed herself a peanut butter and jelly sandwich on toast, Wilder focused the binoculars on the feeder.

"Who's the classy bird, black with a brown head?"

"That's a cowbird."

"He looks like he owns the place. I wonder if he's got a little pair of binoculars so he can watch us while we eat."

"They aren't very nice. They lay their eggs in other birds' nests and when they hatch the baby cowbirds grab most of the food away from the other babies. Or they just throw the others out of the nest altogether."

"Handsome and heartless. I've known people like that." Wilder put the binoculars back feeling somehow disillusioned. "Say, do you know anyone named Henry?"

"We had a dog named Henry."

"Oh, thanks. Eleanor Bean called me Henry."

"She probably just forgot your name."

"Probably."

Marilyn brought her sandwich and two glasses of iced tea over to the table under the window and they were both just sitting down when Mrs. Wooten breezed in the back door. Wilder stood and greeted her.

"Lewis, hello." She came and took his two hands in hers and held them. "You maybe don't remember, there were so many new faces, but I did meet you just after you moved here. Of course, I left for Maine soon after that so I didn't get a chance to know you better but I'm so glad to see you again. I've heard so many good things about you and I hear you're doing wonderful things for our museum. We're just so lucky to have you."

Wilder felt breathless after this effusive greeting but managed to thank her and offered her his chair.

"Oh, no. You just sit right down and eat. I'll get myself something and join you."

She busied herself making a salad, humming as she bustled around the kitchen. Wilder glanced at Marilyn who smiled back at him, her fondness for her mother obvious in her face.

"And how are you finding Nolichucky, Lewis?" Mrs. Wooten asked as she brought over another chair.

"So far, so good. Though, I'm still getting my feet wet, I think."

"Well, and I'm sure the museum's been keeping you busy, too. But don't worry, no one stays in the foot-wetting stage for long in Nolichucky. Why, in another twenty years, people might not even think of you as a foreigner."

Wilder laughed.

"She's right, Lewis. You might feel like an outsider now, but give it twenty or thirty years."

"And where are you from, Lewis?"

"Well, the strangest place I ever lived was West Texas. Did you know you can see a storm coming from a couple of hundred miles away out there? And people raised out there in the wide open spaces get claustrophobic here with the trees and mountains."

"Good heavens. Is that where you grew up?"

"No, thank goodness."

"Well, I imagine it's a perfectly nice place for whoever gets used to it. But I see what you mean, Marilyn," said Mrs. Wooten turning to her daughter.

Wilder felt like he'd just lost the thread of the conversation somewhere.

"Hmm?" he asked, looking first at Marilyn and then her mother.

"It's just that you might consider entering politics someday, Lewis," Mrs. Wooten said. "The way you answer questions."

Marilyn swallowed a bite the wrong way and coughed into her napkin. A short silence followed as Wilder chewed and swallowed a bite of his own sandwich, which had turned out to be chicken salad. He took a long drink of tea.

"I'm sorry, Mrs. Wooten," he said, putting the glass down. "I was born in Ohio. I grew up near Knoxville. And I spent some unpleasant time in West Texas."

"Oh, Lewis, I'm sorry, I didn't mean to embarrass you and I don't mean to pry."

"You weren't prying."

"Well, that's all right, then."

"Oh, pry away, Mom," Marilyn said. "You got more out of him in those three short sentences than most people have. But you'll notice he was still short on specifics."

"Hush, Marilyn. Lewis, I can certainly

understand your not wanting to answer a bunch of nosy questions. I dare say you've had nothing but nosy questions since you arrived. You're right to maintain a certain distance. It gives you a chance to size things up. But it's nice to have a friend to talk to, too, don't you think? Someone more your own age. You must get tired of listening to old ladies driveling on and on about their sainted ancestors and their priceless hair wreathes. That would be enough to give any sane person the heebie-jeebies after five minutes."

She paused for a moment, squinting at a piece of lettuce on her fork. Wilder and Marilyn watched as she picked something off then delicately wiped her fingers on her napkin. "Cat fur. It's an epidemic." She took a sip of iced tea and sighed.

"Well, Lewis, I'm glad Marilyn invited you over. You must have been awfully lonely when you first moved here, though I know you've been working hard and that's always good, too. And George Palmer tells me, I ran into him this morning when I stopped in at the library, that you're a wonderful addition to his congregation. I think George is one of the few truly good people I've ever known. It's a shame he never married."

Wilder let Mrs. Wooten's steady stream

roll over him like a blanket of steam. He sat back and finished his sandwiches, watching the two women. Marilyn seemed content to let her mother carry the conversation, enjoying her recital of summer tales, catching his eye from time to time and smiling. Wilder realized he would never have picked her mother out of a crowd as being the artist responsible for the somber, haunting mountain scenes hanging out in the shop. He'd pictured a gaunt, older woman with a bleak look in her eye. And here she was, more like one of the wrens he could see hopping around on the bird feeder.

"I always thought you must take after your father," he told Marilyn after her mother had wafted upstairs promising to stop by the museum soon to see the changes he'd made. "I've had this image of your mother as being tall and sort of wasted looking."

Marilyn laughed at this description of the antithesis of her mother.

"But you're a lot like her. You just don't have any gray in your hair and you're not quite so chattery."

"I'm sure they both come with age. And believe it or not, I've been told that before."

"Do you mind?"

"No, it's just that it's so obvious."

"Well, not everybody is so obviously like

their mother or father. And there are some children you'd pity if they're destined to turn out like their parents."

Marilyn laughed again. "Like who, for instance?"

"Paul Glaser's children. God, can you imagine some poor kid having to grow up knowing that's all he's got to look forward to?"

"Oh, dear, poor choice on that one, Lewis. Don't you know everyone around here is related? He's my uncle."

"You're kidding."

"Nope. Mom's brother."

"No."

"Mmhmm."

"I've got that sinking feeling."

"Serves you right. But you do have a point, I'm certainly glad I don't have Uncle Paul's paunch and bald head. So, who are you most like, your mother or your father?"

Wilder thought for a minute, scratching his ear. "I used to look just like my father."

"What? You had plastic surgery? You don't look like him now?"

"I guess I do."

"Don't you catch yourself out of the corner of your eye in a mirror sometimes and think you're seeing him? Or find yourself saying things he does that you swore to yourself you'd never be caught dead saying?"

Wilder laughed. "Not my father, no."

"Your mother?"

"My aunt."

"Well now that's just confusing."

"It's not meant to be. My parents were killed in a car wreck when I was eight. My father's sister raised me."

"Oh, that's terrible."

He shrugged. "Long time ago. I got used to it."

"You got used to it? Yeah, I suppose. I'm sorry, though. You don't like talking about it, do you?"

"Oh, well." He crushed the sandwich wrappings into a ball and dropped them onto the table. "What I don't like talking about is my aunt."

"Why not?"

"Probably because I haven't talked to her in about five years."

"Five years?"

"Well, seven or eight."

"Seven or eight, he says with utter calm. My god. Why haven't you?"

Wilder shrugged again.

"If you grew up near Knoxville then she doesn't live more than a hundred miles from here . . ."

66

"Seventy-five."

"And you haven't spoken to her in eight years? You really do have some dark secrets, don't you?"

"Been talking to your Uncle Paul?"

"Answering questions with questions? Well, you've got to admit, at least Uncle Paul is entertaining. Golly, it's too bad there isn't a heath nearby, you could go off and brood now."

"You're pretty entertaining, too. No, I think I'll just go back to work."

He picked up the crushed wrappers and looked around for the garbage. The mood had shifted. Some of the brightness was gone and he blamed his own sourness.

"Thanks for coming, Lewis." Marilyn took the wrappers from him, holding his hand briefly. Her smile was warm.

"You're welcome."

"Come again?"

Well, maybe it was brighter than he thought.

"Thanks, I'd like that."

CHAPTER 4

"Nice lunch yesterday?"

Wilder didn't bother to wonder at Pam's greeting. He would have wondered if she hadn't heard about his lunch with Marilyn.

"Yes, Pam, nice lunch."

"Mail."

"Oh, man, it's about that time again, isn't it? Did you look? Is it there?"

She waved an envelope at him. "Think so. Want me to save you the trouble and open it for you this time?"

"What trouble?"

"Look in a mirror next time you open one of these things. It gets worse every time, I'm telling you. Adding years," she said shaking her head. "Marilyn Wooten won't be so quick to invite you to lunch, you start having worry lines and losing your hair like her uncle."

"Oh, shut up." Wilder pulled the envelope from her hand. It looked like all the rest, no return address and a generic Northeast Tennessee cancellation. He slit it open and pulled out a stack of twenties.

"Two hundred dollars. Like clockwork."

"Guess whoever it is doesn't worry about sending cash through the mail." She leaned over the counter and made a show of inspecting him, opening her eyes wide. "Ooh, you should see . . ."

"There's nothing wrong with me that a little less in the wise-ass department won't help."

She sat back, chuckling. "But the money sure is nice."

"Yup. It sure is." He fanned the twenties in his hand, wishing he could shake them and accuse them of making his life difficult. "Pam, tell me, honestly, do you think there's a connection between this money and the Fox?" He narrowed his eyes at her as he spoke. "And I dare you to make even one remark you'll regret."

She started to smile but stopped. "Truthfully? I don't know. How could I? But why not? The money started showing up after the guy started operating. He steals antiques, he must like them, so maybe he sends some of his ill-gotten gains to the museum. Who knows? Who cares? It helps the budget."

"It's not exactly a line item we can count on, though, is it? Which reminds me, I'm giving a money-grubbing speech to the Rotary Club today."

"Sock it to 'em. Here's the rest of the mail. Cute little package for you."

Wilder looked at the brown box. "No return address, Pam, I don't know if I want to open it."

"Wuss."

"What do you think, is our friend entering a new phase in anonymous correspondence?" He picked it up. "Kind of light, though. Probably not a million bucks."

He pulled out a pocketknife and slit the tape. Under a layer of foam chips, which made a nuisance of themselves all over the counter, was a child's pair of toy handcuffs. Wilder picked them out of the box and held them up, eyebrows raised.

"Kinky," Pam said.

He tipped the box and more chips fell out along with a stuffed animal. A grinning fox.

"Oh."

"Any idea who sent it?" he asked as he scooped everything back in the box.

"No."

"Well, I guess it doesn't really matter."

"Lewis, if it's any, what-do-you-call-it, consolation, people kind of like the Fox. It's not like a lot usually happens around here and he's been spicing things up. And he's, I don't know, elegant with those notes he leaves. And no one's really getting hurt except a bunch of people with plenty of insurance who should have better locks on their doors anyway."

"Paul thinks someone's going to end up dead."

"Paul thinks 'Law and Order' is a documentary. No, you've got to look at it this way. The Fox gives us a touch of class. Something we don't get a lot of around here. He's a bona fide folk hero, you know? And so what if people think he's giving money to the museum?"

"Except they think he's me."

"Nobody does seriously." She waited a few beats. "Except a few sleazoid-types down at the bar who want to shake your hand and discuss technique."

"Ha bloody ha." Wilder picked up the rest of the mail and the box. "I'll be upstairs." He hoped it didn't look as though he was stomping up to his room.

From his office door he tossed the mail, box included, into his in basket and immediately regretted it when the foam chips spilled out, dancing across the desk and floor. Swearing, he chased them down and corralled them again. A few stuck to his shirt and hands. Like little rumors, he thought. If only rumors were so easy to grab and smash. He threw the crushed chips into the wastepaper basket and took three deep breaths. Time to compose, both himself and whatever he was going to say to the Rotarians.

Anonymous donations aside, the Nolichucky Jack, like all but very few of its kind, was in constant need of fundraising. Wilder knew he was luckier than many small museum administrators. The museum's board members were required by the by-laws to raise money, which was not so unusual. But what Wilder blessed the members for every night in his prayers was their willingness, aptitude, and frank pleasure in raising funds. He loathed it himself.

But, as Dr. Ramsey, Lillian Bowman, and George Palmer often told him, and especially just before asking him to address one of their community organizations, he was one of the museum's best advertisements. He might not like talking about himself, but he glowed when he talked about the museum. Or so Lillian said. Wilder thought it more likely that he just worked up a sweat.

He had a spiel suitable for most occasions that he changed around depending on the audience and what props he took with him. Rotarians might not be as charmed by needlework and baby shoes as the Garden Club. The women had gotten a kick out of the cigar mold, though.

As he packed what he hoped were some sure-fire artifacts in a sturdy box to take with him, he went over the basics of the speech in his head. Adding a bit about the museum as a business being an asset to other businesses would be a good idea, and a rundown on the history of Nolichucky businessmen supporting cultural endeavors in town. It occurred to him that before long he was going to have to come up with more than just a few new lines. Sooner or later he would have addressed every social club in town. And most of their members more than once. Nolichuckians were definitely joiners. But the speech probably still had a few good meetings left in it.

With the Rotarians under control, he retreated to the attic to lose himself in a therapeutic dose of inventory work. To hell with the Fox and all rumors and jokes.

"I'm running behind, Pam," Wilder called later, rushing past the reception desk, artifact box tucked under one arm.

"As usual. Your jacket."

"Damn. Hold this." He shoved the box at her, raced back up to the office and grabbed the tweed jacket he kept on a hanger behind the door. He pulled his tie from the sleeve and choked himself with it on his way back down.

"I'll be at the . . ."

"Rotary meeting."

He snatched the box on his way out the door, negotiated the steps two at a time and jogged on his way. As he swung into Main Street he caught sight of Marilyn coming out of the café.

"Hey," she called to him.

"Hey, yourself," he said jaywalking to meet her.

"You're all gussied up. You look practically radiant."

"That happens when I tie my tie too tight."

"So where are you off to?"

"I'm on my way to eat a large free lunch with the upstanding business and professional leaders of our community and then I'm going to tell them why they should give me lots of money."

Marilyn looked him up and down.

"I thought you hated that kind of thing."

"I do. I'd much rather be working on the labels for the old underwear exhibit." He shrugged. "Once I get warmed up it isn't too bad. And most of these guys haven't set foot in the museum since the opening night wine and cheese party ten years ago. Who knows, maybe I'll hit the right note and some nut will clasp me to his bosom and say he'll fund the museum for the next ten years."

"Dream on, then you'd have to spend all your time doing something you were actually trained to do, like preserving my great-grandmother's garter belt. Besides," she added with a wicked gleam in her eye, "I thought the Fox was taking care of the museum's money problems these days."

There was a small, constrained silence in which Marilyn looked as though she might try to kick herself.

"What's in the box?" she asked several watts too brightly.

"Stolen silver."

"Oh, hell, Lewis, I'm sorry."

"It's show and tell for the Rotary club; a vulcanizer for making rubber dentures, a tiny gold pistol to be carried in a lady's handbag, and your great-grandmother's garter belt. Look, I was already late before I stopped." He started walking backwards down the sidewalk. "Will you come for supper tonight at my place?"

"Yeah, sure, I'd love to."

"Outstanding. Spaghetti at seven, then." He turned and ran.

"Lewis," George Palmer made his way over to Wilder during the back-patting aftermath of his presentation, "I want you to meet someone."

"Matchmaking, George?"

"You've heard the phrase 'where the big possums trot'? Well, this is one mighty well-grown marsupial. Deep pockets." Palmer pointed out a large man, silver-haired, maybe mid-fifties, enjoying someone's joke.

"He looks like he's got about twenty extra teeth in his mouth."

"Best behavior, Lewis."

They started across the room and the man spotted them. He met them halfway, his right hand already out ready to shake Wilder's, a fat cigar in his left.

"Don Sherrill," he said, gripping Wilder's hand. "You got a winner here, George." He put his cigar in his mouth and clapped Palmer on the back. "Thanks for bringing him over to meet me." He turned back to Wilder and blew a smoke ring. "Great speech, Lewis. You're a good salesman. You know, you almost had me going there for awhile."

Wilder smiled, wondering why Palmer had melted into the distance and what Sherrill was talking about.

"What I mean to say is, you've already got exhibits, right? It seems to me, then, you're pretty well set. You're the curator. What is that, custodian of the past? That's a nice phrase. Well, you just go on keeping the dust off the old stuff you've got there and that'll be fine. But I say look to the future. What's past is past."

Sherrill emphasized this profound bit of philosophy by waving his cigar around. Wilder retreated a half step to be out of the cigar's range and made an effort to listen without grinding his teeth.

"But you can't go on living in the past. Now look, I know something about what you might call the good old days and they weren't so good. Why, do you know what the infant mortality rate was a hundred and fifty years ago? Technology, high technology, that's where people ought to be putting their money these days. It's bad enough we're slipping behind the Japanese, now we've got to compete with the Chinese and who knows but the Mexicans or the Russians will be next. We've gotten soft. And we're letting kids get soft in the brain. Liberal Arts is a thing of the past. And I say let the dead bury the dead."

Wilder let his mind wander during the last part of Sherrill's harangue hoping that if he didn't listen he wouldn't have to restrain himself from pushing the cigar into the back of Sherrill's throat. He wasn't sure he could do that without attracting attention. He brought Sherrill back into focus as he heard him wind down.

"And what line of business are you in, Don?" he asked with no interest in hearing the answer.

"I own the Lincoln-Mercury dealership over in Stonewall. That's about seventy-five miles west of here. The wife and I've been coming up here for years, summers and hunting seasons, mostly. And I've never missed a Rotary meeting in all my years as a member so I came along here today. They let you do that, you know. Doesn't matter where you are in the world. Rotary is everywhere."

"Just like assholes," Wilder murmured. "Excuse me, will you Don," he added in more audible tones.

"Whoa, wait a minute, though, Lewis. What's this I hear about you having a second job?"

"I don't know, maybe you have me confused with someone else."

"Haha! It's a joke, don't you get it? Second job, the Fox, anonymous donations?"

"Oh, yeah. Excuse me," Wilder said and went looking for George Palmer.

CHAPTER 5

"So what did George say when you found him?" Marilyn asked, licking stray spaghetti sauce off her thumb.

"He quoted Shakespeare at me. 'Villain and he be many miles asunder.' "

"That's George. The sauce is ready, how about the noodles?"

Wilder took a fork and dredged a few strands of spaghetti out of the steaming pot. He deftly flicked them towards the ceiling where they stuck.

"Ready."

Marilyn looked at the ceiling and then at Wilder who was busy draining the pan.

"I can see this is going to be a real adventure in eating."

"It's called 'Wilder dining.' That's a neat trick, isn't it? An old army cook taught me that when I was working as a short-order cook. When they stick, they're done."

"How do you time soft-boiled eggs?"

"I never eat them."

"That's probably good."

He held her chair for her.

"Ooh, thank you. I didn't hold your chair for you at my place."

"This is a class joint."

"I can tell because it's got pasta stuck to the ceiling. You want me to light the candle so we get the full effect?"

Wilder leaned over her shoulder and lit it himself, brushing her cheek with his fingers as he straightened back up.

"Well, that was more fun," she said.

He brought a green salad and a crusty loaf of bread to the table then filled two plates from the pots on the stove. The smell of warm garlic bread mingled with the savory steam rising from the plates as he put them down in front of them. Marilyn watched as he poured a glass of wine and handed it across to her.

"So where did this jerk, Sherrill, come from?"

Wilder drained his own glass and inspected its emptiness in the candlelight, then looked at her.

"Stonewall."

"What?"

"Sherrill comes from Stonewall. It's a medium-sized town, just this side of Knox-

81

ville. It's where I grew up."

"Oh. So, it's not him that's bothering you so much as where he's from."

Wilder shrugged.

"Well, it had to happen sometime, Lewis. You can't live this close and not expect to run into someone from your hometown sooner or later. You didn't know each other, though?"

"No."

"I wonder if George knew you were both from Stonewall when he introduced you?"

"He knew. George has this idea that my taking the job here is just my subconscious' sneaky way of prodding me toward a reconciliation with Aunt Katherine. Don Sherrill was supposed to be a subtle hint that home is closer than I think."

"George knows about your aunt?"

"Yeah, well, George and I talk sometimes. I think I've become his mission in life."

"That's what happens when you're the first new parishioner in recent history. George is probably bored with the rest of those tired old Episcopalians. When were you a short-order cook?"

"You know, I think that might've been my true calling in life. When I was in college I even wrote a paper on the art of short-order cooking."

"What class was that for?"

"Anthropology of Art. It got rave reviews."

"I'm sure it did."

"It did. Believe me, I knew my stuff. I rose in the ranks from lowly dishwasher to the highest possible degree, Salami King. I could be trusted to run the kitchen, solo, on a Friday night and not confuse orders for seven hamburgers medium-rare, three well-done, two polish sausages, one with kraut, one with kraut and mustard, six orders of fries, two of onion rings, a fish sandwich, and a small salad, extra dressing on the side all at the same time. I kept those waitresses hopping. Why are you laughing, I'm perfectly serious."

"You're really much more entertaining than Uncle Paul."

"The difference being that I don't make things up."

"Right. Did you ever sweep any of those hopping waitresses off their feet?"

Wilder waved his fork as if dismissing entire ranks of wait staff. "They were mostly airheads."

"Is that a sexist remark?"

"Not at all."

Wilder made a pretense of eating as he amused Marilyn with tales of his salad days, but rearranged more of the food on his plate than he ate. As soon as Marilyn finished he cleared both plates from the table. He started water for coffee while she excused herself to find the bathroom.

When the coffee was ready he poured it into two stoneware mugs and carried them into the living room. He put them down on the low bench he used as a coffee table. He sat down, then jumped up again and went over to an antique walnut sideboard that held his stereo equipment. He slipped in a CD and turned it on. The sound of a guitar and then the plaintive voice of a fiddle filled the room and they wove a melody around the rippling harmony of a hammered dulcimer.

"I wish I could play like he does," said Marilyn from the doorway.

"Him who? Which one?"

"The guitarist. That's Hart Warren. He's from Nolichucky. Boy, did I have a crush on him when I was in high school."

"He doesn't live here anymore?"

"Not that boy. He shook the dust of Nolichucky years ago. Maybe he stops through from time to time, but I don't think he was ever satisfied with the tame life we've got to offer around here."

"So, do you play an instrument?"

"Not really. I taught myself to play a

recorder, but I haven't played it for years. I tried teaching myself the bagpipes when I was in college but my roommate wasn't thrilled when I practiced. Did you buy this from me?"

"Yeah. I got it in your shop the first time I went in."

"It's a good CD. I had a Music Appreciation professor who would have described it as having a great vitality that stirs the very roots of one's soul. He was a pompous ass, but he pretty much knew what he was talking about. I don't remember you coming in and buying it."

"That was before I became infamous and could still walk down Main Street incognito."

"That dumb stuff really bothers you, doesn't it? The rumors aren't that rife, are they?"

"They're sure as hell annoying. And it doesn't help that your uncle hunts me up and asks me where I was every time this guy makes a haul. He came into Willie's last time looking for me, for Christ's sake. Even that jerk Sherrill had heard them. He asked me about my second job."

"Ah, another piece of the puzzle falls into place. So which bothers you most, Sherrill being from Stonewall, his lamebrain joke, his attitude toward the museum, or Uncle Paul's congenital lack of tact?"

"You forgot Sherrill's cigar and all those big white teeth. Why are you still standing over there? Your coffee's over here." He wiggled his eyebrows at her.

"I'm appraising your living room so that I might gain an appreciation of the real Lewis Wilder," she said, screwing her mouth into a prim moue and putting her nose in the air.

"Probably not worth it." He sipped his coffee and watched her.

Marilyn turned her appraising look on him then slowly surveyed the room. The ceilings were low throughout the house due to its humble beginnings. This one was painted white. Bookcases hid two walls, their shelves full from top to bottom. The other walls were the color of faded butterscotch. A pen-and-ink sketch of two iguanas hung next to a watercolor of irises and lilacs, both over a battered wooden desk. The sofa and a worn, inviting armchair were upholstered in fading blue. The floors were bare wood.

She walked over to one of the bookcases and ran a finger along several shelves. Thurber, Twain, Wodehouse, Margaret Meade, *Help for the Small Museum, Introduc-*

tion to Archaeology, back issues of *Museum News.* She hesitated, her finger tapping the spine of a Bernie Rhodenbarr mystery by Lawrence Block, then moved on to Dick Francis, the Sharpe series by Cornwell, Dylan Thomas, Austen, *One Fish Two Fish.*

She sat down in the armchair in the corner between the two bookcases, letting her head nestle into the soft back cushion.

"You could spend a lot of time here, all alone, perfectly happy."

"Do you do palm reading, too?"

Marilyn ignored him and leaned forward. "What's in the aquarium?" She peered into the tank sitting on the coffee table. "They're newts."

"Yeah," he got up and went over to squat down next to her, peering in alongside her. "I'd rather have had a cat but newts don't have fleas."

"My brother used to keep newts. But they didn't look like these. He used to find them out in the woods."

"I found these out in a pet shop. They're South American fire-bellied newts. That one's Spot and this one's Tiger."

"You can tell them apart?"

"No, but they don't know that."

She put a hand on his neck and her fingers played idly with his hair. "So does your aunt have pretty, dark wavy hair, too?"

"She did until I moved in with her and then she went gray."

She pulled a bit of his hair and sat back in the chair again. "Well, this is nice, what you've got here. Do you feel like it's home? I mean, six months isn't all that long to feel settled in yet."

"I guess. These are my things. I live here."

"But does it feel like home?"

He stopped trying to catch the newts' attention and turned to look at her over his shoulder.

"You know, the other day when we were talking about my mother being glad to be home and I said something about how, after being gone awhile, it's always good to get back home? Just something I figured anyone could relate to, but later it occurred to me, maybe you don't know how that feels."

He shifted around so he was sitting on the bench next to the newts, facing her. She cocked her head at him.

"Prying?" she asked.

"No. This is home and every night I'm glad to come back to it. It would be nicer with a cat. Especially a cat that could pop open a beer can and remind me to bring home milk for breakfast. But it'll do. Satisfied?"

She smiled. "Whatever turns you on."

"Well, that's another story entirely. Why don't you come sit on the sofa and we can drink our coffee and entertain the newts?"

So she did.

The telephone rang. Wilder swore softly into the nape of her neck, which is where his lips had wandered after spending a little time with her earlobe.

"Sorry," he said, "no answering machine." The phone was on the wall just inside the kitchen door. He caught it on the third ring.

"Hello?"

There was silence then the caller hung up. Wilder looked at the receiver for a moment as though it ought to have been more responsible before hanging up himself.

"Wrong number?"

"Heavy breather without the breathing."

"Well, that's an improvement."

He put his left hand on the back of the sofa and vaulted over it, landing neatly on the seat next to her. She stared, then laughed.

"Do you practice that move?"

"I've only tried it once before, but that was without someone sitting on it and it tipped over backwards. You make a good counter balance."

"I have a reason for living." She'd kicked

off her shoes and turned sideways, propping her back on the arm and putting her feet in his lap. "Lewis?"

"Hmm?" He stopped studying her argyle socks and looked at her.

"Why haven't you talked to your aunt in all this time?"

He didn't answer right away. He rubbed her feet, then let them slip from his lap as he stood up. He crossed over to the sideboard and leaned back against it with his hands in his pockets.

"We had a disagreement."

"That must have been a hell of a disagreement."

"I've got a hell of a temper. So does she."

"I'll keep that in mind."

"Anyway," he said after a pause, "the longer it's been the easier it's gotten not to."

"You think so? I read body language, too. You're like a seesaw. You're either being charming and talking about this, that, and nothing in particular or you're clamming up and looking like you're strung out on something."

"How flattering."

"So what gives?"

"Not much."

They stared at each other across the small room.

"Well, maybe it hasn't been so hard for you not to talk to her. You don't make a habit of talking much to anybody, do you?"

"There seem to be plenty of people around town willing to do that for me."

"Don't take those dumb jokes seriously."

"Tell your uncle that."

"Well," Marilyn stirred herself, "let me help you with the dishes and then I'd better be getting home."

"I'll get the dishes."

She sat awhile longer but his thoughts had gone somewhere else. The CD ended. Coughing in a leave-taking sort of way, she stood to go.

"Sunday night we're having clam chowder. Would you like to come? Mom makes a mean clam chowder."

He shook himself, bringing things back into focus, and smiled. "Yeah? Thanks. I'll bring some of those neat little crackers."

She took her jacket from the peg where he'd hung it. Wilder took it from her and helped her into it, then turned her around, zipped it, and chucked her under the chin.

"Gee, thanks, Mom."

He pulled her to him and kissed her.

"There, is that better?"

"Mmm. Much. But don't worry, I won't spread it around town."

"Damn."

The phone rang again as Wilder headed for the kitchen with the coffee mugs.

CHAPTER 6

Wilder found space on the counter for the mugs and fumbled the phone to his ear.

"Hello?"

Again, silence and a hang up. He tsked at the phone and banged it down harder than he meant to.

As he started clearing up the kitchen, he wondered why he hadn't let Marilyn help with the dishes. Possibly, he thought, for the same reasons he liked her. She was bright, curious, and perceptive. He considered banging his head against the refrigerator to see if that would wake him up to what an idiot he was.

Instead he opened the refrigerator and took out a small jar. He unscrewed the lid and stirred the contents around with his finger. "Time to buy more," he said and rummaged in a drawer for pen and paper. Finding them, he wrote down "mealworms." After a second he added below that "oyster crackers" and "milk."

Whistling softly to himself, he carried the jar to the living room. He extracted two worms and dropped them into the aquarium.

"Supper time, boys."

He squatted down to see if the newts would come out for their evening meal. They did, sliding out from under a rock and swimming around. He watched them for awhile then bid them happy hunting and went to finish the dishes.

He let TV engross him the rest of the evening. The Crocodile Hunter had more immediate and interesting problems than his own. Some of his had big, white teeth, too. Nice to find something in common with a guy like that. But after the hunter had said good night, and reruns and the Weather Channel began to pall, he took himself off to bed.

Sometime after four A.M. he woke up. He wondered if Vernon was back prowling around. Or maybe howling around. He lay still, listening. Nothing out there. Maybe the wind. He punched his pillow up and rolled over, willing himself back to sleep. Maybe if Vernon were here and breathing in his face he'd drift off as though on the breath of angels. Maybe if Marilyn were here. Maybe he shouldn't be so quick next time to blow her off. Maybe he should just stop thinking about it. Thinking about anything. His arms and legs felt cooperative. They were ready to nod off. But his brain was up and at 'em. He told it to sod off.

Four A.M. was a dangerous time, a time when his mind had a mind of its own. It wandered places he wouldn't have taken it. A friend who suffered from migraines told him once that she would never keep a gun in the house because she knew she would use it. Wilder sometimes felt like that about four A.M. Three rules he had for restless nights: never take his mind seriously in the darkest hours, trust no decisions it made for him when it insisted on waking him up and haunting him, and no guns. Not that he'd ever really teetered that close.

Sometimes he tried distracting his brain by reading something ponderous enough to fell an elephant. The danger then was in waking his head up so completely that the rest of him might as well follow and then the next day was shot.

"No pun intended," he muttered as he felt for the switch to his reading light. The sudden brightness was hard on his eyes but he ignored their complaints and rummaged on the bedside table for the *Scientific American* he kept there for emergencies. He pulled it from under an overdue library book and flipped it open. A likely article met his eye, 'Phototropism in Temperate Zone Mollusk Production.' He sighed and settled back. And was awake enough to enjoy the article. Hell. He tossed the magazine aside and abandoned himself to morbid thoughts.

Maybe George was right. Of course, with George around, who needed an overactive subconscious, a midnight brain sneering recriminations at him for his lack of remorse? Remorse for what, he tried sneering back. Well, so he'd cut himself off from everything and everyone when he left. She would have been better off without him in the first place. So maybe he missed her. He was heartless, callous, and impenitent. Why was he even thinking these things? So he left. So what? People go. And none of it mattered. Or hadn't. Maybe she missed him. Some weekend he should bite the bullet and drive over. Not too soon, though. Maybe she wouldn't recognize him. Hah. Funny thing, but the Fox rumors never slunk around in the dark like this, disturbing his sleep. Only Aunt Katherine. Of course if she heard the rumors . . . Oh God, that was all he needed. And now the two, rumor and remorse, twined together, coiling around . . .

CHAPTER 7

"What time do you expect him?"

"If you turn around you'll find him breathing down your neck."

The man turned from the receptionist's desk to find Lewis Wilder standing behind him.

"Those are some quiet shoes you've got there, Mr. Wilder."

Wilder smiled. "What can I do for you?"

The man put his briefcase down and stuck out his hand.

"Chuck Nelson. I'm a travel writer and I'm in the area doing research, you know, gleaning nuggets of information on this part of Tennessee and North Carolina for a tourist publication. I'm hitting the high points, of course, but I'm also looking for the little off-the-beaten-track gems, the hidden treasures, and I've been told that Nolichucky, and your museum here in particular, shouldn't be missed. I was hoping maybe you could find some time to show me around and answer a few questions."

"Sounds like a great idea for an article, but I'm afraid you've picked a rough day for a visit. We've got a hundred and fifty seventh and eighth graders due to start arriving in about half an hour. They'll be coming through in shifts most of the day, and even with volunteers, with a load of kids like that we're all going to have our hands full."

"How about I just tag along behind?"

Wilder rubbed his ear and wondered with amusement if Chuck Nelson had ever been confined in a small space with group after group of large, loud, children.

"Well, sure, but what exactly are you interested in for your article? You might want to look around the museum on your own, first, while it's quiet before the kids get here, sort of orient yourself. The exhibits are straightforward enough. And Pam or I'll be happy to answer any questions."

"Actually what I'd like to do is get the human interest angle, if you know what I mean. The man and his museum, the personal story, that sort of thing. I'd really like to interview you."

Wilder looked at him skeptically. "Are people who read travel magazines interested in the people who work behind the scenes?"

"You'd be surprised."

Wilder tried to change his skepticism to surprise. He wasn't sure he'd succeeded.

"How about this?" Nelson asked. "Do the kids take a lunch break? I'd be happy to combine business with pleasure, take you to lunch. You know, they always say food tastes better when somebody else is paying for it."

"Depends on the restaurant," Wilder said.

"Hah! That's great. I can tell you're just what I'm looking for. What do you say? Twelve? Or is one better for you?"

"Mr. Nelson . . ."

"Chuck."

"Chuck. I appreciate the offer . . ."

"Oh, come on, no buts allowed. This'll be great, do you some good. Put the man and the museum on the map."

"Thanks, Chuck, it's a great idea. But this man and this museum have only been together about six months. You'd get a much better story if you focus on the people in town who got the museum going in the first place. They're as colorful a bunch as you'll ever meet. Now there's some great human interest."

"You're not local yourself?"

Wilder was beginning to get tired of Chuck Nelson. He tried smiling with all his teeth like Don Sherrill.

"Pam can give you the names of the museum's board of directors. Most of them work right here in town and I'm sure some of them will be exactly what you're looking for and happy to help you. Talk to Lillian Bowman. She'll blow your mind. And she lives just down the street. The chairman, Dr. Edward Ramsey, is out of town until next week but you ought to be able to find any of the others easily. But now, really, the hordes will be descending before you know it and I've got a few things to do before they get here." He stuck his hand out, gave Nelson's a firm, quick shake, turned abruptly, and headed up the stairs.

"Damn." Wilder hung his jacket behind the door. His rotten night was already threatening havoc for the day. Nothing like biting the hand that wanted to feed him.

He was pulling together museum activity sheets for the students when he heard someone coming up the stairs. He stuck his head out the door and saw Chuck Nelson. Nelson grinned when he saw him.

"We never decided. Twelve or one?"

Wilder shook his head at his dogged luck. Whether it was good luck pursuing him with a chance for him to redeem himself or just another hobgoblin getting in line and waiting for him to screw up, he wasn't sure. "Make it twelve-thirty."

"Great. I'll meet you back here. Say, you know, you've got a great gal down there." He waved the list Pam had given him. "She says you're a nice guy. This'll be great."

Wilder watched him bounce back down the stairs. "Great," he said when Nelson was gone. "Just great."

"Great," Pam said. "That was Charlotte. She can't make it." She was hanging up the phone when Wilder came back down with his stacks of activity sheets.

"Who's Charlotte?" he asked.

"Volunteer," Pam said with an exaggerated sigh.

"Oh, right. There were two volunteers scheduled, though."

"Yes, and Shirley is already here. But we've got five groups of thirty coming, each staying an hour. Rough night? You look tired."

"Yeah, thanks for noticing."

"Anytime. So, we'll definitely need your help with the kiddos now that Charlotte isn't coming." She watched him straightening the stacks of papers. "Through lunch. Sorry."

Wilder looked at her. She didn't look sorry. He wasn't either. He grinned. "Remind me to cry later."

The first group of seventh graders trooped in at nine-thirty, thirty children, variously enthusiastic, irrepressible, bored out of their skulls, and sheep-like. Wilder and Shirley, the volunteer, spent the morning walking around answering questions and keeping an eye on things. Not all the exhibits were in cases, and just as glass attracted fingers and nose prints, some of the freestanding artifacts were magnets for curious hands.

The activity sheets Wilder gave the students were designed to lead them on a self-guided exploration of the exhibits. Except for the occasional pencil-fencing duel, the morning groups obligingly followed their printed instructions around the museum. As with any group, there were some who had trouble reading, some who wouldn't, and a few who inhaled the information and wanted more.

At eleven-thirty the eighth grade groups started arriving. Being a whole year older, they saw themselves as too sophisticated to enjoy touring a museum. As a result they ended up being far less sophisticated than the seventh graders and generally less cooperative. And the eighth grade teacher apparently saw the field trip as her afternoon off.

Shortly after noon Shirley and Wilder crossed paths outside the Victorian parlor. Shirley was explaining to a hormone-laden duo that the courting couch was for looking, not test-driving.

"Shirley, I've nominated you for honorary zookeeper. How are you holding up?"

"I'll get Pam to spell me when she's finished eating. Grab a quick bite and a bit of a sit. It'll get worse as the afternoon goes on. We might be surprised but I doubt it. Downhill from here, I'd say, bless their tiny little hearts. But don't worry, this doesn't phase me. I used to be a lunchroom monitor."

"Have you thought about taking up alligator wrestling?"

"Pshaw. I've known some of these little darlin's since they were in elementary school. And their parents. Don't worry, Lewis, our nerves might be in tatters by the time they've all come and gone, but the museum will still be in one piece."

She patted him on the back and stalked off. If she were willing to exaggerate she could claim to be five feet tall and a strapping one hundred pounds. Wilder watched her go and decided she was his new role model.

They were saying goodbye to one group, keeping some of its number from tripping members of the next group on their way in, when Chuck Nelson reappeared. He beamed and mingled with the students at the back of the pack. Wilder tried to combine a warm smile with a steel eye as he welcomed them and explained museum etiquette. Shirley circulated with their activity sheets and a ready snarl. Then Wilder held his breath for a second and turned them loose on the museum.

"Hey, Lewis, great," Nelson said, making his way through the now milling students. They seemed to be having trouble locating the exhibits until Shirley pointed a few in the right direction and prodded several others.

"Very neatly done. So, how does Willie's sound? I understand you like to eat there."

Wilder had been distracted by a boy spitting his gum into the apple butter kettle, but turned around at hearing this bit of newsgathering. Nelson was grinning at him.

"Well, I'd avoid the chili if I were you."

"Hah!"

"Look, Chuck, I'm going to have to duck out on you. I'm sorry, but we've ended up shorthanded and there's no way I can get away."

"So what time will the tours be over?"

"You're persistent."

"I always get my interview."

Wilder ran his hand through his hair and looked around. Three students were sitting splay-legged on the floor in front of the pioneer-life exhibit talking on cell phones. He sighed.

"They'll be gone by three-thirty."

"Great, tell you what I'll do. I'll take a walk, see who else I can talk to, take a few pictures, and you know, soak up some of the small-town atmosphere. Catch you later." He cocked his finger at Wilder and made a sound like a popgun.

Wilder, Shirley, and Pam were out on the porch, in various stages of collapse, after returning the last of the students to a teacher who seemed reluctant to reclaim them.

"Here's your pal," Pam said, nudging Wilder.

Wilder had closed his eyes, hoping his head would stop pounding or maybe just explode quietly and leave him alone. He opened them again to see Chuck Nelson bounding up the steps.

"So, you want to grab a cup of coffee at the café? Or we could go over to your place. I walked past it earlier. Looks great."

"No," said Wilder. "Let's just go up to my office and get this over with." He turned and went into the museum without waiting to see if this suited Nelson. Halfway up the stairs, with Nelson tromping up behind him in time to the throbbing in his head, he excused himself and went back down to find Shirley and Pam.

"Hey, you two, thanks for your unfailing unflappability. I couldn't do it without you." He stood there for a second. "Either of you got an aspirin?"

Pam went to the reception desk and produced an economy-size bottle of painkillers and doled out two for each of them. Shirley brought three glasses of water.

"Thank you. Oh, god, he's still up there, isn't he." He climbed the stairs again and when he reached his office, he found Nelson sitting at his desk, either the same grin or another just as irritating plastered to his face. Wilder hcsitated at the door, trying to think what was wrong, other than Nelson sitting in his chair.

"How did you get in?" he asked.

"Turn knob, open door," Nelson said. "Simple."

"It wasn't locked?"

Nelson shook his head.

"But the door was at least closed, right?" Well, hell. All those kids all day long and the office unlocked. He glanced around and saw nothing obviously amiss, sighed, scooped a stack of papers off the chair opposite his desk, and dropped into it.

"You're not an easy guy to pin down." Nelson swiveled from side to side in Wilder's chair, taking in the small room.

Wilder made an effort to be polite. "Not so tough most days. You caught me on a bad one is all. If I'd known you were coming . . ." He left it at that with a tired lift of one shoulder. "Did you talk to Lillian Bowman?"

Nelson pulled a notebook from a jacket pocket and flipped through it. "Sure did and you were right, well worth talking to. She's a character, sure enough. She says, let me see." He peered at his notes, the tip of his tongue between his lips. "Yeah, she thinks you're doing a great job here and that you're in your element." He chuckled and looked across at Wilder. "But she thinks your hair is sometimes on the unruly side."

Wilder stared at him. "Well, that's nice. Lillian's nothing if not precise." He was working hard at not showing his impatience, either by snapping at Nelson or, now, by running his hand through his hair. "But did you get the kind of information you were looking for about the museum?"

"Oh, yes, I sure did. I like your office, by the way. It's compact. Like you. So how'd you get started in the museum business?"

Wilder wondered if his mouth was hanging open. He couldn't remember ever being interviewed by a travel writer, or any writer for that matter, but he'd never imagined it being like this. He was still trying to frame an answer that didn't include the words "get the hell out of my unruly hair" when he heard Jim Honeycutt coming up the stairs singing "Louie Louie." It was his theme song for Wilder.

"Hey, Lewie. Oh, I'm sorry, am I interrupting?" He nodded a brief acknowledgment to Nelson. "Hi, how ya doing? Just be a minute, here. Lewie, about the stage for the Pickers' Picnic. You'll help set it up, won't you, week from today? That would be, uh, Friday."

"Sure, Jim. Let me know what time or come get me, either way." Honeycutt nodded again and propped himself in the doorway, an expectant smile hovering between Wilder and Nelson. Wilder sighed. "Chuck, this is Jim Honeycutt. He does maintenance here. Jim, Chuck Nelson. He's writing an article for a travel magazine."

"Hey, no kidding. How ya doing? Say, Lewie, you got a date with that foxxxxy lady, Marilyn, for the picnic?"

Wilder felt like burying his head in his hands. He tried smiling instead. It hurt. "Maybe."

"Say, speaking of foxy," said Nelson, "I heard a story in town today about this string of burglaries by some guy who always leaves a receipt for what he's taken and he signs it 'the Fox.' But this is the best part, you'll love this, Lewis, the story goes that you're fencing the stuff for him. Hah! Is that great or what?"

Wilder wondered if they could hear him grinding his teeth.

"Yeah, yeah," Honeycutt, nodding, eagerly jumped in. "That's a new one on me, but I'll tell ya, I've heard wilder. Get it? Wilder. Ain't that a hoot? You know what the latest one I heard though, is, see, it's a whole gang of these guys and Lewie here is the ringleader. What a hoot! I mean, what a hoot! But the best part is that Lewie here just rolls with it all. He's a good old boy." He clouted Wilder on the shoulder. "See ya, Lewie."

Wilder rubbed his shoulder and looked at Nelson, still in his chair, still grinning.

"What?"

"So, people call you Lewie?"

"No."

Nelson left soon afterwards, telling Wilder he thought the whole day had been great. The interviews were great. The article would be great. Wilder said great and kept himself from slamming the door. He didn't know how he could be both numb and exhausted at the same time but he was. He felt as though he'd been playing tug-of-war with Nelson, using his last unfrayed nerve for the rope. At least he hadn't hanged himself with it.

He decided to call Marilyn. A dose of gentle kindness and maybe a little something else might do more wonders than a beer and more aspirin.

"Oh, Lewis," Marilyn's mother answered the phone. "She's gone out for the evening. Would you like her to call?"

"No, that's okay, it's not important. Tell her I'll call back." He hoped beer and aspirin did the trick.

Time to call it quits for the day. For the week. He grabbed his jacket, clattered down the stairs and asked Pam if she minded locking up. Heading across the back lawn he remembered he still needed to get milk and a few other edible things and detoured toward Main Street.

It was a nice evening and people were out walking. Wilder greeted a few he knew and nodded at others. At Mrs. Daniels' market he took a hand basket around and couldn't work up enthusiasm for anything more than a box of Grape-Nuts, the milk, a bunch of bananas, and a couple of cans of soup.

"That'll be ten dollars and fifty-three cents, Lewis."

Wilder felt for his wallet. He didn't have it with him.

"What's the matter, hon, leave your bill-fold behind?"

"Huh?" He madly patted all his pockets. "No. I had it." Damn. The unlocked office door. One of the kids must have rifled his jacket pockets.

"Hey, c'mon. You're holding up the line."

"Hon?"

"Sorry, Mrs. Daniels. I'll put it all back."

"No, that's all right. You just don't worry. You're good for it. You pay me next time you're in."

"Hey, Wilder, why don't you just steal it?"

He didn't turn around to see who it was. He picked up the bag of groceries, thanked Mrs. Daniels again and left. Maybe he'd just stay in bed all weekend. Or under it.

As he was passing the Western Auto, feeling less like greeting anyone or nodding, a red Bronco pulled into the curb. The driver honked an obnoxious tattoo. Wilder couldn't resist turning and glaring. A deer carcass was tied across the top of the Bronco.

The driver honked again and Wilder figured it was some drunken hunter either celebrating his superiority over the poor dead creature on his roof or trying to flag down medical aid because he'd shot himself in the foot. He was cheering up with the latter thought when the driver jumped out and hailed him.

"Hey, Lewis!" It was Don Sherrill.

Wilder felt a small zipping sensation run around his brain and down his spine as his last nerve began to unravel, but he gave his head a shake and made an effort to remain civil. "Don."

"What do you think of my baby up there, huh?"

"It's dead."

"Well of course it's dead. I shot it. Ain't it a beauty?"

Wilder didn't answer.

"Aw, now don't tell me you're one of those bleeding heart animal rights whosamabobs. Son, you've got to loosen up. You're too danged concerned about everything. Don't you know about everything in moderation for godssake? Now look, we're having a party tonight, celebrating the opening of bow season, and I saw you walking along there looking like you'd just buried your mother and so I stopped to pick you up and bring you along to have some fun. What do you say? Come on, hop in."

"No. Thanks anyway."

"Now, don't hand me that. Bows and arrows oughta be right up your alley, you're into all that old crap. Come on, I won't take no for an answer. Do yourself a favor."

"No, really, but thanks."

"What's the problem? We've got booze, eats, women. What more could you want? Hop in. It'll be great."

Wilder saw someone waving at him from the Bronco. He squinted his eyes to see beyond the reflections on the windshield and saw the woman, call-me-Barb-and-let-me-pinch-your-ass-while-we-dance, grinning in the front passenger seat. He looked back at Sherrill. "Are you drunk?" he asked.

"What? Hell no."

"Then you must be stupid. Listen, Sherrill, I don't want to go to your party. I don't want to celebrate killing and maiming season. I wouldn't join you and Big Bad Barb on a church picnic . . ."

"Now just a doggone minute . . ."

"You think I'm too concerned, well I think you're an asshole. If you were drunk there might be some excuse. As it is you can just go take a flying . . ."

"Well aren't you something. Who the hell do you think you are? I'll tell you what you are, you're an over-educated, intellectual . . ." he sputtered, pop-eyed. "Why, I oughta . . ."

Wilder was enjoying himself. Sherrill might have been, too, but as he was building up steam, looking as though he might blow a gasket, Wilder saw him hesitate and look around. He followed Sherrill's gaze. Nolichucky had its share of drunken brawls and public misunderstandings, but usually not in front of the Western Auto at five-thirty-five on a mellow Friday evening. People at the other end of the block were gaping.

Sherrill, the veins in his neck still bulging, gathered the shreds of his dignity and slipped back into his truck. Wilder closed his eyes and massaged his aching forehead. Then he heard a low chuckle and looked over his shoulder. Paul Glaser was leaning against the front window of the Western Auto.

"You going to slap the handcuffs on, Paul?"

"No, son. I'm only after the drunks tonight. The disorderlies can go on home.
With their wives."

Wilder felt sick. "His wife?" Glaser nodded, smiling. Wilder looked at the ground
for a minute shaking his head. Then he said
good night to Glaser and headed for the alley midway down the block, a handy escape
route from the still-enthralled audience up
and down the sidewalk. At the opening to
the alley he found Chuck Nelson, eyes alight
from drinking in the spectacle.

"Soaking up the wholesome small-town
atmosphere?" Wilder asked, brushing past
him.

"Hey, Wilder, I never got a picture. Mind
if I get one now?" Nelson called, holding up
his camera.

"Christ," Wilder muttered and kept walking.

CHAPTER 8

Wilder slept late the next morning. After he woke he lay in bed staring at the ceiling. It went through his mind that he might feel purged after his exchange with Sherrill, psychologically or mentally or something. But he only felt deflated and a fool. He peeled himself out of bed around ten-thirty when the phone rang. No one was there. He slammed the phone down and got dressed.

The ordinariness of housework might have a soothing effect on someone under stress. It didn't on Wilder. He put clean sheets on the bed and changed the water in the newt tank and felt just as low. He drew the line at dusting but decided to throw a load of laundry in the washer. As he was going through pockets and tossing clothes in the machine he remembered his missing wallet. Damn, he should have reported it to Paul last night when he saw him. And he should have called the credit card company. Hell. He dumped the rest of the load in, started the machine, and went to call Glaser's office.

The phone rang again before he could pick it up. Another silent one. Swearing, he disconnected and dialed.

"Sheriff's Department," a woman's voice answered.

"Is Paul Glaser in?" Wilder asked.

"No, sir. Can another officer be of assistance?"

"Yeah, well, yes. Is it worth reporting a stolen wallet?"

"It's worth reporting, sir. That doesn't mean you'll have much luck getting it back." She sounded kind but realistic.

"Swell. What do I need to do, come in and sign something or can you just do it over the phone?"

"Oh, say, wait a sec, is this Mr. Wilder? Lewis Wilder?"

"Yeah," Wilder said, wondering how suspicious or paranoid he sounded.

"Your wallet was turned in. Sheriff Glaser has it, sir."

"Why?"

There was a pause on the other end. "Well, sir," the woman said then, confirming by her tone of voice that he sounded like a paranoid crank, "I expect he's planning to return it to you."

Wilder heard a rap on his door. He stuck his head around the corner to see who it was. Glaser was framed in the door window waving his wallet like a small trophy. "Sorry, thanks a lot," he told the patient woman and hung up.

He opened the door and stepped aside to let Glaser in, his hand out to take the wallet. "Thanks, Paul. Who turned it in?"

"How long's it been missing?" Glaser hung on to the wallet and settled himself on the sofa.

Wilder stood looking at him, itching to snatch the wallet from his fat fingers and push him back out the door. Glaser returned his look from under lazy eyelids and stretched his legs out, laced his hands behind his head, still with the wallet, and smiled. He looked comfortable enough to become a permanent fixture. Wilder gave up and slumped in the chair opposite him.

"Sometime yesterday. It was in my jacket in the office. I forgot to lock the door. We had about a million junior high kids through. I figure one of them helped himself."

"You think? Whyn't you report it?"

"I only missed it last night and I had other

things on my mind."

"Oh, yeah, I reckon."

"Besides, I just did. I was on the phone to your office when you showed up." He held his hand out again. "May I have it, now?"

"Sure. Why don't you check and make sure nothing's missing."

Wilder took it and wondered why Glaser's eyes on him as he flipped through it annoyed him so much. Or made him uneasy. He tried to remember how much cash he'd had, but it looked about right. Wonder of wonders, the credit cards were there. License, insurance card, library card, stray addresses, and accumulated scraps that might or might not be important if he ever bothered to look at them. "Looks like it's all here. Too bad they didn't clean half the crap out of it for me," he said, tucking it in his back pocket, thinking he probably ought to be smiling. He didn't bother to say that the contents had been sifted through. Glaser had probably shuffled through it himself.

"You don't look entirely satisfied."

Wilder sat back and made himself smile. "Sorry, rough night. Thanks for bringing it over. So who did turn it in? Where'd they find it?"

"Garbled story," Glaser said.

Wilder waited then prompted, "Yeah?"

120

"Just one more anonymous crime, Lewis."

Wilder looked at Glaser. "Speaking of anonymous, I've been getting anonymous phone calls."

"Call the phone company."

"And mail," he added, remembering the toy fox.

"Besides the money?"

"This was addressed to me, not the museum."

"Any of these, either the phone calls or the mail, threatening?"

"No."

"Is it blackmail?"

"Oh, ha ha. No, forget it, Paul. I'm sure it's just some jerk's idea of a joke."

Glaser held up his hands as though warding off Wilder's jab. "No need to get personal, Lewis." He let his hands fall into his lap again. "Seriously, though, let me know if it continues or if it gets to be anything more than annoying." Then he put his right hand over his heart and an earnest look on his face. "But in the meantime, think of it as just one more interesting detail in your murky life's story."

"Oh, for Christ's sake, Paul."

Glaser hauled himself to his feet, chuckling, and let himself out.

Wilder spent the rest of the day snubbing

the bright sunshine creeping into his living room. He slouched low in his overstuffed chair and tried to read.

Sometime late in the afternoon Dr. Ramsey called from Chicago. Afterwards Wilder couldn't concentrate at all and he left his shirts sitting in the dryer, getting wrinkled.

Sunday, after three more silent calls he unplugged his phone. He left the house early in the evening and didn't take his oyster crackers to the Wootens' for clam chowder as planned. Instead, he got in his car and drove out of town on the old stage road.

Driving the eccentric mountain roads of Upper East Tennessee could be breathtaking. In the springtime, around every corner and over every rise, drifts of blooming redbuds and wild dogwoods met the eye. Summer drenched the countryside in shades of green and the autumn lit flaming touches of red and orange. But after dark on any moonless night, unfamiliar roads were breathtaking in a different way.

Wilder had never driven the road he was on before. The curves and sudden hills hid his view ahead so that around every bend and at each crest he held his breath as the car plunged into apparent nothingness. The shoulders were either unmarked or non-existent. The road's edges, when not dark with trees, were dense with honeysuckle vines smothering fencerows.

A crow leaving Nolichucky would have flown fifteen straight miles and reached the same spot it took Wilder thirty-two tortuous ones to travel. But he found the mailbox and the house he was looking for. He drove past it several hundred yards to a farm lane where he pulled in and left his car behind a row of Swiss bales. He returned on foot.

After watching from the shadow of an oak, he circled around to the back of the house and let himself in.

CHAPTER 9

Monday morning Wilder let himself into the museum with the barest of greetings for Marcie and glad for her wise mother's sense of when to ask questions and when to postpone them.

Marilyn called him there mid-morning.

"It's too bad you didn't make it last night. I might have been able to supply you with an alibi."

"What?"

"An alibi for the Fox."

"I forgot the clam chowder, didn't I. Marilyn, I'm sorry."

"He broke into a house about thirty miles from here. Belongs to a preacher. The whole family was at a revival at their church when it happened. You know who they are, the ones who have the daughter who's been sick and they took her to Nashville, but now they won't let the doctors do anything because it's all in God's hands or something. By the way, where were you?"

"I was working."

"Not at home."

"No."

"There were no lights on at the museum."

He didn't say anything.

"All right. It's none of my business. But it was good chowder and it could have used those crackers."

"I'm a rat. I am sorry."

"Are you all right?"

"Probably. I suppose you heard about the run-in I had with Don Sherrill on Main Street Friday night?"

"Talk of the town. It was a little out of character, wasn't it?"

"It might raise a few eyebrows in the ladies auxiliary knitting circle."

"Mild Lewis Wilder goes wild on Main Street."

"Can you come over tonight? I don't deserve it, but I'd like to see you."

"I don't know if I ought to be seen with you. I have my reputation to consider."

"There is that."

"I'll bring the leftover chowder."

"Thanks."

That afternoon Wilder was on his hands and knees inside one of the large freestanding exhibit cases, cleaning the inside of the glass.

"You look good in there."

The voice came from behind him and it was distorted through the glass. But he recognized it. Don Sherrill walked around to the side of the case, flashing his white teeth, waving.

"Lewis, I've come to bury the hatchet. I'd like to apologize and to say that I'm not always such a, well, you said it best, such an asshole. Come on out and I'll buy you a drink. Haha! Just kidding."

Wilder crawled out of the case and stood up, wiping his hands on his cleaning rag. He was having trouble dredging up any common courtesy for Sherrill.

"What can I do for you?" he asked, hoping the answer might be to show him the quickest way out.

"I've got something for you. Look, have you got an office or something somewhere? I don't think we'd both fit in that case."

Wilder waited a beat before answering.

"Sure." He tossed the cloth into the case and led the way upstairs.

"This is quite a place you got here," Sherrill said, staring around as he followed. "I guess you know I don't go in much for museums myself, but I can tell when I see a class operation. And I know a thing or two about antiques, for all I don't give a hoot for them.

"I'm a salesman, see, and a good one. I make it a point to know what other interests my potential customers might have. People who buy Lincolns can afford antiques. They might also be into UT football or hunting or Cajun cooking. I keep up on all sorts of things so I can make them feel comfortable, like they're dealing with a friend, someone who takes an interest in them as people, not just a quick sale. It works."

"How do you know what your customers are interested in?" asked Wilder, not feeling interested himself. He unlocked the office door, took a chamber pot off the extra chair and offered the chair to Sherrill.

"By listening and being sensitive. Ha! I can tell by the look on your face that you don't believe it. But it's true. And to be honest with you, that's why I'm here today. Now, you see, I know that I've been out of line. Your talk to the Rotary club last week was better than a lot I've heard. And I was out of line to mount my hobbyhorse like that. And you were right, I was drunk Friday night and, truly, I'm sorry.

"See, I know what it's like to move into a small town and be treated like a damn foreigner. It happened to me when I moved

127

to Stonewall. My wife is from Stonewall and I'm not. I never will be. I'm sensitive to that. And I can see that you might be having the same sort of problems here. And I'm ashamed if I've added to them."

Wilder studied Sherrill's face and was surprised to see something that might be shame there. It kept the teeth in check, anyway. He was even more surprised when he realized he was feeling something like empathy for Sherrill. He shrugged one shoulder and gave him half a smile.

"You are a good salesman. Consider your apology sold."

Sherrill relaxed in his chair. "I've got something you might like to have for the museum." From one of the large cargo pockets of his jacket he pulled a cloth-wrapped bundle. He handed it across the desk to Wilder. "See what you think of that."

Wilder weighed it in his hand. Though small, whatever was inside was heavy and solid. He looked at Sherrill but couldn't read anything there now. Feeling a familiar tingle of excitement, he put the package in the middle of his desk and folded back the wrapping.

A low whistle escaped him when the object lay exposed before them. It was a pipe, carved from green stone in the shape of a bird, six or seven inches long, smooth and cool to the touch. It looked to be Hopewell. It was exquisite. He looked at Sherrill again.

"Don't ask me where it came from," Sherrill said spreading his hands.

Wilder paused, trying to interpret the gesture and the words. That was the first question he would have asked and if Sherrill didn't want to answer that one, he thought he'd better tread carefully with the next one.

"Don't ask because you don't know?"

Sherrill just stared at him. Next question.

"Or is this a little like don't ask, don't tell?"

"Does it make a difference?"

"Yes."

"Why?"

Wilder took a deep breath and started in on what he hoped wasn't a slippery slope. "The museum has a general policy to accept only those things which have a bearing on the history of this area. For instance we wouldn't accept a Plains Indian war bonnet. But something like this pipe is probably appropriate."

"So what's the problem?"

"No problem, so far. If you know where the pipe came from, then that information adds something to its historical value. And," Wilder turned the green pipe over in his hands then looked up at Sherrill, "well, if you know, but won't tell me where it came from, it makes me wonder about ethical questions, if you know what I mean." He wondered if Sherrill did know what he meant, whether he was aware of the illegality of certain ways of collecting Indian artifacts. Whether he would explode at the implication of what he'd just said.

Sherrill's eyebrows drew together and he pursed his lips. Wilder imagined he could see and hear the wheels grinding in his head. Then, as though galvanized by whatever decision his brain had churned out, Sherrill stood up.

"I'll get the information for you. Will that do?"

Relief at this mild and reasonable reaction swept Wilder back in his chair. "Sure." He swaddled the pipe in its wrappings and held it out to Sherrill.

"No, you keep it here, Lewis. I'll get you the info. But say, will I get some kind of a receipt or something?"

"How about a loan agreement until you get whatever information you can? Then we'll do it up right with a donation form." Wilder unwrapped the pipe again and couldn't help stroking it. "You do know this is an exceptional piece, don't you? Are you sure you want to part with it?"

"Damn right I do. I'm on my way back to Stonewall tonight but I'll be coming back up on the weekend for the Pickers' Picnic. You ever been to one of them? They're better than a Rotary meeting any day. I'll bring the information with me then."

Wilder fished two copies of the loan form from one of his desk drawers and started filling in the blanks. He stopped and looked up at Sherrill. "I owe you an apology, too, Don."

"Bury the hatchet, Lewis, and pass the peace pipe. A man can't afford to have enemies in this world." He nodded toward the pipe on the desk. "I'm glad you like it."

Wilder handed him the forms to sign. "Admit it, Don, it's better than a dead deer."

Sherrill barked a laugh and pocketed one of the signed forms. He waved as he left the office, calling back, "To each his own, Lewis."

Wilder listened to Sherrill's footsteps descending the stairs. Then he rewrapped the bird pipe and locked it in the desk drawer. Sherrill didn't strike him as a pothunter. He couldn't picture him tiptoeing around, stalking legitimate archaeologists and plundering their sites. He didn't see Sherrill taking enough hands-on interest to hunt up sites on his own, either. Still, there was something not straightforward about the pleasant green pipe. He patted the keys in his pocket, and whistling birdcalls, he went back to polishing the glass case.

CHAPTER 10

Something Wilder liked about Nolichucky was its general lack of pretense. Several blocks beyond the museum, in the opposite direction from Main Street and across the four-lane, sat an unprepossessing package liquor store with a drive-up window. The owner handed out lollipops to children shopping there with their parents.

Wilder made a side trip there on his way home Monday night and bought a six-pack of Killian's Irish Red Ale. He eyed the Guinness but decided it would probably overpower clam chowder.

The evening was warmer than usual for early October. When he got home he put the beer in the refrigerator and took himself back out to the front steps to wait for Marilyn. He sat on the second step from the top, propping his elbows behind him on the porch. It was a beautiful evening and reminded him of other porch steps and other seasons. His favorite had been old green steps, crowded in spring with heavy lilacs and humming bees.

He spotted Marilyn as she came around the side of the museum. She hadn't seen him yet and kicked her way through the drifts of needles under a stand of pines. The setting sun caught her hair, lending it a hint of red. When she looked up and saw him she waved.

"What's that funny little smile for?" she called as she got closer. "What are you thinking about?"

"How nice it is to just watch something gentle walking toward you and not shoot it."

"Oh." She stopped short.

"And about how surprising people can be."

"Maybe I should just leave the chowder," she said, reaching forward to put the bag she'd been carrying on the steps at his feet.

Wilder caught her hand in his.

"No. That's the limit of my idiocy for the day. Stay. Please."

Marilyn drew herself up. "I think that will have to depend, then," she said, "on whether or not you have the oyster crackers."

The crackers were crisp and the Killian's

was cold, perfect complements to the leftover chowder.

"After supper," Wilder started to say around a mouthful. He washed it down with a swallow of Killian's. "This is good chowder, by the way. It's right up there with some I had Friday, November 21, 1997, and that was killer chowder." He ate another spoonful. "Would you like to take a walk?"

"After supper, would I like to take a walk?"

"Yeah."

"Do you keep track of every bowl of clam chowder you eat?"

"I try. Sort of the way some people keep track of birds. Do you want to take a walk?"

"Sure."

"I'd like to see Nolichucky through your eyes."

"To get a saner perspective? Then I'd like to show you."

The telephone rang. Wilder looked over his shoulder at it and muttered something under his breath. He turned back to Marilyn. "How much do you want to bet that either no one answers or it's a wrong number?"

"Do you get a lot of those?"

"A few." He dropped his napkin on the table and went to answer it. "Hello," he snarled. It was George Palmer. "Oh,

George, sorry," he started to apologize for his initial greeting.

Palmer cut him off, the usual warmth missing from his voice. "I want to talk to you."

Wilder kicked himself for letting the phone dictate his moods. He tried again to apologize and explain. Palmer didn't respond. "Well, look, George," he said, "there's someone here now. Can I call you back?"

"No. I mean I want to see you and talk to you. Stop by tomorrow morning before you go to the museum."

Wilder hesitated before answering. "Yeah, sure."

Palmer cleared his throat.

"Anything else?"

"No. See you in the morning." He hung up before Wilder could say goodbye. Wilder blinked, then hung up on his end.

"Something wrong?" Marilyn asked, catching the unsettled look he thought he'd cleared from his face before turning around.

"No." He told himself he wasn't lying to her. That he didn't know that anything was wrong. That George was feeling cranky. But he didn't sit back down at the table, either.

"How about that walk?"

"You haven't finished yet."

"I'll reheat it later."

Marilyn raised her eyebrows and picked up her sweater. Wilder covered his bowl with a saucer and put it in the refrigerator. He flicked off the light, grabbed his own sweater off the sofa in the living room, and locked the front door behind them.

Stars shone through wisps of high-flown clouds. Smoke rose from one or two chimneys. The warmth of the Indian summer day had faded with the sunlight. They walked through the museum grounds, stopping beside an enormous tree stump to shiver into their sweaters.

"You're seesawing again," Marilyn said. She leaned against the stump and looked across the lawn.

"Hmm?" Wilder was watching a curl of her hair and feeling jealous as it smugly caressed her cheek by her right ear.

"This morning you were down, over supper you were up, after that phone call you went down again."

"Oh."

They both sighed, at which they both laughed, and then sighed again.

"Do you want to talk about your argument with Don Sherrill?"

"No." They were quiet again. Then Wilder prompted, "Take me on a tour of your childhood."

"Oh, no, now I'm going to feel self-conscious. What do you want, should I do it like a tour bus guide? Or would you rather have 'This is Your Life, Marilyn Wooten'?"

"How about starting with 'once upon a time,' that's my favorite beginning."

"Oh, yeah, right. You'll probably fall asleep. Okay. Once upon a time this tree," she turned around and spread her hands on the weathered surface of the stump, "stood straight and tall. God, I haven't thought about this tree in years. My brothers and I were always trying to climb it." She thought for a minute then shook her head. "We never got very far. Sometimes we ate picnics out here.

"I remember one summer when my friend Maureen was convinced this tree, why this one, I don't remember, but she insisted she knew that it was planted by pirates to mark the spot where they'd buried some of their booty. She dug. We dug. We finally gave up but she kept digging, it seemed like all summer. She was sure if she dug deep enough she could push it over and find the treasure."

"And did she?"

"That never happens in real life, Lewis." She ran her fingers over the weathered rings. "I cried the day they cut it down."

"Part of you went with it."

She looked at him out of the corner of her eye. "Some people don't understand that kind of thing. But at least I have my memories."

He mimicked her sideways look. "Memories are nice. So what'd they do with it? Must've made a hell of a lot of firewood."

"Actually that was cool. You'll never guess. Uncle Paul took a section of the trunk and made a cupboard out of it. He cut it in half lengthwise, and hollowed out the rotten middle part, then hinged it back together so it could open and shut, and he put shelves in it. He had it in a corner of his office for a long time. I guess it's still there. He used it as a liquor cabinet."

"In the Sheriff's Department?"

"Yeah, and before that. When he was an insurance investigator."

"Oh. That explains it."

"Explains what?"

"Nothing really. I guess he's just always been a professional nosy guy."

They started walking again, Wilder trying to picture Paul Glaser making a wet bar out of a diseased tree trunk. The man had talents he hadn't suspected.

"What are your brothers' names?"

"Keith and Paul."

"Older or younger?"

"One of each. Tit for tat?"

"What?"

"Have you got brothers or sisters?"

"No. Did you always live in the house you're in now?"

"We'd have driven Mom and Dad crazy in that little place. No, she and I moved in there after Dad died and Paul and Keith were off on their own. We grew up in the house Lillian Bowman lives in now. That's why we played around the museum and your place so much. It was empty then, no one was living there. We liked to think it was haunted."

"Did you ever see a ghost?"

"We were too chicken to look for one. What's that?" Marilyn stood still and listened.

"What's what?" Wilder looked up and down the sidewalk they'd come to.

"I heard a skittering sound behind us. Like claws, like an animal running along, but there's nothing there."

"Probably a rabid ghost squirrel," Wilder said. "Oh, no, geez, look."

A pop-eyed dog dashed out of the hedge next to the sidewalk, stretched to its fullest height and lunged at Wilder's ankle. They stood rooted in amazement as the minuscule animal struggled with his pant leg. Then the needle-like teeth found their ultimate goal and Wilder said something like "ah," but with more feeling, and kicked his leg sideways sending the dog orbiting over the hedge. There was a noise suggesting it had landed in a collection of flowerpots.

"God," said Wilder with some emotion. "I'll tell you what I did have. I had a cousin with a dog just like that." He looked at his pant leg, now perforated, and his ankle, now spotted with blood. "What a stupid excuse for a dog."

"Are you all right?"

"Yeah, it's just a nip. Maybe I'll get lucky and it was rabid and they'll have to shoot me to put me out of my misery."

"No, that was Boyd's dog. He makes sure its shots are up to date because it's a bloodthirsty little species of vermin. It's genetically more like a rat than a dog."

"That's something like what I told my cousin about his dog. We didn't get along very well."

"You and the cousin or you and the dog?"

"Not with either one of them."

"Did they live nearby?"

"Down the street from us in Cincinnati. Then he came to visit every summer after I went to live with Aunt Katherine."

"How come you didn't go live with him after your parents died?"

"I guess my parents thought Aunt Katherine was a safer bet. She was in their wills as my guardian. His parents weren't very stable. His mother was my father's and Aunt Katherine's older sister. She was an alcoholic."

"That sounds like a sad family, an alcoholic mother and a micro-dog."

"Yeah, pretty depressing all the way around. His parents used to send him to live with Aunt Katherine every summer so I would have more family around, so we could be like brothers. So they said. I always figured it was so they could have the summer off while someone else put up with him. Or because they didn't want him to lose out on any of Aunt Katherine's money."

"Were they afraid she'd give it all to you?"

"Well, she would have."

"How do you know?"

"She told me."

"But now she won't? Was that the argument you had with her? Over money?" She sounded disappointed.

"Not really."

They started walking again, Wilder with his hands in his pockets and his thoughts somewhere else. Before they got to Main Street he steered them into the alleyway running behind it. It was a more street-like alley than some, though just as narrow. It gave access to the apartments above the Main Street businesses and to the few houses that had been built back from the street decades before and ended up closed in by progress.

"We used to ride our bikes down these alleys at twilight," said Marilyn. "The granite paving blocks jiggetted the handlebars out of our hands if we went fast enough. We pretended we were explorers. The town seemed so big back then. Endless. Limitless. Are we headed somewhere in particular?"

"No. I just like these alleys. Probably for the same reason you used to ride down them. They're places out of time. Wait a sec." He stepped over to the back door of one of the businesses and tried to open it. It was locked.

"What are you doing?"

Wilder went to the one window in the back wall. It was boarded up from the inside with no gaps to peer through. Then they heard a sharp yipping from inside.

"Jesus, he's got the twin in his back room," Wilder said, backing away from the

143

window.

"Large rats make good watch dogs. Why does it look like you're trying to break into Boyd's? You're making me nervous."

Wilder turned and looked at her. "Oh, no, I'm sorry." He put his arm around her shoulder and pulled her to him. "I'd just love to see what he's got in his back room."

"Well, I'm sure he'd show you if you ask."

"Not what I'd be looking for. I was just wondering if he has any stolen antiques hidden away back there." He looked at her and saw he wasn't making her any less nervous. "Not that I'd recognize a stolen antique," he added.

"Oh, of course not."

"So," he said starting down the alley again, hoping a change of subject and scenery would ease her disquiet, "what are your brothers doing now?"

"Keith is an electrical engineer out in California and Paul's a forest ranger in Virginia."

"That's neat. What did your parents say when he wanted to be a forest ranger?"

Marilyn shrugged. "That's what he always wanted to be. That or a snake handler at the zoo."

"Amazing."

"Why? Is that so different from wanting

to be a museum curator?"

"That wouldn't have been my aunt's first choice. She wanted me to be a brain surgeon."

"You usually have to go to medical school for that."

"Is that why I keep failing the boards?" He kicked a stone. "I was accepted at a few."

"Did you go?"

"Nope."

They came out behind the church across from the bookshop. Wilder looked up at the lighted dormer windows hoping for a glimpse of Marilyn's mother flitting past, maybe with a paintbrush between her teeth.

"So how come you've never stretched your wings and left Nolichucky like your brothers?"

"Who says I haven't? I went away to college and then I lived in Nashville for about five years. That's where I learned what I know about the book business. Then old Plez was ready to sell-up and retire. You ever met Plez?"

"Not a name that rings a bell."

"Short for Pleasant. Pleasant Lee. Isn't that awful? Poor old guy. No wonder he buried himself in books."

"Did he have a brother named Precise? And a sister named Pure?"

"Yeah, and a cousin named Insane. No, I think he was an only child. Or maybe he took pity on any siblings that came along and put them out of their misery before they were old enough to suffer what he did. Anyway, I came back and got a loan and bought the bookstore. Best move I ever made. So what did you want to be if you didn't want to be a brain surgeon?"

"You'll blanch."

"No I won't."

"I hesitate to say."

"No, come on."

"Robin Hood."

"Well, geez, no wonder you don't spread your life's story around. Don't tell that one down at Willie's. I take it, though, we're talking about a pre-adolescent fixation? Something you've outgrown? It might be safer just to say you played Davy Crockett."

"My cousin would have liked that. But he always insisted on being Davy, on account of being named David, and we never liked to give him the satisfaction."

"Who's we?"

"Friend of mine and me."

"Did you drop him, too?"

"You're awfully blunt, Maid Marilyn."

"One of my many charms."

Wilder leaned against the wall of the

church and felt the rough bricks against the back of his head. She was right. When he'd dropped out of his aunt's life, he dropped everyone else associated with Stonewall, too. He reached for Marilyn's hand and reeled her in until she was leaning against him, her back to him, and they were both looking up into the Nolichucky night. She crossed her arms over her chest and he put his arms around hers.

"I don't think I ever knew what I wanted to be. Realistically, anyway. I mean, Canadian Mountie probably wasn't ever really in the cards. But Aunt Katherine wanted me to be a doctor because my father was a doctor."

"Why?"

"Long story."

"You'll notice I'm not going anywhere."

"Aunt Katherine thought the world of my father and mother. Saw the good in what he was doing and in the encouragement my mother gave him."

"And?"

"And it's complicated."

"Once upon a time . . ."

"Yeah, yeah, okay. See, my grandfather left his farm and his money to Aunt Katherine because she never married. The way he looked at it, Aunt Doris, that's David's mother, was taken care of because she married well, and my father, being a doctor, was going to do all right. So he left everything to Aunt Katherine. Not fair, maybe, but that's what he did. Aunt Doris resented it. My father didn't care, but he never made much money either. He felt a need to provide as much free care as he could to people who couldn't afford it and who would've otherwise fallen through the cracks. There's a large and mostly poor population of transplanted Appalachians in Cincinnati, and I think he must have felt something particularly for them because there, but for the grace of God and Grandfather, who was something of a financial wizard, our family might have gone.

"When my parents died Aunt Katherine treated me as if I were her own son. She was great. No question. But she also wanted me to be my father all over again. She wanted to pay my way through medical school and then settle enough of my grandfather's money on me when I turned twenty-five that I could continue what my father was doing and never have his money worries.

"And I gave it a lot of thought. I tried to want to do it. But I said no. And a few other things. Loudly. Because she's not a person

148

you can say no to easily.

"And we haven't spoken to each other since. Or, to be fair, I haven't spoken to her since, which amounts to the same thing. And I guess I've been an incredible jerk for about eight years now. Or maybe I just always was one."

"Because you didn't become a doctor?"

"Oh, no, that was the right decision. I'd make a lousy doctor. But I shouldn't have . . . I don't know." He was quiet for a minute and rested his chin on her shoulder. "I shouldn't have not gone back."

"I don't see how you didn't. I can't imagine cutting off someone I've loved and who's loved me and cared for me."

"It wasn't easy, but it wasn't hard, either. I don't know if I can explain it, but it was like tentacles or something, all her expectations, her blindness to the fact that I couldn't be my father. She was trying to squeeze me into a mold that I didn't fit. I was suffocating. I had to get away. And maybe it has something to do with losing my parents like that. I'm sure that's what a psychologist would say. If you lose the people you most care about once, maybe it's not so hard to do it again. Anyway, it didn't bother me. It was liberating. Maybe too intoxicatingly liberating. I don't know. I loved it and didn't look back. Until recently." He cleared his throat. "As you seem to have noticed."

"So what's got you thinking about her now?"

"Oh, let's see, take your pick. No, most recently it's that damned travel writer. It never occurred to me I might show up somewhere in print, and even though I doubt Aunt Katherine reads travel magazines, who knows? I feel like a car wreck where they don't release the names until the next of kin is notified. I guess I'm not as callous as I thought I was, but it doesn't seem right that she might hear I'm around from some dumb magazine article."

"Or some dumb rumor."

"Christ. That one occurred to me in the middle of the night last week. Have you heard the latest? I'm fencing the stuff for the Fox."

"Yeah, I kind of like that one. So what are you going to do?"

"I guess I'll have to grow up and go see her."

CHAPTER 11

Wilder stood in the middle of George Palmer's study and watched him avoiding eye contact and fidgeting with the papers on his desk. Palmer picked up his coffee mug and took a swallow. It was too hot and burned his mouth. He banged the mug down, sloshing coffee onto the papers.

"For goodness sake, sit down, Lewis."

"I thought maybe you wanted me on the carpet."

"You think I'm going to chew you out like some school boy?" Palmer looked up. His gray eyes were tired.

"It sort of sounded that way on the phone last night."

Palmer took another mouthful of the scalding coffee. He grimaced and pushed the cup away. "I'm disappointed in you, Lewis."

"It happens to the best of people, George."

"You're not funny. Sit down."

He sat in one of Palmer's chintz-covered wing chairs so popular with the old ladies of the parish and unsuitable for the bulky men. Wilder had no complaints. He crossed his legs and composed his face so it wouldn't show his rising sense of unease. He wished he could radiate a state of calm that would encompass George. Peace be with you, you old goat. Palmer's body language was screaming volumes.

"Oh, try to be human."

"What?" Wilder was startled.

"How can you be indifferent to what's going on?"

"Why don't you tell me what you think is going on?"

Palmer sank his head into his freckle-spattered hands, massaging his temples, then looked up again.

"You aren't doing yourself any favors lately, you know. Foisting that journalist off on Lillian and the rest of the board, brawling on Main Street."

"That's exaggerating a bit, isn't it?"

"You didn't come to church on Sunday. And Paul seems to think there's something significant about you not eating clam chowder at the Wootens' Sunday night." Palmer raised his chin as though challenging Wilder.

This wasn't going well. Wilder looked out

the window behind Palmer and watched a squirrel gnawing at something it held in its paws. Nuts. Palmer was a kind man with kind thoughts and intentions. Wilder didn't like the tension welling up between them. He didn't know where it was coming from but he didn't feel like rolling over, either.

"That's getting more personal, George."

"Look, Lewis . . ."

"No, George, you open your eyes and look. You know I'm not hiding anything. I'm not keeping secrets. But I don't see any reason to trot my personal life out in front of everyone, either."

"Then you shouldn't be found arguing in full voice on Main Street."

"That was my mistake. It won't happen again."

"Are you ignoring what Paul is implying?"

"Wasn't that your advice?"

Palmer stared at him.

Wilder shrugged and looked away. "Okay, George, if you insist, I'll say it. I'm the Fox."

He might just as well have tossed a small bomb at Palmer. The shock of his statement rocked Palmer so, that he gripped the edge of his desk, his mouth hanging open. Wilder had never noticed how many fillings he had.

"That's the story so far, George," he said, hoping he wasn't going to be responsible for a stroke. "There's nothing in it."

Palmer wilted in his chair. "I don't see how you can take this so calmly."

"I think you know I don't, but if it makes you feel any better, sometimes I can't eat."

"Stop joking. I worry about you."

"Don't."

Wilder watched for an improvement in Palmer's troubled expression. There wasn't any. He decided to cheer him up.

"I have a piece of good news for you, George."

Palmer raised his eyebrows. That didn't seem to reflect any corresponding rise in his spirits, though. Wilder thought for a minute.

"Okay, two pieces. First, Don Sherrill came to see me yesterday. We apologized to each other and he's made a donation to the museum."

"Huh. Well, that is good news. You know, he isn't as boorish as he first comes across. It's such a shame. I think it must be a defense mechanism that operates when he's feeling unsure of himself with someone. What did he donate?"

"Actually there might be a problem there." Wilder scratched his ear, which didn't contribute anything to his thinking but was somehow comforting. "He's coming back up over the weekend and I'd better not say anymore now, except if you don't mind, please don't say anything to anyone else."

"Ah, you're bribing me to get back on my good side. All right, I'm open to corruption. What's the rest of your good news? God knows we could use it."

Wilder drew a deep breath and felt his heart flop over. "I'm going to talk to Aunt Katherine. I'm going to go see her."

"You're going to go home. Say 'home,' Lewis."

"I'll see her, George, and then I'll see."

Palmer's face suffused with a warm glow. He nodded his head several times. "I should think it would be a relief to finally make that decision. Remind me to lend you a copy of Longfellow's 'Mezzo Cammin' which he wrote just before returning home after a long absence. I think you'll find his thoughts and imagery apropos. When do you plan to go?"

"You know, contrary to what you and Marilyn seem to think, I don't spend a lot of time in anguished brooding."

"Lewis. When?"

When? Now that it came down to it, Wilder realized setting a date hadn't entered his head. A moment of panic struck him, but he overcame its stifling effects and answered Palmer.

"I think I'll waffle around a bit longer."

"I've got some interesting news for you. I don't know whether it's good or bad." Susan stopped in Wilder's office on her way to the attic Wednesday afternoon with a box of catalogued photographs.

He looked up from the description he was writing of a pair of crotchless pantaloons. "I have broad shoulders. Lay it on me."

Susan eyed the article of clothing on his desk. He could see her adding it to the mental record she once told him she was keeping of odd artifacts he took an interest in. She smoothed a loose strand of graying hair back behind her ear.

"My sister was here visiting for a long weekend and I took her on a tour of the area because it was her first time here and all. She's from Michigan, near Lansing. Well, north of Lansing. It's just a small town. Anyway, one of the places we stopped was Barter. Do you know where that is?"

"Yes." He didn't, but if he admitted that, Susan would digress from her intended path, and knowing her narrative peculiarities as he had come to, she might never find her way back. Susan was a valuable volunteer. He wouldn't for the world hurt her feelings. But she seemed unable to stick to the point of any given story without some-times backtracking as far as Genesis.

Susan looked skeptical.

"Yes. Yes, I do." Wilder hoped he sounded confident enough and that she wouldn't now stop to ask him just where he thought it was.

She looked at him sideways but continued. "We went into the museum there. It's just a little place, sort of tacky. Not as professional as ours. But they try hard and it's interesting in an off-the-beaten-track sort of way. And I got to chatting with the people there and happened to mention the writer who was here last week. You remember him?"

"What do you think?"

She smiled. "Just checking. Anyway, do you know that he didn't stop through there? I'd have thought that was an obvious place for him to stop, considering the article he's supposed to be writing. The place is full of history and it reeks with human interest." She stopped, waiting for a comment.

"Maybe he hasn't gotten that far yet?"

"Well, that's what I wondcrcd, too. But I mentioned him again at several other places we stopped, and in fact after awhile I made a point of asking everywhere we stopped." Susan was like that, very thorough, which was why she did such an excellent job with

157

the photographs and why she carried on such appallingly long conversations.

"And?"

"When my sister and I set out to see the sights in an area, we see them all. He hasn't been anywhere but here."

"Maybe he started here and then just gave up."

"You mean after your exhibition on Main Street? I considered that."

"Thank you."

"So what do you think?"

"I really don't know. What do you think?" This might have been a dangerous question to ask, considering Susan's long-windedness, but Wilder also knew from experience that she had already considered every conceivable angle and would by now have everything distilled into an intelligent and succinct answer.

"He wasn't a writer."

"Just an eccentric tourist then, you think?"

"Eccentric only in that he managed to bring every conversation he had here around to you."

"Oh. How do you know that?"

Susan shrugged. "In this town? It's not hard to find out something like that."

"Then why haven't I heard it?"

"You just did."

"So I did." He looked at the pencil in his hand and wished he were the sort of person who thought more clearly or at least gained comfort from chewing a helpless pencil to rags. He sat back in his chair, rubbed his hand over the lower part of his face, knitted his brows, and pondered this latest development in his idyllic small town life.

"I hate to sound as though even I entertain suspicions about myself, but was he police, maybe?"

"No. My neighbor Deborah's cousin, Shorty, is in the sheriff's department and he checked around."

"Are there a lot of people in on this?"

"Well, there were some, naturally, who thought he was here undercover investigating the rumors that you're the Fox."

"Oh, naturally. Christ."

"But most of them were just as glad to find out that he wasn't any sort of police, because, as they say, it's more fun to wonder than to know."

"Well, then, I guess my reputation remains safely in shreds. Thank you for stopping in, Susan."

"You aren't going to let any of these rampant rumors keep you from the Pickers' Picnic, are you?"

"I'm helping set up the stage Friday afternoon."

"Which doesn't answer my question, but we'll let that slide." Susan gathered herself and her box of photographs for the ascent to the attic. She turned around before leaving the office.

"Doesn't any of this begin to get to you?"

Wilder looked up from the measuring tape he'd started stretching around the waistband of the pantaloons.

"Should it?"

Chapter 12

By all accounts, the Pickers' Picnic in Nolichucky was the cat's meow. Or whatever the current expression would be. Wilder had heard it compared to the annual World's Fair in Tunbridge, Vermont, and the Fly-In Fish Boil held each July on Washington Island, Wisconsin. He'd never been to either of those and could only guess if it rivaled the annual festival in Buffalo Gap, Texas, that he'd enjoyed so much but couldn't remember the name of. The all-woman volunteer fire department there had made such an impression on him that other details were forever foggy.

Excitement ran high in the days leading up to his first Pickers' Picnic. The dry summer had been followed by a dry autumn and it suddenly occurred to people that for the first time in years they might have an expanse of green grass to sit and dance on instead of the more usual wallow of mud.

For weeks Wilder had heard musically inclined people making plans to polish up their instruments and tune up their voices. His ear sometimes caught the muffled strains of undercover jam sessions around town as people exercised their picking fingers.

The lawns around the museum were the closest Nolichucky came to having a centrally located public park and Wilder gladly offered to help set up the tarpaulin-covered stage there. And when he was asked often enough by a wide enough range of people if he were planning on not missing the picnic he finally said no, meaning that no, he wasn't planning on missing it and yes, he would be there.

Thursday evening came and for once he didn't feel like sitting at home alone. He tossed aside the new issue of *Museum News,* put on his jacket, and stepped out onto the front porch. The spicy smell of the changing season and crisp air gusted around him in little eddies. He thought of Marilyn as she'd turned the corner of the museum the other evening and of her smile as she'd caught sight of him. He pictured her sitting here with him listening to the pickers on Saturday. And then he realized the complacent trap he'd fallen into, just assuming the two of them would end up at the picnic together.

Only a few dates and already he was taking her for granted. Was that a good sign because he obviously felt comfortable with her or bad because it showed him what a cocksure moron he was? He decided that issue was too complicated and maybe suggestive to go into and a better idea was to go see her and actually ask her to the picnic.

As he passed Lillian Bowman's house his ear caught a wisp of lively music. He stopped under the dogwood tree opposite her front window and gazed in wonder at the tableau lit up before him.

Lillian was sitting poker-backed at her old upright piano, her fingers pouncing on the keys. She'd told Wilder half a dozen times over the six months he'd been in Nolichucky how a soulless retired banker had paid her twenty-five dollars to haul the piano out of his basement. It was her favorite morality tale of triumph over cultural Philistines.

Charlie Ramsey stood beside Lillian, so intense with his electric bass he looked to be playing it with his whole body. Charlie was Dr. Ramsey's nineteen-year-old son who wore one gold earring and repaired cars down at the police garage. A clone of

163

Charlie's, wearing a madras sport coat and a long, moth-eaten beard and shoulder-length hair, was bowing and scraping a fiddle.

But most arresting was Paul Glaser in a pair of faded overalls playing the bass fiddle. He reminded Wilder of the stuffed bullfrogs he'd seen once in a junk shop, each dressed in a tailored suit of clothes and arranged in some intriguing pose.

The tune ended and Glaser leaned his instrument against the wall. He produced a clarinet from behind a chair. Charlie separated himself from the guitar and picked up another fiddle. An amazing rendition of Gershwin's "Promenade" followed.

Over the sonorous wail of Glaser's clarinet Wilder heard footsteps approaching and he looked around. Ed Ramsey must have arrived home from the medical convention in Chicago earlier in the day. He was out for his usual evening stroll with his Irish setter. Wilder wondered whom he'd spoken to since he'd gotten back and what he'd been hearing. He stepped away from the tree and greeted him.

"Christ, Lewis. I didn't see you standing there. Why are you lurking under Lillian's dogwood?" Wilder gestured with his chin toward Lillian's window and Ramsey turned and took in the spectacle in the parlor. The setter set about making itself familiar with Wilder's pant legs and shoes.

"That's why they're so much better than the rest. They practice. Of course the others practice, too, so maybe it's the rapport. Wonderful rapport between those four. Have you ever heard them play?"

"No. I had no idea they played at all." Wilder stepped back beyond reach of the dog's leash. "Do they do Gershwin at the Pickers' Picnic?" The dog gave Wilder a dispirited look and threw itself down to chew on Ramsey's shoelaces.

"They manage to slip something in once in awhile. Wish we could step inside and hear them properly. But we shouldn't bother them while they're practicing." Ramsey hauled the dog back to its feet and away from his own. "Besides, Ralph here likes to chew on Lillian's legs. I mean her piano's legs. And they're playing 'Walking the Dog' so I'd better go do it. And of course you'll hear them on Saturday. See you then." Ramsey turned to continue on his way.

Wilder dragged his eyes away from the captivating sight of Paul Glaser's rapport and headed off in the opposite direction. But Ramsey turned again and called to stop him.

"Oh, Lewis. I haven't quite caught up on things since getting back. I forgot to ask you, you didn't have any problems Sunday night, did you?"

Wilder hesitated. "No."

"Good. Thanks for filling in for me. Not a word, though, eh?" Ramsey waved and went on.

CHAPTER 13

"Why, Lewis, Marilyn didn't tell me you were coming over this evening." Mrs. Wooten met him at the door with a smear of cobalt blue across one cheek.

"I just sort of stopped by. I hope I'm not bothering you."

"Not at all. She's on the phone and I'm working. Come right in." Wilder stepped inside and closed the door. "She's upstairs, go on up. I'll just start some water for the tea."

He started to tell her not to bother on his account but she had already wafted into the kitchen. He could hear Marilyn's voice somewhere overhead, so following her animated tones, he found the door to the staircase and climbed to the apartment above.

There were picture frames hanging on the walls on either side of the enclosed stair. Wilder eyed them, expecting to find a brief

167

photographic history of the Wooten family. He chuckled when he saw what was there instead. The frames held fragments of old wallpaper and chips of paint that must have been uncovered as the house was restored. And there was one frame that turned out to be a window giving a look at the original lath under the new plasterwork.

Wilder studied each frame on his way up, delighted with the Wootens' approach to interior decorating. Walls full of family photographs had always made him uncomfortable. Maybe they were too sentimental. Or personal. His own family had never gone in for displaying pictures of themselves to themselves on pianos and along staircases. Photographs of unusual fungus formations, maybe. Then again, he mused, he wouldn't mind looking at boxes full of pictures of Marilyn as a child.

The door at the top of the stairs was open and he found Marilyn there sitting sideways in an overstuffed chair, her legs over one arm, her back supported on the other. She was laughing into the telephone and twisting the cord around one finger. The blue in her tattersall shirt brought out the blue of her eyes. He noticed that her corduroys were the same color as his living room and she had on argyle socks again. When she caught sight of him, she waved him over.

"Wait, I want you to say hello to someone," she said into the receiver. She handed it to Wilder. "Here."

Wilder took the phone and put it to his ear. He listened for a minute before saying hello. Then he switched hands and put the receiver to his other ear, scratching the first ear. "Oh, well, yeah, hi." He handed it back to Marilyn and went to look out the dormer window across from the top of the stairs.

While Marilyn continued her conversation Wilder tried to figure out the layout of the second floor. It looked as though there could only be three rooms. This room, the middle one, they obviously used as a living room. It was comfortable and cluttered and almost as full of books as the shop downstairs.

The other two rooms must communicate off this one; there wasn't any room for a hallway. He knew there were three dormer windows so each of the two side rooms must have one. But with the whole upstairs being snugged up under the roof like this, he marveled that neither of the Wootens had permanently angled spines. Or brain damage. He idly wondered which was Marilyn's room.

She talked on for several more minutes

and ended up making happy plans to meet at the airport the next evening. Wilder pretended he wasn't listening.

"Don't you know who that was?" she asked after she hung up.

"Heartburn, I think he said his name was."

"Hart Warren," Marilyn tsked.

"Oh, yeah, the guitar player."

"He's coming in tomorrow for the picnic. I can't believe it. I haven't seen him in years." She smiled and chattered, apparently unaware that Wilder didn't share her enthusiasm.

"Fond memories?"

"Oh, I don't know. Not like that. We weren't ever really a thing. But, well," her face lit up again, "sure, it'll be great to see him. I can't wait for you to meet him. And hear him. So what's new? What brings you out this evening?"

"Where's your bathroom?"

"That's why you came?"

"No, while you were on the phone I was just trying to figure out your floor plan up here and I realized I didn't see anything that looked like one unless it's in one of the bedrooms. Assuming those are both bedrooms."

"See that door?" She pointed to a corner of the living room.

"Jesus."

"It's oddly shaped and the cause of many bruised heads and comments like yours."

Wilder raised his eyebrows. "I'd been wondering if you wear safety helmets to bed. Your mother's making tea. I tried to tell her not to bother."

"She always makes tea this time of night."

"Oh, that explains it." Wilder, hands in his pockets, wandered over to the sofa. He ducked his head in time to avoid the ceiling, plucked a sleeping cat off the only cushion not holding a stack of books and sat. The cat rearranged itself on Wilder's lap without bothering to open its eyes and drifted back to sleep. Wilder's bemused eyes came to rest on Marilyn. "Nice cat."

Marilyn's eyes danced. "He's got fleas."

"But anyway, warmer than a newt. Do you have any of Heartburn's music up here?"

"Hart's? Sure, I've got one of his solo CDs. You wanna hear it?"

"Only if he's as good as your Uncle Paul."

"Oh, well. No one's as good as Uncle Paul." Marilyn levered herself out of her chair and went to rummage through a shoebox full of CDs. "When did you hear him?"

"He's over at Lillian's practicing and I caught a few bars on my way over."

"With Charlie Ramsey and Hoot? Yeah,

they're not too bad. You should hear them do Debussy. Their tone really improved after Ralph chewed on Lillian's piano a few times. Must be something with the resonance. They'll have to haul it up on stage Saturday. It's the only one she'll play now."

"What do they call themselves?"

"They haven't got a name. Lillian doesn't like anything Uncle Paul suggests, Uncle Paul ridicules Lillian's ideas, and they both hate anything Hoot or Charlie come up with. The only time they get along is when they're playing. So no one brings up a name anymore."

Mrs. Wooten appeared with a fragrant, steaming pot and three mugs on a tray. Marilyn found and started the music. Mrs. Wooten poured the tea and then took her mug with her into the room on the left. Through the door she left ajar Wilder could see several easels and many spatters of paint.

Marilyn caught his eye and smiled. She handed him a mug so he wouldn't have to disturb the cat. Then she settled back in her chair and they sipped and listened as invisible fingers tickled a twelve-string guitar.

"He's good. I'd like to see his fingers moving that fast." Wilder was impressed and, after watching Marilyn's reaction to her phone call, something else, too. "Does he make a living at it?"

"During summers and holidays, I think. Last I heard, in real life he's a high school math teacher. This is the first time he's made it back for the picnic in years."

"Where's he live?"

"North Carolina. Charlotte. He can hop on a flight and fly direct tomorrow evening."

"How is he getting from the airport, Marilyn?" Mrs. Wooten called.

"He asked if I could run over and pick him up. You won't need the car, will you?"

"No." This came mumbled through a brush she now held between her teeth as she rubbed at something offensive on her canvas.

"Does he still have family here?" Wilder asked.

"A few cousins and some several-times-removeds scattered here and there. You know Herb Lundy, don't you? He's married to Hart's mother's cousin's daughter or something. And I think Boyd of the killer dogs must be kin somehow. He's a Warren, anyhow, and tall like Hart and has about as many freckles. Why?"

"I was just wondering if he needs a place to stay." He made a nonchalant show of inspecting the cat's head for fleas that didn't look like it was fooling Marilyn.

"Or, are you being disingenuous and really wondering if he's staying here? I offered him the sofa bed."

"Oh." Wilder chucked the cat under the chin, transferred it to the back of the sofa and stood up. "Well, thanks for the tea and the cat. And the music. Maybe I'll see you Saturday."

"He's just an old friend, Lewis. It was the polite thing to do."

Wilder smiled, he hoped carelessly. But Marilyn was looking at him and probably right through him again.

"He's staying with one of his cousins."

Then Wilder felt an odd sensation and realized he was blushing. He looked at the floor and coughed. "Sorry, it wasn't any of my business."

Marilyn came over to him and put her hands on his shoulders.

"Thanks for being jealous. I'm flattered. But you know what? I'm jealous, too. I'm jealous because there are things I'd like to try to share with you, but so much of the time you seem to keep me on the outside. There are so many things about you that I like, but there's a whole lot more there that you only ever let me catch a glimpse of. You say you don't have any secrets. But what am I supposed to think?"

Mrs. Wooten had started whistling as soon as the conversation turned serious. She was now attacking "La Marseillaise."

"What is it that you think I'm hiding? It seems to me I've been pretty forthcoming lately."

"Where were you Sunday night?"

He looked her in the eyes, but he didn't answer. Marilyn shook her head. Wilder kissed her good night and left.

CHAPTER 14

Friday it rained just enough to give the pessimists a rosy cynical glow. Saturday dawned as clear and bright as any of the optimists could have hoped for.

Ed Ramsey arose and ate his breakfast of shredded wheat while reading the local weekly, hot off the presses. He took off his glasses and polished them when he came to the report of the Fox's activity the previous weekend.

Charlie Ramsey drifted in. He joined his father for a cup of coffee, then excused himself to lend Hoot a hand in moving Lillian Bowman's piano. They loaded it onto an old railroad freight wagon and pushed and pulled it around to the stage set up on the museum grounds. They arrived there in time to see Lewis Wilder fetching his paper from the middle of his small yard while wearing a faded red tartan bathrobe.

Hart Warren woke up feeling groggy and

pasty-tongued on a sofa in a cousin's mobile home. He sat up and was joined on the sofa by three smaller cousins who had turned on the TV, which was what had waked him in the first place. They bounced him the rest of the way out of bed and he went to find the telephone.

Lewis Wilder's phone rang while he was brushing his teeth. He spat and went, still lightly foaming, to answer it. No one was on the other end. He stalked back to finish with his toothbrush, then he called George Palmer.

"George, can you hear me?"

"Yes. Trouble with phone goblins again?"

"I suppose that's one explanation for it. Have you got plans for the picnic?"

"Of course I do. Martha and I are going together."

"Who's Martha?"

"Who's Martha? Marilyn's mother."

"Oh, right. I guess I never think of her that way."

"What way? As having a first name or as being someonc I might like to spend time with? What about Marilyn?"

"You've already got her mother, don't be greedy."

"Wise guy. I thought the two of you . . ."

"She's got heartburn."

"Hart Warren, that's right, I heard somewhere he'd be in town. Fine musician. Good with numbers. Amazing fingers. Nothing that boy couldn't do when he set his mind to it. I don't think he's a guest of the Wootens', though. I think you ought to call Marilyn. In fact you two should have made arrangements days ago. I'm surprised at Marilyn but that's just typical of you. You tend to put important things off. Like going to see your Aunt Katherine. By the way, when are you going?"

"You'll be the first to know, George. 'Bye."

Wilder stood with his hand still on the phone, thinking about his short conversation with Hart Warren the other night at Marilyn's. Warren had known who he was. That wasn't impossible. Warren might be in frequent contact with his cousins and keep up on the latest gossip. Which would account for the irritating joke he'd made about the Fox.

Or maybe he'd just been in recent contact with an emphasis on Marilyn. But Wilder was sure he could give Marilyn credit for being more sensitive than to feed Warren all the current misinformation. She hadn't just before handing him the phone, anyway. And it would have been a strange topic of conversation for people making transportation arrangements.

Still, the whole thing rankled. And, whether out of jealousy or spite or because he was turning into a paranoid neurotic, he'd never asked Marilyn to the picnic. Swell, now the nose he'd cut off could be his date.

"Oh thou child of many prayers. Life hath quicksand, life hath snares." Where the hell had that come from? Longfellow if he remembered right. At least George would be pleased. Longfellow was his patron saint.

Well, hell. In for a nose, in for a noose. He tucked in his shirt, calmed his hair with a brush and set out for the Wootens'.

He found Paul Glaser standing across the street from the bookstore, surveying the front.

"You're running late, son. Some speckled, long drink of water just went in. Carrying a guitar case. Hope you got your reservations in early or I'd say he's got you beat."

"George seems to think he's a fair-haired boy, but that maybe I still have a chance," Wilder said.

"He does, does he? Well what does George know? He's in love with nineteenth-century romantic poets and quite possibly my sister."

Wilder, now less resolute, dallied, with his

hands in his pockets. He hesitated to go on and risk rebuff but wasn't quite willing to slink back home. He stood next to Glaser and they both stared across at the bookstore.

"I heard you playing night before last at Lillian's."

"Mmph."

"Marilyn's keen on your Debussy."

"She would be."

"Paul, did you know Boyd Warren sells fake antiques?"

"Mmph."

"Have you ever questioned him about the burglaries?"

"Too obvious."

"What, and I'm not?"

Glaser turned and looked him up and down. "Hell, son, you're not from around here. Fair game."

On that inspiring note Wilder decided it was time to make a move. In imitation of one of Glaser's own more or less communicative grunts, he made a guttural noise deep in his throat and left Glaser to interpret it as he liked. He crossed the street, took the steps two at a time, and entered the bookstore.

Wilder didn't know the man leaning his elbow on the counter, gazing into Marilyn's eyes. But the guitar case and general length

180

of the stranger were good clues. He and
Marilyn looked up, happy and breathless
with laughter, as Wilder came in. Wilder
chalked up one point for himself when the
pleasure didn't fade from Marilyn's face
when she saw him. He didn't look that
closely at the stranger's face.

"Hey, I just tried calling you. This is Hart
Warren. Hart, Lewis Wilder."

Warren unfolded himself, shaking the
creases out of his legs and arms on the way
up. He held out a hand and Wilder stepped
forward to shake it.

"He really is just a little feller, ain't he?
He's just your size, Marilyn."

"Hart! Tact is not one of Hart's strong
points, Lewis."

"That's all right. Actually I'm tall for my
height."

Warren laughed. "Pleased to meet you.
Marilyn tells me the three of us are sharing
a picnic this evening after she closes up
here."

Wilder glanced at Marilyn's face and
caught a brief flicker there of something he
couldn't quite make out. He was startled
but recovered.

"Yeah, I'm looking forward to it." He stole
another glance at Marilyn and she seemed
pleased. "I'm bringing the drinks and some

chips and a blanket, right?"

"Sounds good." It sounded good to him, too. He liked this kind of ad libbing. "I'll bring sandwiches and deviled eggs," she added. "Hart can take care of the dessert and the entertainment. I'll lock up here at five."

"I signed up to go on from six 'til seven so we can eat before or after. Or straight on through if there's enough."

"Isn't it open stage until seven?" asked Wilder.

"Well, they decided to have everyone sign up ahead of time so there's some organization to the thing. I guess it's got kind of wild some years."

"Any idea when Paul and Lillian will be on, then, Marilyn?"

Marilyn shook her head. "Signing up is news to me. I've always sort of enjoyed the skirmishes between acts. We can call one of them up, though, and find out."

Wilder turned and looked out the window. "No need, Paul's still across the street staring this way. I'll go ask him. Where do you want to meet?"

"We'll come up your way. Hart probably hasn't seen your place since . . ."

"Since the tenants weren't quite so respectable," Warren laughed.

"Then I guess I'd better go do the dishes and shovel out the dust. Nice meeting you, Hart."

Wilder left the bookstore unenlightened about Hart Warren's or his own role in the present or future scheme of things, but lighthearted about the evening's prospects. He crossed the street and stood once more with Paul Glaser.

"Were you lip-reading through the window?"

"I notice Marilyn remains inside with the musician."

"You have keen powers of observation. When are you and your group playing?"

"The sooner the better. I like to set some tone for this affair."

"You know about signing up this year?"

"Yes I do. Some joker penciled in his name for the opening slot but I took care of that. We'll be first up like we always are." With that Glaser ambled off.

By one, with the sun shining high, the crowds were already setting up lawn chairs and digging into coolers and picnic baskets. Some people stretched out on their backs in the warm grass. Others visited back and forth, calling to neighbors and waving. Wilder made several false starts at straightening his living room and finally decided he didn't care if Hart Warren tripped over a stack of old newspapers. He went to join the sunshine and bright crowd.

Booths had sprung up around the perimeter of the grounds, selling boiled peanuts, cotton candy, funnel cakes, corn dogs, soft drinks, and an endless menu of other junk food. People running the booths waved and called to Wilder as he strolled past. They were all members of the civic organizations he'd made speeches to over the months. He stopped at the Garden Club booth and bought a cup of iced tea from Eleanor Bean to see if she would call him Henry again. She didn't seem to recognize him at all today and he continued his circuit, ending up back on his own front porch.

He was amazed at the appeal all this held for so many and such a varied crowd. Thin-haired families were down from the mountains mingling with school board members and county commissioners. Immense young mothers with their round children stood with Ed Ramsey and the off-duty sheriff's deputy to wait for sugar-dusted, piping-hot funnel cakes. George Palmer and Martha Wooten had their chairs set up right in the middle of it all. It was one enormous family picnic. Everyone included. Everyone belonging. Standing alone on his porch, Wilder didn't feel part of it.

At one-fifty a thin, sallow man stepped out on center stage and started tuning his fiddle. He backed off at one-fifty-five when Paul Glaser and his quartet moved in and commandeered the microphones. The music started at two.

Wilder found he could hear well enough from his porch. But hearing Glaser's quartet and seeing them make love to their instruments were entirely different things so he eased his way through the crowd until he could see Lillian's poker back and her priceless piano.

They opened with Hoot singing accompaniment to "Milk 'Em in the Morning." That ended with resounding applause. They were obviously considered a class act. Or maybe it was the shining day and the brilliance of the crowd lending the sheen of perfection.

A string of fiddle tunes followed, one tripping into the next. Wilder had heard of "Flop Eared Mule" and "Dog in the Mustard" and wondered if he was hearing them. Paul Glaser took on a whole new persona on stage. Hoot and Charlie probably always looked as though they were being swept away by their inner harmony.

The audience was like a wavering field of

unlikely wildflowers. It didn't remain still for more than a few minutes at a time. People wandered in and out of the smaller family groups, over to the concession stands and back again. Some stood, some danced, some slept. Wilder glanced across to see how George and Marilyn's mother were making out. Then he wondered if they ever did. Then he told himself to grow up.

Ed Ramsey was there with them, keeping time by patting Martha on the shoulder. Then Ramsey turned as if drawn by Wilder's eyes and excused himself from the couple. He headed in Wilder's general direction but wasn't making much headway. Wilder had choked on a bite of toast reading his own paper that morning and had a fair idea what Ramsey might want to talk about.

He stood his ground through an excellent bit of Gershwin sandwiched between "Turkey in the Straw" and "The Tennessee Waltz." He looked up when that ended, wondering how long it could take the man to negotiate the legs strewn across the lawn. Dr. Ramsey, popular man-about-town that he was, had been waylaid by Eleanor Bean. Wilder silently thanked her for the reprieve and faded off in another direction.

Glaser's group finished its set with a bluegrass version of "Norwegian Wood."

Debussy hadn't shown up. Wilder felt cheated and wondered if by mentioning it to Glaser earlier he had ensured it not being played. He seemed to have that effect on Glaser. Thinking about unpleasant old coots made him remember that Don Sherrill should be in town for the weekend. He hadn't heard from him but supposed he was somewhere in the crowd.

The next group on stage was not so inspired. Wilder concentrated less on the music and more on keeping an eye out for Sherrill. He saw Edith Daniels out from behind her grocery counter. He wasn't sure he'd ever seen her legs before. Boyd Warren from the Antique Mart was eating a mustard-covered corn dog and admiring some teenage girls lounging recklessly. Wilder wondered where Hart was. With the amount of space he'd take up either standing or stretched out he shouldn't have been hard to miss. Maybe he was tuning up his guitar somewhere. Maybe he was with Marilyn.

Palmer and Martha Wooten got up to stretch their legs. They came to join Wilder leaning against the giant tree stump.

"Lewis, I'd like you to meet Martha."

"Oh, George, Lewis and I are old friends."

"I'm making proper introductions. He

didn't realize you have a first name."

"And all this time I thought you were just painfully polite. Well, my goodness. Of course you should call me Martha."

"Thank you, it'll be my pleasure."

"George tells me you're planning to take a trip?"

Palmer clapped his hand on Wilder's back. "Yes, when are you leaving, Lewis?"

Wilder smiled. "Nothing confirmed yet."

"Procrastination is the thief of time."

"I'll keep that in mind. By the way, have you seen Don Sherrill at all? He was supposed to be here this weekend."

"I think I saw his wife. Do you know her?"

"Barb Sherrill?" asked Martha. "Oh, Lewis wouldn't want to know her. She'd eat him alive."

Wilder couldn't help laughing at Martha's tart comment. "Oh, I've met her and it was definitely memorable."

"Well, I shouldn't say such things, should I? But didn't you know? She's the real hunter of the family. All those heads on the walls of their cottage? Hers. She's shot bighorn sheep in the Rockies and she's been all over Africa. I heard next she's going for a record grizzly in Alaska."

"Wow."

"Well, yes, not exactly Garden Club material," Martha said. "Then again, I've never in my life been a member of a Garden Club so who am I to cast poison ivy at anyone?"

"Well neither have I," said Wilder, "and I've always been just as happy. But if she's here, he must be, too, so I guess I'll go scout around."

Ed Ramsey arrived at the stump just as Wilder's flannel shirt blended into the distance.

After the uninspired band, a group of middle-aged cloggers came on stage. The chunky women wore short, blue gingham skirts with full petticoats and bright red panties that showed when they twirled on the toes of their white patent leather Mary Janes. The men had matching beer guts and red gingham shirts. Wilder wandered through the crowd seeing no sign of Sherrill or his elephant-gun-toting Amazon. Or Hart Warren. Ed Ramsey was now talking to Charlie and Hoot. Wilder took the opportunity to retreat to his porch again.

He was sitting on the steps, drinking a beer, when the telephone rang. He sat listening to it. Before it stopped he'd abandoned the beer and headed for the museum and a better refuge.

"Many people in today?" he asked Pam on his way past the reception desk.

189

"You can't hear the music as well in here," she said, not bothering to look up from her magazine.

"I'll spell you if you want to go out there for awhile."

"What's the matter, you don't like it?"

"Just thought I'd take a break."

"No, you go on upstairs or wherever you get your thrills. I stood outside and listened to Charlie and Hoot and them earlier on, and it won't be too long before we close up here anyway."

"Any messages?"

"Nope. Here's the mail."

"Thanks."

He climbed the stairs, leafing through the stack of envelopes and circulars and post-cards. Junk museum mail wasn't any more interesting than any other kind of junk mail. Sometimes he got free samples of orange-scented floor cleaning compound. It was a nauseating product. He fished around in his pocket for his keys and dropped several pieces of mail. He unlocked the door, retrieved the envelopes from the floor and tossed everything on the desk.

Leaning back in his chair, hands clasped behind his head, he took in a slow, deep breath. He loved this poky office. The walls might have no windows, but every file and record and artifact within reach became a window he could look through and see the least details of another time.

He felt content. Here was peace and quiet. And a beautiful green bird pipe. He unlocked the drawer and took out the wrapped bundle. He opened the package and made a nest of the cloth wrappings in the middle of the desk for the bird. It nestled there with its sightless eyes and watched him open the mail.

Slipped in with the ads for sling psychrometers and micro-crystaline wax specially formulated by the British Museum was an envelope from Palmer. Wilder snorted when he saw what was inside. "Here," he said to the bird, "see if you think Longfellow's as hot as George does." He unfolded the poem Palmer had sent and read it to the bird.

Mezzo Cammint
Written at Boppard on the Rhine August 25, 1842, just before leaving for home.

"Half of my life is gone, and I have let
  The years slip from me and I have not
    fulfilled
  The aspiration of my youth, to build
  Some tower of song with lofty parapet.

Not indolence, nor pleasure, nor the fret
   Of restless passions that would not be
    stilled,
   But sorrow, and care that almost killed,
   Kept me from what I may accomplish yet;

Though, halfway up the hill, I see the Past
   Lying beneath me with its sounds and
    sights,
   A city in the twilight dim and vast,

With smoking roofs, soft bells, and gleam-
    ing lights,
   And hear above me on the autumn blast
   The cataract of Death far thundering
    from the heights."

Wilder finished reading and sat, not seeing the poem in his hand or the desk or the
walls around him. He stirred himself and
refocused on the small bird. "Where did you
come from and where do you belong, little
green friend?" he murmured.

Someone chuckled. Wilder's attention
snapped to the open doorway. Hart Warren
lounged there, hands in his pockets, smiling. He didn't say anything, just stood there
looking at him. Was there an unpleasant
brightness in Warren's eyes? Or was he just
looking for a reason to dislike this guy?

He felt an irrational urge to defend himself against Warren. Instead he returned his stare and laid the poem down over the bird still nestled in its wrappings. He leaned back in the chair and pushed away from the desk, not wanting to give Warren the satisfaction of seeing his unease.

"Relax, Lewis." Warren eased himself away from the door frame, stretching. He yawned and looked around, nodding.

"Pretty amazing what they've done with this place." He turned his back on Wilder and made a study of the titles in the bookcase. He turned around with *The Graveyard Preservation Primer* in his hand.

"You read all this shit? Oh, hey, no offense. I mean, I used to get off on logarithms." He put the book back and walked over to the filing cabinet. "Good security, here, too. That's good." He gave each drawer a rattle. "I see you even lock up the files. You afraid Lillian Bowman might come in and rifle the records? Or is there a more, shall we say, sly reason for the good care you take?"

Was there a sneer curling around the edges of his smiling words? Wilder felt the space between them constricting.

"Oh, sorry, Lewis. Bad joke. Marilyn told me you were sensitive about that. No offense."

"That's okay. No big deal," Wilder said, trying to shrug off the joke and its effect at the same time. "You been enjoying the music?"

"Not especially. I caught that old fart, Marilyn's uncle. Not too bad. That Lillian's an incredible old lady, and Hoot and Charlie are coming right along." He stopped fingering the beadwork on the lid of a Victorian sewing basket and turned toward him with what Wilder could only think of as a leer. "I'd rather catch Marilyn."

"Oh, well, I'd've thought you could've done that years ago. Why'd you wait so long?"

Warren laughed. "I like my women more mature. I was just waiting until she was ready to be," he paused for effect, "plucked. What? You don't like that?"

"I'd be surprised if Marilyn did."

Warren came over to the desk and shoved the in and out baskets aside so he could perch on the corner and stare down at Wilder. Wilder felt the space in the office shrink a bit more.

"Well, now, I wouldn't have thought much in this old world would surprise you at all," Warren said.

"What's that supposed to mean?"

"Make of it what you like. I just thought that a historian might find human nature sort of jading after awhile." He moved his hand to pick up Palmer's poem. Wilder slid forward and covered the paper with his own hand. Their eyes locked. The room became suffocating.

Then Marilyn's head popped around the corner.

"There you are. Pam said to let you know that she's ready to lock up and were you two planning a slumber party up here or what?"

She came the rest of the way into the room and looked from one to the other of the men. Warren smiled and pulled his hand back from the paper. Wilder gathered the poem and the bird in its wrappings and tucked them under his arm.

"You two go on. Tell Pam I'll be down in a minute," he said.

Warren got up and stood behind Marilyn with his hands on her shoulders. "Hold on tight to your little friends, Wilder." He laughed and went out.

Marilyn raised her eyebrows. Wilder gave her a corner of a smile and shook his head. He didn't move again until he heard them both going down the stairs. Then he re-wrapped the pipe and started to lock it back

195

in the desk. Out of the corner of his eye he caught sight of his jacket behind the door where he'd left it hanging the day before. He retrieved it and zipped the bird into an inside pocket. Don Sherrill might turn up yet. In any case, good as Hart Warren estimated the security to be, Wilder suddenly felt it wasn't good enough.

Before locking the door he took another look around the office. It was the right shape and size again. He wondered if he'd imagined the tension, invented it. He rubbed the back of his neck. There were some things better left unthought. He locked the door and followed the others downstairs.

Music swelled toward them as the three stepped out the front door. The crowd was buoyant as ever. Marilyn reclaimed her picnic basket from behind a porch rocker. Warren made a gallant show of taking the basket from her. She let him have it and with a smile linked her arm in Wilder's and the three of them set off through the sea of revelers towards Wilder's low quarters.

In the confusion of crossing the crowded grounds Wilder examined his own befuddlement. The signals he was getting from Marilyn didn't seem to be mixed. But he was certainly mixed up. He hadn't felt this kind of jealousy, if that's what it was, since he was a teenager. It wasn't an ennobling feeling. He told himself to look on the bright side. After all, Hart only had a basket on his arm. He had Marilyn.

She gave his arm a squeeze and he turned to smile at her. But she had already caught Warren's eye and was winking at him so Wilder settled for returning her squeeze with whatever message it sent. But the last of the day's fiddling and plucking, he decided, would come none too soon for him.

Almost home and Ed Ramsey finally caught up. The three were brought up short when he materialized from behind an obese couple placating their sullen child with cotton candy. His eyes were stark, and Wilder fancied, feverish. Maybe he wasn't benefiting from his afternoon of music in the sunshine. Wilder empathized.

"The paper," growled Ramsey.

"Excuse me a minute, will you?" Wilder said to Marilyn and Warren. He and Ramsey went a short distance away and held an animated, though quiet, conversation that lasted a bit longer than just a minute. When at last Wilder turned away from Ramsey he saw Warren, his arm encircling Marilyn's waist, exchanging pleasantries with Eleanor Bean.

"Well, it is just so nice to see the two of you together again," Miss Eleanor was quavering.

Wilder started back to his place alone.

Chapter 15

The phone was ringing again as he unlocked the front door. He thought about ignoring it again but instead picked up the receiver and listened without speaking.

"Hello? Hello. Lewis, Don Sherrill here. I've been trying to reach you. Bad news, I can't get away this weekend after all."

"Oh. I heard your wife was here and I assumed you were, too."

"No. Damned shame, too. I always like the Pickers' Picnic."

"Your wife didn't bring the information with her?"

"Hm? No, of course not."

"Business booming?"

"What? Oh, yeah."

"You could put the information in the mail."

"No. I'll be up again soon. You just keep that little beauty under lock and key and don't let that Fox fellow get his hands on it.

Or am I speaking to the wrong guy about that? Ha! Ha!"

"Right. So I'll see you when I see you." Wilder banged down the receiver. "Jerk."

He went to the kitchen and put the chips and drinks he'd bought earlier for the picnic into a large paper bag. Through the kitchen window he could see the end of a long-handled tool moving around on the other side of the hedge. Grady, ignoring the festivities and finding peace in his garden. Or maybe he was doing a tango with his hoe among the cabbages.

He was in the living room stuffing a blanket in on top of the chips when Marilyn and Warren arrived.

"Sorry for the delay, Lewis," Marilyn apologized. She glanced at the bag. "Where are the chips and I'll go get them."

Wilder stopped jamming the blanket and indicated the bag.

"Oh."

Warren, his head grazing the ceiling, was making a tour of the place. He lowered himself far enough to peer into the aquarium and came face to face with one of the newts. He recoiled and continued his prowl. Wilder ignored him.

It couldn't have escaped Marilyn's notice that their picnic à trois was going over like a lead balloon. In an apparent effort to lighten the atmosphere she turned to Wilder.

"We just saw George," she told him. "He asked if we were looking for you, and said if we found you to tell you, 'time and the world are ever in flight.' "

Wilder's eyes narrowed a fraction but he otherwise remained expressionless. Marilyn floundered on.

"He said you would know what he meant and wished me good luck. As conversations go, it reminded me of you. Sort of flaky, you know?"

As efforts go, Marilyn's didn't get very far.

Wilder looked over at Warren sneering at his iguana picture. He turned around and walked into the kitchen and on out the back door.

"Evening, Grady."

"Evening, Lewis."

"Would you mind keeping an eye on my place for a day or two?"

"Nope."

"Thanks."

He stepped back inside, closed the door and walked back into the living room. Warren was sitting in the easy chair with his feet up on the coffee table next to the newts. Wilder stepped over his legs and went through to the bedroom. Marilyn followed him. Without speaking he took a soft zippered bag from the shelf in the closet. Marilyn watched as he sparsely packed it. He brushed past her to get what he needed from the bathroom.

"Would you like me to feed the newts until you get back?" she asked.

He looked at her. "Sure, Grady's got a spare key." Then, stepping back over Warren's legs, he carried his bag into the living room. He picked his jacket up off the sofa and felt the weight of Sherrill's pipe still in the pocket. He thought for a minute. Still holding the jacket he went over to the phone. He called information, asked for Sherrill's number in Stonewall, and dialed it.

"Don? It's Lewis Wilder. Turns out I'm driving to Stonewall tonight. May I stop by your place and pick up the information while I'm there?"

"You're coming all this way just for that?"

"No."

"Oh. Well, sure. I guess that'll solve all our problems, won't it? I'm on Sheffield just off 11E as you come into town. 2349. You can't miss it, name and number's on the gate. What time?"

Wilder glanced at his watch. "Seven-thirty

or eight."

"Okey-doke. You couldn't bring some of that music down with you, could you?"

"Sorry, I've had enough picking and plucking for awhile."

Marilyn stood near the front door holding the picnic bag. Warren appeared to have dozed off in the chair.

"You want to wake him or shall I?" asked Wilder, picking up his own bag.

"I'm awake. What time is it? What the hell is in Stonewall that's so important? Marilyn, where did I leave my guitar?"

"Get yourself a handler, Hart."

Someone knocked at the door. Wilder opened it to a woman with a child struggling to throw the grip she had on his wrist.

"I just want you to know," the woman huffed, "that you shouldn't leave cans half-full of beer sitting on your porch where any passing child can get ahold of it." She glared at Wilder while trying to keep her footing and held an empty can out to him. The child hiccuped.

"Thank you," he said, taking the can. She looked as though she expected more from the encounter than Wilder's thanks. He closed the door in her face.

"Will you at least stay for a sandwich?" Marilyn asked.

"Let him go, Marilyn. Leaves more for us."

"You're about to miss your cue, Hart."

"Shit." Warren leapt to his feet and dashed, averting disaster by hurdling the stumble-gaited child.

Wilder took the empty can to the kitchen.

"Lewis?" Marilyn still stood by the door with the picnic bag. "I suppose you won't be gone long enough for me to miss you?"

He didn't answer.

"Are you running to something, or away from something?"

She said it so softly he wasn't sure he was meant to hear it.

"How much do you know about Hart?" he asked instead, coming back into the room.

"Why?"

Wilder shrugged. Looking around he spied a book he'd started and never finished reading. He slipped it into an outside pocket of his bag.

"I just wonder what brought him back here."

"And how long he's staying?"

"You sure you don't mind feeding the newts?"

She shook her head.

"I might be back tomorrow night."

"Spend some time with her, Lewis."

"I'll see."

"Say hello for me?"

"Sure."

Their remarks to each other were stiff and seemed to Wilder to be carried on across a widening chasm. Marilyn sketched a wave to him and walked out the door.

Outside Hart Warren was wowing the crowd with his intricate fingers. Wilder didn't stop to listen but headed for his car. He caught sight of Marilyn crossing the lawn and his eyes followed her. She joined her mother. Palmer wasn't there. Wilder wondered at his absence, then turned and bumped squarely into him.

"Sorry, George."

Palmer fixed him with a piercing eye. "Ed Ramsey . . ."

"I've talked to him."

"Marilyn . . ."

"She's with her mother."

"Lewis . . ."

"Now, George. I'm going now."

CHAPTER 16

Half an hour down the road, Wilder shook his head to clear it. Marilyn's question kept rattling around in there. Was he running to something or away from it? He wasn't even sure that he was running. Had he run before, when he'd left Aunt Katherine and Stonewall behind? He supposed he had, though his own memory of it was more like someone accepting wings of freedom than fumbling with some mean escape.

He'd stormed out of Aunt Katherine's life knowing he'd never want to go back. To hell with it all. When he'd eventually realized that he might like to go back, the inertia of his self-imposed exile sapped any incentive. Comfort and the ease of doing nothing were a lullaby. He'd never quite been able to bring himself to light the dynamite under his current sense of ease.

But he could picture several people right about now running around with spent matches and great bursts of excitement as they watched his small corner of the world fluttering down around them in pieces.

He stopped in the next town for a cup of coffee and to pull his brains together. There was a choice of McDonald's or a homey-looking place called Granny's Cup of Tea. Granny's looked pleasant and more palatable. Anonymity won out and Wilder pulled into McDonald's.

Over a Styrofoam cup that might as well have been steaming bilgewater as coffee for all the notice he took of it, Wilder considered what he was doing. He'd left Marilyn behind with his new archenemy, the fair-haired, smiling and beguiling, guitar-picking wonder. He was driving to Stonewall, up Aunt Katherine's drive, and knocking on the door he'd slammed shut eight years ago. But stopping first to see a man he'd rather throttle than pass the time of day with. Christ Almighty. He wondered what he should say for openers to his aunt. Hi, I may not be a brain surgeon, but some people like to think I'm a serial burglar?

He swallowed some of the coffee. At least Don Sherrill would provide a buffer. He could put himself at the mercy of a boor before facing the shock of the known and grimly anticipated. He consigned the rest of the coffee to the garbage and headed west. The sun was setting. It was unspectacular.

As he drove, Wilder wondered how Stonewall itself was faring. It had always been a bustling sort of town. Parts of it were charming. Most of it was undistinguished. He had no special feelings for it one way or another except he'd always enjoyed the joke of its name.

Tourists stopped in Stonewall thinking something significant must have gone on there during the Civil War. The confusion came from assuming the town was named for General Stonewall Jackson. In fact it was named for the stone wall a farmer named Jonas Grundy built around his cow pasture. He'd pulled the stones out of his cornfield, cursing one every time he broke a plow bit. The wall, when it was high enough, did the job it was meant to do.

A century or so later, when there weren't any cows left to keep in, the wall was pulled down and sold piecemeal to people from Nashville wanting weathered flagstones for their patios.

Wilder remembered another joke about the town's name, one his cousin had thought up.

"What if he didn't build a stone wall," David had said. "What if he built a stone outhouse. You'd be living in Stone Out-house, Tennessee." And that's what he'd called it, out of their aunt's earshot, from then on.

Wilder followed 11E into Stonewall and turned off on Sheffield. Palmer was right about Sherrill and big possums. This was a neighborhood where they didn't just trot, they swaggered. Sherrill was right, though, and he had no trouble finding the place. He just couldn't drive up to it. An imposing pair of closed gates supported by massive brick pillars met him as he turned off the road. In the pool of light shed by an over-head security light he could see a six-foot tall wrought iron fence disappearing into the darkness on either side of the pillars.

Unimpressed by the show of wealth and annoyed at the inconvenience, Wilder turned the car off and got out. The gates were locked. He looked for an intercom or a doorbell or something that would let Sher-rill know he'd arrived. He found it on one of the pillars under a brass plate warning off solicitors. Expecting to hear Sherrill's over-jolly voice boom out at him from the speaker, he leaned on the button. Nothing happened.

The paved drive swept in an arc toward the house looming several hundred feet in the distance. Sherrill must not have bothered drawing the curtains; he could see lights blazing through the windows and another shining over the front door. Wilder wondered if the button he'd been pressing wasn't working. He stood for a few minutes considering what to do. He could just go on to Aunt Katherine's and call Sherrill from there. Set something up for the morning. He glanced at his watch. Only seven-twenty. There was a small gate to the left of the drive meant for foot traffic. He tried it and found it unlocked. Good, a reprieve and Aunt Katherine could wait.

He decided to move his car first, though, in case the bell was working but Sherrill had just run out to get something. He drove it back to a turnout he'd seen not far along the road, locked it and put on his jacket. Then he walked back and let himself in through the small gate.

The outline of the house reared up against the night sky. It was big and, as Wilder got closer he realized, ugly. It was a circa 1970 pseudo plantation mansion. The roofline lacked grace and the proportions were all wrong. Six columns pretending to be white marble were wasting their energy supporting a pediment too flimsy for their mass. The whole thing gave an impression of ungainliness and too much money poorly spent.

Wilder crossed the concrete porch and rang the doorbell. He waited. He rang the bell again. Either Sherrill really wasn't home or he was in the shower and couldn't hear the bell. He lifted the heavy brass knocker and let it fall. Not that it would do any good. If Sherrill couldn't hear the bell he wouldn't hear the knocker. He peered in one of the sidelights. Nothing stirred.

It was still only seven-thirty. Wilder stood on the edge of the porch and looked out across the expanse of lawn. It stretched away, uninterrupted and flat, into a distance rimmed by large trees and dense bushes. Traffic noises from beyond the trees reached his ears. He sat down on the step, waiting to hear Sherrill's car coming up the drive.

Wind blew through the treetops and scudded a piece of trash across the grass. A truck backfired. If the concrete step had been warmer Wilder might have fallen asleep. If sitting there had been less boring he might not have been inclined to. He roused himself and walked out onto the lawn to look at the stars. Orion was there. Cassiopeia. The Big and Little Dippers. Draco the dragon would be nice to find, or the Pleiades, but he couldn't remember where to look for them.

By now it was ten minutes to eight. He rang and knocked again with no results. Wondering how long he should hang around waiting, feeling restless, he strolled along the front of the house. It was too dark to see more than the shapes of the stiff shrubs planted below each window. Instead he looked in the windows, marveling at the Sherrills' taste in wallpaper and furniture. He trailed his hand along the wall as he turned around at the corner and headed back to the porch. The surface of the mass-produced bricks felt too smooth. No amount of time would mellow them.

He sat on the step again, wondering why he bothered, then reminded himself he had a good reason. He was stalling. He waited some more. But at eight-ten he decided the hell with it and stalked off down the driveway.

As he neared the gate he saw something white propped between two of the vertical bars, resting on one of the horizontal cross braces. It was an envelope that hadn't been there when he'd gone in. A message from Sherrill? He looked around but saw no one. He picked up the envelope expecting to find it addressed either to himself or Sherrill. It was addressed to the Fox.

"What an asshole." Wilder ripped the

envelope open and read the enclosed message. "I have just blown the horn. The hounds will soon be loosed."

"Jeeesus what a moron." Jamming the envelope and note into his pocket he yanked the gate open. He fumbled in his pocket for his car keys and in bringing them out the note escaped, was caught by a gust of wind, and blew back through the gate. Fuming, he stooped down and reached back to catch it.

The gate slammed shut, catching his left arm and smashing it against the brick post.

CHAPTER 17

Stunned and sickened by the sudden pain, Wilder stumbled to his knees and would have fallen except that his upper arm was still pinned by the gate and the rest of him was in an uncomfortable embrace with the brick pillar. He gulped and caught his breath. And then he did fall as the gate swung open again. He pitched sideways and came to earth on his shoulder.

A gust of wind must have blown the gate shut. Except that the wind was blowing in the opposite direction. Wilder heard a car start up and accelerate away. It couldn't have been a person who'd slammed the gate. But a person had left the note. And Wilder didn't know who might have been or might still be there beyond the pool of light. He scrambled to his feet and looked around for any sign of a lurking menace. Then he thought better of heroics and beat it to his car.

Once inside, all doors locked, he explored his upper arm with tentative prods. He rolled the shoulder, tried wiggling the fingers. They waved back at him. No doubt he would have a tremendous bruise but he appeared to be intact.

And this was supposed to be the tame part of the evening. What more could an encounter with an estranged aunt bring? He'd had his share of butterflies in his stomach over the years. The feeling he had now was more like weasels in his guts. With increasing misgivings and the weasels stepping up the tempo of their hornpipe, he turned the car around and drove on to see Aunt Katherine.

Wilder's misgivings had nothing to do with his memories of the Wilder homeplace. It had been heaven and a haven for a child cast adrift in the world. Katherine Wilder had continued in the tradition of her father and his father who had built the place in the 1890s. She kept a few riding horses, several sheep to picturesquely crop the grass, and varying numbers of ducks and geese. She hired a caretaker to keep the animals and tend the modest orchard, grow masses of flowers and enough vegetables to offer the surplus to friends and provide pickles and chutneys for the church bazaar.

Her male forebears envisioned themselves as gentlemen farmers. In reality her grandfather had been something high up at the bank and her father a shrewd lawyer with a lucrative practice. Katherine maintained the illusion of a working farm not because she suffered the paternal delusions but because she liked the place and had the money to do it.

Wilder liked the place, too. He had read *Charlotte's Web* in the hayloft and been comforted along with Wilbur "by the sameness of sheep, the nearness of rats, the love of spiders, the smell of manure, and the glory of everything." The pond had been the ocean for his pirate vessel and the Mississippi River for his raft. The orchard was his Sherwood Forest and every apple tree had felt his bare feet and shins in its branches. Owls and whippoorwills had taught him to whistle as he listened at his window on still summer nights.

His misgivings reared up at the thought of crossing the threshold of the house and reentering his life as his aunt saw fit. As he turned off the highway and up the old gravel drive, shadows familiar even in the dark rose to meet him and his breath quickened.

The house sat on a knoll overlooking the rest of the rolling acres of the farm. Maples, black walnuts, and oaks stood nearby, stretching their limbs toward him. He was drawn forward like a magnet. The wide front porch wrapped around to one side, and before he knew it he was standing there with his overnight bag and no idea what to say when she opened the door. He rang the bell and his cousin David Collins opened the door.

Wilder was at an even greater loss for words than he'd anticipated. Collins wasn't much less dumb.

"Well, well," he finally managed to say.

"Well, well," echoed Wilder. What was this great ass, the bane of his childhood, doing here? As a jealous, spiteful child Collins had delighted in saying his smaller cousin resembled the runt pig Wilbur in more ways than size. The coincidence of Wilbur and Wilder varying by only two letters was an endless source of fun.

Now Collins filled the doorway, his presence adding one more sour note to the discordant evening. Things could only get worse from this point and Wilder considered turning around and forgetting the whole misbegotten venture. Then he felt a perverse trickle of relief worm its way through him. He wouldn't have to face Aunt Katherine alone. Provided she were here. He didn't intend spending any time with Collins.

"Hello, David."

"Hello, Lewis. Hail the return of the prodigal nephew." Collins, recovering from the shock of finding his long lost cousin on the doormat, became effusive and obnoxious.

"Is Aunt Katherine home?"

"Well, she's not out arranging for a fatted calf, if that's what you're wondering. But God, how amazing. Do you want to come in?" Collins made no move to let him in.

Wilder heard someone calling from somewhere inside. Footsteps came down the hall towards the door. Collins smirked and stayed where he was, blocking Wilder's view and that of the person now approaching.

"What's so amazing, David? Who is it?"

"Presenting, dear Aunt Katherine," Collins intoned, "the once and future nephew." He stepped aside with a sweeping gesture in Wilder's direction.

Katherine Wilder stopped where she was and stood staring at him framed in the doorway. Wilder looked back. Neither spoke. Whatever their thoughts and emotions after the years of separation, they were neatly masked. But their eyes took in the details of each other's aging and possibly an understanding of what those years hadn't been able to change. Then Katherine held out a hand to Wilder and he stepped inside.

"This calls for heartwarming welcome-home-drinks all around." Collins slammed the door and ushered the two ahead of him, happy in his role as convivial host to this couple of mutes.

"So, what'll it be? How about a dram of Drambuie?"

They were paying no attention to him, so Collins shooed them into the living room and rushed off to get the glasses and something suitable for the occasion.

Katherine more or less dropped into the first armchair she came to. Wilder crossed over to another chair and was about to sit when the fireplace caught his eye.

"Aunt Katherine, you've got a woodstove insert." For all the times he'd wondered what his first words in eight years would be to this woman who had lovingly raised him and endlessly meddled with his life, "you've got a woodstove insert" had never occurred to him.

The words brought her attention snapping back. She sat up straight and smoothed the wrinkles from her skirt.

"You thought I'd never stop letting the fireplace 'suck the heat right out of the room' as you so tirelessly used to put it?"

She fixed him with a challenging eye. They'd had memorable discussions on that subject.

"And do you think I'm still foolish enough to answer a question like that?" He glanced around the rest of the room, not keen on hearing her answer.

The room looked much the same as when he'd left. The inevitable difference of things growing old and more worn didn't matter here. Aunt Katherine would not part with her grandparents' furniture for the sake of vogue novelty. Old slipcovers might fade away, but the foundations were as steadfast as her own. Putting his bag down beside a chair, which he seemed to remember in a previous life being striped but was now covered in marvelous, verdant, floral vines, he sat and realized how tired he was.

"Things do change, Lewis." Katherine's voice was soft and even, just as he remembered it being. He wished she'd keep talking.

But Collins came surging back carrying a tray with three glasses of Drambuie and the bottle.

"Libations for my little cousin," he announced, making a point of standing over Wilder and looking down at the top of his head. The effect of the slur was lost because

Wilder wasn't standing. Collins presented them each with a dainty liqueur glass, then arranged a small table for the tray. Wilder and Katherine suspended their openers as Collins fussed around the room. He then arranged himself on the sofa, one long arm along the back and one leg crossed over the other.

"So Lewis, did you leave the wife and kids out in the car or aren't you married?"

Wilder took a sip and leaned back into the cushions, amused for the time, by his cousin. He let Collins' ridiculous banter wash over him and watched Katherine's eyes watching him. They were deep-set eyes, like his father's had been, like his own. Their strength and intelligence belied the rest of her looks, which suggested she was a slight wisp of gray-haired feminine fluff. Katherine Wilder would not blow away with the next puff of wind or adversity. She wore like iron. Wilder had never dreamed of being glad to see Collins. But looking at his aunt, he was thankful again for his cousin's presence giving him a chance to slip in without fireworks.

When she'd finished her drink, Katherine stood up. Wilder stood, too.

"I'm going up now. Lewis, I'll put clean sheets and towels in the spare room for you." She nodded toward his bag. "I assume you intend to stay a day or two."

Wilder went over and kissed her on the cheek. She put her hands on either side of his face and held it for a minute, studying it.

"We'll talk in the morning," she said. "You're looking thin, Lewis."

He stood in the door as she walked up the stairs. When he turned around again Collins was standing in front of the fireplace, a less jovial expression on his face.

"You're looking short, Lewis."

As Collins smiled to himself and poured another drink, Wilder picked up his bag and went up to bed.

CHAPTER 18

The face barely able to look out of the mirror at Wilder the next morning couldn't have spent a good night. He splashed cold water on it, hoping to revive it. He thought about pinching his cheeks to put some color in them, not wanting to upset Aunt Katherine's appetite by going down to breakfast looking like the pale underbelly of a slug. Then again, she might enjoy that. Give her something right off the bat to start on. He dressed, taking his time because his arm was indeed very bruised, hoping she hadn't taken up bear hugging.

Katherine was already sitting at the kitchen table when he went down. She looked up from the newspaper, an obvious blind. It was open to the sports section, a section Wilder knew she took interest in only as liner for the cat pan. He stopped in the doorway.

"Don't be so melodramatic, Lewis. Come

in and sit down. Eat your breakfast." She shoved a box of Wheat Chex across the table to a place set and waiting for him.

Wilder smiled at her familiar cantankerousness and sat.

"Where's David?"

"At church. Where I would be, too."

"Sorry."

"Are you? That's an interesting thought."

"Well, you don't need to stay home on my account."

Their eyes met over the top of the cereal box. Katherine sighed.

"Oh, Lewis."

Wilder poured a bowl of cereal.

"The milk is in the icebox."

He fetched it, poured it, returned it. Then he sat and forced himself to eat.

"David's got quite a business going, you know."

He thought about saying no he didn't know but decided he'd better accept the statement in the spirit it was given. She appeared to be offering a neutral subject as an olive branch. Or maybe she was using Collins as a safety buffer, too.

"That's great. What is it?"

"The Alternative Energy Co-op. He sells solar cells, windmills, fireplace equipment . . ."

"Woodstove inserts?"

She looked up. "Yes. He does. He also acts as a broker for firewood and corn. The corn is for cornstoves. That's what they burn instead of wood."

"Ah."

The everyday trivia of the Alternative Energy Co-op seemed to fascinate Katherine, at least she was able to recount enough details of the business to avoid having a real conversation. Wilder pretended to listen while he ate, but his eyes strayed around the familiar walls of the kitchen and more often to the windows and beyond. She kept track of his progress, though, and as soon as he put his spoon down she stopped chattering.

"All right, why have you come?"

It was a straightforward question. There was no sign of rancor in her voice. But he noticed she hadn't added the word "home" to it. He also noticed her hands were shaking slightly. Emotion? Stress? Was she so old? Was it Parkinson's? He was stalling again. And he still didn't know what to say or how to start. It would be so much easier if they would just fall into each other's arms and sob. But it would be hell on his arm. And her sense of dignity. He looked at her, feeling hopeless and hollow, and shook his head.

"Well, I think I know." She bit off each word as she spoke it. "And I'll have you know that I don't appreciate it."

That was why she was shaking. It was suppressed anger. She must have already heard the rumors and was ready to bite him in two and shred the pieces. Now would be a good time to show he'd matured. React calmly. Soothe the wild aunt. Like hell.

"I thought it might help if I came and told you myself. Obviously not. But if you know why I'm here, then why did you ask?" He felt his cheeks getting hot. "You don't believe any of that shit do you?"

She drew her breath in as though he'd slapped her. "What did you say?"

"Or is it just your reputation you're worried about?"

"It has nothing to do with my reputation. If I choose to be anonymous that's my business."

That sounded odd. Something had jumped off track here, but before Wilder could figure it out Katherine began raging.

"And just how did you find out that money is coming from me? That is my confidential business and neither you, nor anyone else, has any right to that information. I want to know . . ."

She puffed up in her outrage so that she resembled a ruffed grouse ruffling. Wilder had forgotten how she looked in her glory. She was wonderful and he laughed with real pleasure.

"What are you laughing at?"

"I'm sorry," said Wilder, shaking his head again.

"And stop shaking your head at me as though I'm some sort of unbelievable specimen."

"Aunt Kate the Great." He sighed. "Are you telling me you're the one who's been donating two hundred dollars to the museum every month?"

She deflated a bit. "You didn't know?"

"Never occurred to me."

She wilted in her chair, looking around her as though expecting a different answer or at least some back-up support from the cupboards and stove. "You didn't know?" Wilder shook his head. "Hell's bells."

"Can I get you anything, Aunt Katherine?" he asked, feeling solicitous now and alarmed at how much her anger had taken out of her. "Some tea maybe?"

"There's a crow in the pantry, I think, dear," she answered.

"You've never eaten crow in your life."

"People do change, Lewis."

227

"Not much," he said, smiling. "Aunt Katherine, I had no idea the donations were from you. They've been wonderful for the museum." And less so for me, he thought. "But why anonymous?"

"I didn't want to be accused of meddling in your life again. Let me ask you this, would you have accepted the money if I'd sent it to you rather than the museum?"

He knew he should say yes. But she was brighter than that. He looked down at his bowl, shoved it aside. "I don't know. How did you know where I was?"

"Wait a minute," Katherine said, ignoring his question and working on one of her own with narrowing eyes. "If you didn't come here to berate me for interfering in your life, again, then why did you come? What are you so eloquently concerned I not believe and what has it got to do with my reputation? You've never called even once in the last eight years. For all you knew, I was dead."

"Not you, Aunt Katherine."

"Why not? People die all the time."

"I know."

"Yes, well. You do. We both do. But what could possibly be so important for me to hear now?"

Wilder stood up and walked over to look

out the window above the sink. He cradled his bruised arm. He didn't want to spill the rumors now and start another eruption. Maybe he shouldn't have come. But she did care about her reputation and rumors always had a way of sprouting and twisting and living an ugly life all their own. But it would end up being such a long story and it was all so stupid. Maybe first things should come first.

"I came," he said, "because I wanted to see you." He turned to face her. "Because I've missed you and I love you."

"Well, we'll leave it at that for now." Then her expression softened. "But that's why I was glad he told me where you were."

"Who?"

But the telephone rang and Katherine ignored his question again and went to answer it instead.

"That was David," she said when she came back. "He won't be home until tonight. He hasn't been home often lately anyway. Maybe he has a girl somewhere. He's divorced, you know. Or I guess you didn't know. It happens so often these days, though. I'll start a kettle for tea, or would you rather have coffee?"

"Tea's fine."

"Then let's go sit on the back porch."

"Isn't it kind of cool for sitting out there this morning?"

"David winterized it."

"Oh, of course."

Wilder followed his aunt to the newly energy-efficient porch and they sat in the comfortable, old rattan furniture, looking down past the remains of her summer garden to the pond. His eyes followed a line of rail fencing that disappeared over the next hill. He'd like to have asked how long his cousin had been staying here but didn't want to take a chance on ruffling the feathers again. Katherine was on a parallel wavelength.

"How long would you like to stay?" she asked.

Wilder cocked an eye at her. "I would like to stay longer," he said with careful emphasis. "But I should go home tonight or early in the morning."

"Home? Well, that's good, Lewis. I'm glad you like it enough that you call it home. I've never been to Nolichucky. Tell me about it."

"It's pretty. Or, most of it is anyway. You'd like the old houses. There are some good people there."

"It's awfully small, isn't it?"

"The town itself is. But there're a lot of

people living all around out in the county."

"And you like your job? You like the life of a small-time curator?" She smiled sweetly.

"Yes." He could smile sweetly, too.

"Good. I'll go get the tea."

"Good."

Good god, he thought, just like old times. But what else had he expected? He told himself to behave and then, when he saw that his knuckles were white from gripping the arms of the chair, he told himself to relax. Crossing his arms, he bumped his bruise and swore.

He ought to call Sherrill sometime today, he supposed. Though maybe after last night he would just pack the bird up and send it back to him and forget the whole thing. Could it have been Sherrill who left the note and slammed the gate? That would take an incredibly sick sense of humor. Or maybe Sherrill was the Fox and he'd just stepped into the trap by accident? No. Even in the dark no one could have mistaken him for Sherrill. He shivered, despite Collins' winterizing.

The doorbell rang and Wilder heard Katherine call out that she would go. Then she was laughing and he could hear her talking to someone.

"No, the cat didn't have kittens again,"

she was saying. "It's more like something the cat dragged in. I'll be out in a minute, you go ahead and see what you can make of it."

Oh, god, he thought. Now what? He stood up, ready to greet whoever this was she was springing on him with such glee. He expected to see one of her old friends and prepared to be clucked over in astonishment. Instead he saw a friend of his who could not have presented a better picture of stupefaction.

Rodger Meade had been his best friend. He'd lived down the road, the only son among six daughters, in a house that rarely saw a moment's quiet or a coat of paint. If Wilder had played Wilbur in his cousin's malicious mind, Rodger Meade had played Lurvey, the hired hand. Meade's father had been the hired caretaker of the Wilder farm, which prompted Collins' inspired name-calling. (He'd tried once calling Meade "Fern" and regretted it immediately.) But to each other Wilder and Meade had always been the indisputable heroes of the world. They were Tom and Huck, Stanley and Livingston, the Wright brothers, Robin Hood and Little John.

And here he was, more powerful through the shoulders than he had been and beginning to thicken through the waist, face half hidden by a magnificent red beard, and his mouth hanging open.

"Close your mouth, Rodger. There's a fly been buzzing around."

"Lewis. God." Meade staggered over to a chair and sat down. "Sorry if I'm incoherent."

"I have that effect on people."

"God, I never expected to see you. What, uh," he gave his beard a scratch, "what are you doing here?"

Wilder smiled and shrugged and sat back down.

"Just happened to be in the neighborhood after ten-odd years?"

"More like seven or eight but, yeah, something like that."

"Does Dave know you're here?"

"Met me at the door last night."

"Man. I'd like to have been the fly on the wall for that reunion."

"How long's he been here?"

"Why?"

Wilder shrugged again, as if the question didn't matter.

"About eighteen months."

"Mm."

"Well, gee, so how've you been?"

Katherine returned at that point. Meade

jumped up and took the tea things from her. Wilder stood and offered her his chair. Thanking him, she sat in another.

"So, what do you make of it, Rodger?" she asked as she handed him a cup.

"Katherine, I'm struck dumb."

"There, Lewis, you've wrought a miracle. Rodger is never without something to say about anything."

Wilder noted that Meade had graduated from calling her Miss Wilder. And he saw the fondness in her smile for his old friend. It mirrored his own feelings and they both unbent a bit now that he was here. The edge was taken off last night's questions and suspicions still creeping around in his brain. The hot cup of tea felt good in his hands. Aunt Katherine's cat wandered out and threaded itself between two potted plants to stretch out in the pool of warm sunlight on the wide windowsill. Wilder sat musing over how suddenly and unexpectedly pleasant everything was.

"He's running a museum in Nolichucky, Rodger. You should go up and visit him sometime. Now that you've resurfaced in our lives you'd like visitors once in awhile, wouldn't you, Lewis?"

"Hm?" He realized he'd been watching them talk and had no idea what they were talking about.

"I think I startled him, Rodger. He's a bit edgy. There's something on his mind he hasn't told me yet. Maybe his conscience is bothering him about something."

"Bound to be, Katherine," Meade said cheerfully. "How about I take him out for a walk around the old place, stir up some memories to make him homesick and bring him back more often?"

"That's a good idea. I wouldn't ordinarily like to say it, but I'll admit it to you, Rodger, I have missed him." She reached over and patted Wilder's hand.

They left Katherine on the porch with the tea and the cat and walked down past the garden. Meade kept up a steady patter of reminiscences and small jokes interspersed with questions about Wilder's job and his life in Nolichucky. Wilder strolled beside him, making appropriate sounds and re-signed himself to being grilled about his long absence. He probably owed a certain amount of penance.

They stopped by the pond and watched a pair of mallards paddling in the water.

"So you never married?" Meade asked.

"No."

"You mean, in all those years, you never met anyone to match Linda Armstrong?"

Wilder laughed. "Linda Armstrong? Oh, god. I haven't thought of her in years." He thought of Marilyn, now, and sighed.

"You were pretty stuck on her."

He picked up a pebble, chucked it in the water, and wished he hadn't because it made his left arm ache all over again. "I was very stuck on her. She never looked twice at me. Linda Armstrong. Geez."

He turned away. The wind was blowing cold and lifted the hair off his forehead.

"Does your dad still do all this?" He gestured at the garden put to bed for the winter and the fences running in crisp white lines.

"No. He died three years ago."

"I'm sorry."

"One of my brothers-in-law took over."

"Well, that's nice." He nodded toward the house. "Does she still keep horses?"

"If you'd kept in touch you wouldn't have to ask."

It was the first hint of rebuke from Meade, but Wilder didn't turn fast enough to catch any sign of it in his face. He was smiling again and recalling the time they'd dug an algae-coated, mud-beslimed rock out of the pond and delivered it to Katherine as a doorstop. She'd sent them each a proper thank you note and put the rock to work at the stable.

They found it still there, apparently still useful for holding the door open on fine summer days.

They stepped out of the wind into the sheltering grove of cedars planted around the stable. Wilder gave the rock a loving kick and stood, hands in his pockets, staring down at it.

Katherine Wilder had never liked the horse barn being so far from the house and invisible behind the trees. She had a horror of the horses being caught in a fire that she wouldn't notice or be able to get to in time. Nothing had ever been changed, though. And the massive timbers used in its construction one hundred years ago were probably rooted forever.

Meade pulled the door open and they went inside to be enveloped in the warm smells of horse, sweet alfalfa hay, and worn leather. Wilder breathed deeply and the memories evoked by the familiar scents came crowding in. Curiosity brought one of the horses to peer over the half-door of its stall to see who had arrived and might have brought an apple. Wilder went over and rubbed the long face, feeling a contentment long forgotten reawakening.

"Do you still ride?" Meade leaned comfortably against the wall.

"No, I don't ever seem to have the time. Or the horse."

"Yeah, I know what you mean. I make do with Dick Francis novels these days."

"You never liked jumping."

"I can always dream. Say, you remember playing mumblety-peg in here on some of those long rainy days?"

"Yeah."

"You still have that Swiss Army knife Katherine gave you for your birthday?"

Wilder smiled and drew a circle on the dirt floor with his toe. He pulled the knife out of his pocket, opened the largest blade and flipped it, landing it sticking upright in the center. Meade grinned and picked it up. He stood, turning it over, admiring the number and variety of blades and the heft of it. Wilder took the opportunity to steer the conversation away from himself. "So what are you doing these days, Rodger?"

Meade looked up.

"Oh, I thought maybe you knew."

Wilder was aware of a subtle shift in his mood. Puzzled, he searched Meade's face. Still the warm smile, the clear, high brow, but Meade's eyes were focused intently on his own. Wilder looked away, uncomfortable.

"Should I know?"

Meade didn't answer. Wilder shrugged it off thinking he was playing some sort of game, such as make Lewis suffer a bit for his indifference all these years. The horse behind him nudged his arm with its nose and he tried not to grimace. He turned back to it and was stroking it when Meade spoke again.

"How's your arm this morning?"

He froze and the hairs prickled on the back of his neck.

"What?"

"How's your arm this morning?" His voice was flat, cold.

Wilder faced slowly around to Meade and for the first time, looking him straight in the eyes, he realized how long it had been since he had known this man. Meade must have slammed that gate shut.

"You didn't just happen to stop by this morning."

"Hardly."

But why had he done it? For what possible reason? How had he even known he would be at Sherrill's? And just how dangerous was he now? Wilder struggled to make sense of the situation. Meade must be the Fox. Jesus.

"What do you want?"

No answer, just Meade looking at him.

He tried to think what he could do. What options were there? If Meade wanted a fight there would be no contest. His arm would handicap him, Meade was more powerful, and he had his only possible weapon. They were here in the barn, too far from the house so that no one would hear if he yelled. Wilder realized, with a sickening jolt, this whole set-up had been planned.

He decided to try just walking away from it. The Meade he remembered had not been violent. Banking on this memory, he stared at Meade for a few seconds and then turned and started for the door.

Meade made no move to follow. Wilder prayed this would work, or better, that he had been wrong, that Meade was innocent, had planned nothing. Then Meade called after him.

"Don't make it hard, Lewis."

Wilder sprinted. He didn't get far. Someone stepped out as he got to the door and clamped a restraining hand on his left shoulder. Taken by surprise and jolted by the pain, Wilder's reaction was to whirl around and plow his fist into the person's solar plexus. He stunned his assailant, but not long enough to get away. The man grabbed him by the left arm and swung him around toward Meade again.

Wilder felt the pressure in his arm as it was twisted up and behind him. He was aware of Meade watching the struggle and then he felt the bone in his arm snap. Gasping at the sudden rush of pain, he stumbled, pulling the other man off balance and down with him. They both swore and then Wilder's head hit the rock by the door.

CHAPTER 19

"Christ, Lewis, you're bleeding all over our rock."

Wilder groaned and rolled the sore, bleeding part of his forehead off the chunk of granite. Now his cheek was in contact with its cool, rough surface and he concentrated on that feeling, trying to blot out pain and panic.

"Fisher's bringing the car down here." There was quiet for a few minutes as they both listened for the car. "You shouldn't have run, you know," Meade added.

The car drew up outside, the motor left idling. Meade helped Wilder to his feet and propelled him into the back seat, propping him there in the corner. He went back into the barn and returned with a clean rag, tossing it to Wilder.

"Blot your head," he said and slammed the door.

Taking over the wheel himself, Meade

turned the car a jerky one-hundred-eighty degrees which was excruciating for the backseat passenger who thought he might like to either pass out or vomit. The car made its bumpy way down the drive, past the house where Katherine was now folding clean dish towels in the kitchen, unaware of her nephew's enforced departure.

Wilder knew he should pay attention to the turns they made once they were out on the main road. He should make an effort to track landmarks. A vague picture ran through his mind of trying to survive this bizarre kidnapping. Instead he held the cloth to his streaming forehead and closed his eyes. Then, opening them again to the merest slits, he looked at his left arm which, for the hell it was giving him, he expected to find bent at some oblique angle somewhere between his elbow and shoulder. It looked unforgivably normal. He closed his eyes again.

"Wake up, beautiful."

The car had stopped. Wilder, who hadn't been sleeping, just wishing he were comatose, opened his eyes.

"Can you walk in under your own steam or should Fisher get a wheelchair?"

Was this an hallucination? They were at the emergency entrance to the hospital.

"What are we doing here?"

"Looking after your welfare. Come on, get out before I pull you out." Tossing the car keys to Fisher, Meade leaned down and hooked his hand under Wilder's right arm.

Things could not get more bizarre. Wilder felt as though he were watching himself being escorted through those hissing, automatic doors and swallowed up in this unnatural nightmare.

Meade remained in control as they sat down at the admittance desk. Keeping his left hand on Wilder's right shoulder, giving the appearance of offering comfort, Meade answered all the clerk's questions. Wilder was already too stunned to be more amazed when Meade rattled off his address in Nolichucky, his phone number, and the museum's number. He only gaped slightly as Meade recited his social security number and produced his insurance card.

They were told to take a seat in the waiting room. Meade snarled something unpleasant under his breath, then smiled and thanked the clerk. He took Wilder's arm, continuing his grim parody of attentive support, and they found two seats in a corner of the room.

"Welcome to limbo. We can expect to be here awhile." Meade picked up a magazine and began flipping through the pages.

Wilder's heart was pounding in his chest to the same beat as the throb in his arm and his forehead. What the hell, he wondered, was going on? And why was he letting it? His brains must have been scrambled back on the rock. It occurred to him that he could jump up and make enough of a scene that someone might come rescue him from Meade. He dismissed the idea as soon as it came. His hysterics would be put down to trauma and disorientation, or with his luck to paranoia from smoking too much dope. And who would believe that the smiling, affable Meade, who had brought him here in the first place, was holding him against his will?

His head hurt and he didn't want to think anymore. He slumped in his chair and looked around at the rest of the souls damned to the oblivion of waiting for emergency care.

There were a surprising number. Those who weren't staring at the television bolted high up on one wall were staring at each other. They all looked as though they had hangovers, but Wilder put that down either to the interminable wait in the god-awful, uncomfortable chairs or the general effect of hospital miasma. Sound from the television was drowned out by the squalls from a small boy. An old man in the opposite corner coughed so frequently and ferociously it was a wonder he still had strength left to put his cigarette to his mouth.

Time dragged. The small boy and his near-desperate parents were at last summoned. The sudden peace lying in the wake of their departure produced a ripple of mumbled conversations. A woman limped in to join the ranks, saying she reckoned she'd used the power mower in her bare feet once too often. Wilder wished he could either concentrate on a magazine or fall asleep. He looked over at Meade. Meade was asleep.

Wilder eased out of his seat. Cradling his throbbing arm, he went out into the hall to find a phone. It would be quicker to call the police than to leave the building and wander around looking for help considering the shape he was in and what he must look like. There were two pay phones across from the admittance desk. Both were being used. He waited, casting anxious glances back at Meade in the waiting room, wondering where the lethal phantom, Fisher, was. Finally the young man using the phone on the right hung up, a look of delirious joy on his face. Wilder started forward. The young man picked up the receiver again, took a quarter from a mound of coins sitting on the shelf in front of him, and dialed again.

"Grandma, it's a girl!"

Wilder moaned.

A passing nurse stopped and peered into his face.

"Sir, can I help you?" Her voice was gentle. She looked sane.

"I want to call the police," he said.

Her concerned gaze followed his to the occupied phones. She looked back at him and over his shoulder. Then she smiled.

"Well, you're in luck. The best policeman in the county is standing right behind you."

Relief swept over Wilder in a great warm wave. He turned around. Meade was standing there.

Wilder stared at his grinning face. "You shit," he said without particular emphasis and walked back to his seat in the waiting room.

Meade followed, chuckling. He sat next to Wilder again, stretching his legs out and propping his feet up on the magazine table in front of them.

"You really didn't know? What a chump."

"Have you got a gun in case I try to make a break for it?"

Meade shook his head in mock sadness.

"Sarcasm is the weapon of a weak character, Lewis."

"You're the one who had a gorilla hiding outside the barn. My god, what did you tell him? Rip his arm off if he makes a break for it?"

"Yeah, I'm sorry about your arm. Fisher's a Philistine. But I bet you two-to-one the arm was already fractured from the gate last night anyway. And hitting your head on the rock was just pure bad luck." He leaned forward and grunted as he picked up another magazine.

Wilder felt dazed. Was this a joke? Had Meade slammed the gate? And if he had, why? And if he hadn't, how did he know about it? Why had he come looking for him? How did he know anything, it seemed like everything, about him? Wilder began to feel sick to his stomach, short of breath.

"What the hell is happening?"

"Not here, Lewis, not now." Meade yawned.

"What do you mean, not here? I want to know what the hell I'm doing here with you and what the hell you think you're doing and just what the hell you think I've done."

"Lewis, for chrissake," Meade hissed out of the side of his mouth, "calm down. You don't need this now. I don't need this now.

248

Not here. Wait until the doctor's seen your head and fixed your arm." He turned to look at Wilder, as though assessing his appearance for the first time. "You look like hell."

"Fuck you, Rodger." Wilder started to get up.

Meade was ahead of him, though, already standing in front of him, staring into his eyes the way a sheep dog might hold a rebellious sheep, daring it to make a false move.

The nurse, responding to Wilder's raised voice, stepped toward them.

"Is there a problem?" she asked.

Meade's reply was calm, but he answered without turning to look at her. "No. Thank you. But is there a room where we could wait in private?"

The nurse impaled Wilder with a piercing eye. "Yes, I think that's a good idea. Follow me."

She led them to an unoccupied examination room. Without speaking another word, she left them with a clear understanding of their fate should they prove disruptive again.

Affecting the role of magnanimous host, contradicted by the look in his eye and the sturdy shoulder he leaned against the closed door, Meade offered Wilder a seat. Choice was limited to a wooden armchair, a skittery-looking stool on wheels, and the examination table. Wilder was torn between crawling onto the table and passing out or standing there in the middle of the tiny cubicle and confronting Meade on his own two feet. He decided the advantage came in not falling asleep or falling down so he sat on the edge of the armchair and stared at the white sink opposite his knees.

"You want to know what's happening?"

Wilder gave one sharp nod.

"A guy named Donald Sherrill was killed last night. His body was found outside his back door. Looks like the proverbial blunt instrument. Have to wait for the autopsy to know what's really what. You were seen at Sherrill's place, near as we can tell sometime around the time of death. Physical evidence has been found showing you were there. Sherrill's wife says that you and he had violent arguments."

Wilder's already gray face now went pale with shock.

"Why didn't you say any of that to begin with?" he asked.

Meade shrugged. "I like to play my cards close. Now, I want to know exactly what you were doing last night and whether Sherrill was alive when you left him."

Wilder's stomach lurched.

"I didn't even see him. I rang the door bell a few times and waited around for maybe half an hour in case he'd gone out for something and then I left."

"And the episode with your arm in the gate?"

"You're a real sleuth, aren't you? The gate slammed shut when I was picking something up. It swung open again and I got the hell out of there."

Meade stood looking down at Wilder, some of the hardness easing from his face. "Why did you come home?" he asked.

"That's irrelevant," Wilder snapped. And pointless, now, he realized. So much for giving Aunt Katherine a little gentle advance warning. "Who saw me at Sherrill's?"

"Anonymous tipper. What did you do while you waited for Sherrill?"

"Admired his herbaceous borders."

"He hasn't got any. What were you doing on October 1st between the hours of six-thirty and ten o'clock?"

Wilder caught his breath. "What?"

Meade pulled something sealed in a plastic bag from his pocket.

"Is this addressed to you?" It was the note Wilder had found on Sherrill's gate.

"What the hell is this?" Wilder was on his feet again.

Meade remained motionless, returning Wilder's glare with his own steady gaze.

Someone knocked. Meade shifted so he could open the door.

"The doctor can see Mr. Wilder now." The nurse looked at Meade who nodded. "Come with me, then, please."

Wilder moved stiffly past Meade and followed her. An incomplete memory of something he'd read long ago swam into his confused brain as they filed down the echoing white corridor. It was an allusion to clouds, clouds appearing on someone's horizon, gathering until they were black with doom. He turned his head to see Meade following resolutely behind. As they were swallowed by the stainless steel doors marking entrance to the emergency ward proper, Wilder felt the weight of his own clouds gathering.

"God, hospitals make me sick." Meade stopped outside the door to light up a cigarette. Flicking the match into some stunted bushes, he filled his lungs with fresh smoke.

Wilder, standing beside him, exhausted from the hours-long attentions of ministering angels, slid a sideways look at him mixing disbelief and disgust.

"What did you tell Aunt Katherine?" he asked.

"So you finally gave some thought to her, did you?"

"Shut up, Rodger."

Meade took Wilder's right elbow and steered him across the parking lot.

"I told her you'd had an accident."

"She's not stupid."

"No. But she'll hear something soon enough, anyway, one way or another."

"Where's your friend?"

"Who, Fisher? Why? You feeling nervous?"

Wilder kept his eyes forward and refused to be baited.

"He's on a mission," Meade stage-whispered. He, at least, had regained his former good humor.

They came to a dark-blue VW Golf sporting a bumper sticker saying "Blow it out your bagpipe." Meade helped Wilder in on the passenger side then went around and tucked himself into the driver's seat. Wilder tried, with his right hand, to pull out enough of his seat belt before the locking mechanism grabbed it so that he could reach across his immobilized left arm and buckle it down by his left hip. It took more coordination than his muzzy brain and one-handedness could muster, though, and he had surreal visions of himself grappling with two or three boa constrictors. Without comment, Meade leaned over and did it for him.

"So what happens now?" Wilder asked.

Meade merged into traffic with a jaunty wave for the pickup he cut off and glanced at Wilder. "You know, you don't look like you really care. But maybe that's the pain-killers."

"You look like you're having the time of your life."

"Well, and why not? And to show you what a sweet guy I still am, I'll tell you what happens next. Although, I also have to tell you, I'm struggling with this. See, I could arrest you right now on circumstantial evidence for Sherrill's murder, and by golly I bet I could throw in burglary, too." He took a last drag on the cigarette and flipped the butt out the open window. "But I think we'll save that for later. The good doctor says you need some rest because you've had a shock." He smiled at Wilder. "So first we'll go to my place because by now it's almost supper time. And then we'll just see if we can't find out what the hell you've been up to."

Neither of them felt inclined to say anything after that for awhile. Meade whistled as he zipped through the light Sunday evening traffic, giving the impression that nothing could be finer than driving along with an old friend by his side who was probably a murderer and who showed definite signs of losing his grip on reality. He looked over at Wilder every once in awhile and smiled.

Wilder stared through the windshield, his thoughts wandering in and out. He imagined the square bandage on his forehead pulsating in geometric patterns of red and black. His left arm, encased and immobilized against his chest, felt like a chunk of granite left uncarved by the slaphappy, irresponsible artist who'd started this mess in the first place. He wondered where or what Meade called home these days and what he would dish up for supper and if he would mind if instead of eating he just went to throw up and then collapse somewhere. Then it occurred to him that Meade might have a family to whom he would be presented in all his current Technicolor and glory.

"Are you married?"

"Yeah, didn't I tell you?"

"You didn't tell me a damned thing."

"I married Linda Armstrong."

"Shit."

"Watch your language in front of the kids, will you, Lewis?"

CHAPTER 20

"Can you tie your shoes with one hand?"

Wilder looked at the serious six-year-old sitting across the table from him. It was another in the long line of questions that the cotton wool between his ears wasn't processing efficiently. Meade's two sons were taking turns posing creative dilemmas to their one-armed dinner guest. How does one tell the children of a large policeman, who is, incidentally, sitting at the end of the table enjoying the show, to go perform an unnatural act? He wrapped his mind around that problem and made an attempt to answer the question with restraint.

"My shoe isn't untied."

"Well, I have a friend, Benny, he has one hand, well, he has two hands but only one works because something's wrong with the other one and it just kind of hangs there, and he can tie his shoes. Why don't you try?"

Wilder blinked. He would have kept his

eyes on both boys at once but it made him dizzy. When he felt a tugging on his shoelace he realized his mistake.

"There, why don't you try it now?"

"Jeff, for heaven's sake, sit back down and leave poor Mr. Wilder alone. Lewis, I'm sorry. You can see they take after their father."

Linda Meade smiled at her husband. She was seven months pregnant and still looked energetic enough to keep up with anything Meade or the children might spring on her. If she was surprised by Wilder's sudden appearance at their supper table, she took it in stride, including him easily in the general family gaiety.

Meade on the other hand seemed to be going out of his way to make things less comfortable for him than they already were.

"But Mommy, how did he break his arm and how did they put it back on?"

"Charlie, honey, the bone just has a crack in it. His arm didn't come apart."

"Someone snapped it for him, matey, like a twig," growled Meade, closing one eye and with a horrible grin.

"Pirates!" shouted the boys, giggling. They looked with wider eyes and more respect at Wilder.

"Daddy used to be a pirate," said Jeff.

"But only until he married Mommy and she made him mend his wicked ways," shouted Charlie.

"Except his beard. Mommy let him keep his pirate beard," amended Jeff.

Meade beamed around the table, every inch the doting father and husband.

"Lewis, what brings you back to Stonewall?" asked Linda, catching a glass of milk sitting too near the edge of the table.

"His pirate ship," yelled both boys.

"That's enough now, boys," Linda shushed.

"Your mother's right, mateys, when a man has secrets, sometimes it's best to lie quiet-like and wait. We'll get the answer to that question out of him soon enough, and plenty of others, too, you wait and see," said Meade.

"Rodger."

"Yes, dear?" asked Meade in a sweet voice.

"I think you're being rude to Lewis. He looks exhausted."

"That's why I thought he could just stay here, tonight. That all right?"

Linda shrugged. "Sure. If you'll be comfortable enough on the sofa, Lewis, we'd love to have you. And if you can put up with these goofy guys." She turned her attention to cutting the younger boy's meat.

Wilder glanced at Meade who, while Linda's attention was diverted, returned a not so benign glare.

"Actually," Wilder started to say.

"Arrrgh," Meade interjected.

It wasn't worth the effort. "Sure, thanks," Wilder said and slumped further in his chair. He looked across at the little boys staring back at him. Charlie slid down in his chair, mirroring Wilder. Wilder straightened back up, watching as the child did likewise. The boy picked up his cup, his eyes peering over the rim at Wilder. Wilder picked up his iced tea. Charlie blew bubbles in his milk.

"Well, you could probably borrow some of Mommy's pajamas. I think Daddy's are too big for you," said Jeff.

Wilder choked on his iced tea.

"That's very thoughtful of you, Jeff," said Linda. She turned from cutting Charlie's meat to cut Wilder's.

"Mommy, he's a grown-up. Why are you cutting up his supper?"

"I'm being thoughtful, too, dear. How do you think he'll cut his pork chop with one hand? Now, excuse me, I'll be right back."

"Mommy always has to go to the bathroom," Charlie explained.

"Do you have any boys, Mr. Wilder?"

"No, sorry."

"Do you have a wife?"

"No."

"How come?"

Wilder turned to look at Meade.

"Why are you doing this to me?" he asked quietly. "Aren't I supposed to be calling a lawyer or something? Don't I have some sort of rights here somewhere?"

Linda came back in as Meade answered, not bothering to lower his voice.

"Rights? No," he waved his hand, dismissing Wilder's question. "No, that comes after I arrest you, Lewis."

Wilder groaned.

"Daddy, are you going to arrest him? Want me to get some rope? How do you handcuff a guy with only one hand?" the boys jabbered on top of each other.

"Whoa, whoa, whoa. Wait a second. What are you talking about?" Linda asked.

"Well, Sweetie-pie, listen to this, there's something rich in this situation that I just want to savor for a bit," said Meade, leaning back and crossing his arms over his chest. "Here's a guy, who was my best friend. Disappears for eight years without a word. Then one morning he shows up again implicated in a whole string of sophisticated house-jobs in his new hometown. And even though that's just seventy-five miles from here he's never even bothered to let his only loving relative in on the secret that he's there. Oh, and yeah, now he's the prime suspect for a charge of capital murder. And he thinks I owe him an explanation."

Linda's hand came up to cover her mouth. Wilder slumped back down in his chair and fixed his eyes on a spot somewhere to the left of the dish of mashed potatoes. Meade sighed, giving himself a bit of a shake. He put his elbows on the table, looking deflated.

"Sweetie, can you get the boys to bed yourself, tonight?"

"Of course. Come on guys, bath time. Now."

Wilder made a move as if to get up as Linda shooed the boys from the room.

"Sit down," Meade roared. "I don't want you out of my sight for even a minute."

Wilder closed his eyes and propped his forehead in his right hand. Meade lit a cigarette and sat watching him. Wilder just sat, making no further efforts to move or talk. Sounds of Linda and the little boys floated down the stairs to them. Not until Linda returned did Meade realize that Wilder had fallen asleep.

Wilder woke the next morning unsure of

anything except the ache in his arm and the pasty feeling in his mouth. He looked around at what must be Meade's family room. He vaguely remembered Meade taking his shoes off for him and helping him into the sofa bed. He peeked under the covers and was glad to see he was still in his blue jeans and not a spare pair of Linda's pajamas.

What in God's name had he gotten himself into? He was tempted to call George to thank him for his great advice and let him know what a swell outcome it was having. Visions of Paul Glaser dancing in glee around some unholy fire flitted through his mind. And of Ed Ramsey typing out the letter canning him. And Marilyn. This ought to send her into Hart Warren's ready arms. And then of course there was Aunt Katherine. And David. Christ. Just goes to show what you could accomplish in a weekend if you just gave it a try.

He looked around for a clock but didn't see one. There were crayon and finger paint pictures stuck up on the wall above an old roll-top desk. It looked like the desk Meade's father had used. A child's jigsaw puzzle covered the floor in front of the television. Books spilled from the bookcases on either side of the door. More were piled on the end table next to the sofa.

Wilder picked up the top one. *Robin Hood* illustrated by N. C. Wyeth. He flipped it open. How funny. This was the book with the clouds he'd been trying to remember yesterday. "So were the clouds on Robin's horizon gathering apace." There it was. Well, hell. Life imitates art. He looked at the endpaper. His immature handwriting crawled across the page. He'd given this book to Meade for his fourteenth birthday. They'd inhaled the book that summer, memorizing scenes, breathing Sherwood Forest. Was it a coincidence now that it was here? Meade might be reading it to the boys. Or maybe he left it here to let Wilder know he still thought of him as a friend. Maybe he was returning it. Maybe Wilder just needed strong black coffee.

He sat on the edge of the sofa for a minute to no ill effect. His shoes were there, side by side where Meade left them. Now was his chance to show up Benny the one-handed shoe-tier, but he decided to give it a miss. He padded over to the door, wondering how in hell he was going to convince Meade, convince anyone, that he had nothing to do with any of this.

He heard voices in the hall outside the closed door. Deciding he might as well be hanged for an eavesdropper as a thief and murderer, he stood, put his ear to the crack, and listened.

"Daddy, why were you so mad at Mr. Wilder last night?"

"Shh, honey, don't wake him. Because he disappointed me."

"Are you going to arrest him?"

There wasn't an answer right away. Wilder felt a tickle of something unpleasant between his shoulder blades.

"Daddy?"

"No, honey. He's going to help me."

"So he's one of the good guys?"

"He's one of the best guys, Jeff. Go on now, you don't want to be late."

Wilder heard the front door slam and Meade's footsteps retreating to the back of the house. Good. Things couldn't be as insane as they'd seemed yesterday. Meade must have come to his senses and realized it was just a whole string of unlucky coincidences that led to him. Or better yet, the real guy, the real Fox had been caught and he'd confessed. And Wilder was free and clear. Good. He felt as though he'd been wading further and further into a puddle of quicksand.

He turned the doorknob. It didn't move. The door was locked tight. Wilder swore and thumped his fist on the jamb. Robin Hood and his damned black clouds had nothing on him.

Footsteps came back down the hall. The doorknob rattled as it was unlocked. Wilder stepped aside to let the door swing open. Meade leaned against the jamb, leering, holding a steaming mug.

"Good morning, Sunshine."

"Why did you lock the door, Rodger?"

"Trust, Lewis. I haven't got much of that where you're concerned. I don't know you anymore, do I? And I'd look like a real jerk if I let you get away."

"It works both ways, Rodger. I couldn't say I know you either."

"And whose fault is that?"

"Why don't you just arrest me, then, and be done with it?"

Meade looked down at the floor and then back at Wilder, the smile gone.

"Because I hope I do know you. Come on in the kitchen, there's coffee and breakfast."

He turned and walked away. Wilder followed in his stocking feet, shaking his head. It didn't help. But he wasn't in handcuffs. Small favors.

A man Wilder didn't recognize was sitting at the kitchen table reading a newspaper. He looked up as Wilder hesitated in the doorway.

"Lewis, this is Fisher," said Meade. "You wouldn't recognize him because he kind of snuck up from behind yesterday." Meade pulled out a chair on the opposite side of the table from Fisher and waved Wilder over. "Here, you sit on this side so you'll feel safer."

Meade was oblivious to the glares from both sides of the table. He turned to the stove and set about pouring coffee and getting Wilder a plate of scrambled eggs and toast.

"Here you go, Hot Shot. Sink your teeth into that." He took a pill bottle out of his shirt pocket and dumped a tablet out in front of Wilder. "And swallow that with your orange juice. The doc said you'll need it for discomfort and you look pretty damned uncomfortable. Now, Fisher, drop the comics and give us a synopsis of the case so far." Meade sat down, crossed his arms over his chest, and tipped his chair onto its back legs.

Fisher made a production of folding the newspaper and placing it squarely on the table in front of him. He pulled a spiral notebook from a pocket, flipped it open, looked bored, and started reading.

"At nine-twenty-three A.M. October 9, an anonymous call was received at the Stonewall PD reporting a break-in the previous evening at 2349 Sherwood Drive in Stonewall. Caller claimed to have information identifying the perpetrator and claiming perpetrator is the burglary suspect known as the Fox. Caller identified Lewis Wilder, 313 Third Avenue, Nolichucky. Caller placed Wilder at the address between seven-twenty-five P.M. and eight-fifteen P.M. giving details including description of Wilder's clothing, vehicle, tag number, and apparent injury to his left arm in commission of the break-in.

"Caller also placed Wilder at 529 Bacon Branch Road in Embree County at the time of a break-in on October 1st.

"Caller reported Wilder as currently staying at 328 Rockhouse Road in Stonewall.

"Officer Henderson was dispatched to 2349 Sherwood, the residence of Donald Sherrill, arriving at nine-thirty-eight A.M. Henderson found Sherrill's body lying outside the back door of the residence. Preliminary investigation indicates victim was struck on the head from behind. Preliminary estimate for time of death is between seven P.M. and nine P.M. of October 8. There were no signs of a break-in at the residence. Victim's wife, Mrs. Barbara Sherrill, was contacted at their property in Nolichucky. She returned to Stonewall and on preliminary report states that nothing is missing.

"Physical evidence was found placing the suspect, Wilder, at the scene sometime recently. Captain Meade approached Wilder at ten-ten A.M. on October 9, at the Rockhouse Road address provided by the anonymous caller. Wilder's injuries reported as sustained the previous evening were aggravated in a confrontation with Detective Fisher. Wilder was transported to Stonewall Medical Center Hospital where he was treated and released to the custody of Captain Meade.

"Preliminary search of Wilder's address in Nolichucky yielded nothing incriminating. As per Captain Meade, a search of 328 Rockhouse Road has not yet been carried out.

"Mrs. Barbara Sherrill and persons interviewed in Nolichucky report ill feelings between the victim and Wilder."

Fisher closed his notebook with a slap, put it back in his pocket and picked up his newspaper again without waiting for any kind of response.

Wilder hadn't taken his eyes off Fisher throughout his monotonic recitation. He blinked and looked away when Meade thumped his chair back to earth.

"Well, hell, bud. If looks count, it's you." Meade looked pleased with himself and the world. "So, what have you got to say for yourself?"

Wilder wondered what planet he was on or which black hole he'd stepped off into. He was musing further along these lines and pushing his painkiller around in a circle on the table in front of him when he realized the room was quiet. He refocused on Meade and Fisher who had abandoned his paper and now stared at him.

"Hmm?"

"Pay attention, Lewis. I know you were listening to Fisher, and you caught most of the details before your eyes glazed over. As things stand, you're looking guilty as hell, here. So what've you got to say for yourself?"

"I'm not," Wilder said, his voice sounding even to him as though he'd strained it out through two pieces of coarse-grade sandpaper.

"Good. I like to see you showing some grit. Now convince me." Meade leaned across the table and picked up Wilder's fork. He speared some egg and handed it to Wilder. "Eat your breakfast."

Wilder drew in a deep breath. He'd seen

people do that in movies and it always looked as though it cleared their heads and gave them strength. Another illusion shattered. He put the fork down without eating the egg and swallowed several gulps of coffee instead.

"Stupid rumors have been going around since summer that I'm the Fox. I'm not. I hardly knew Don Sherrill. I argued with him once and everyone on Main Street heard it. I didn't threaten his life. He didn't threaten mine. I was at his house Saturday night because he was supposed to give me some information about a donation he was making to the museum. He didn't show up. I left. I don't know anything about anything else."

Meade shook his head.

"Well, there's a little more to it than that, I'm afraid. You're acting very dim about all this, Lewis, and I know you're not stupid. So unless you're lying through your teeth, which is something I've got to consider and Fisher here is counting on, the only other possibility I can see is that you're innocent."

"What a great defense."

"Not too good, is it?"

"And I guess you've talked to Paul Glaser."

"Mmhmm."

"Jesus, I can't believe this." He took another swallow of coffee and cleared his throat. "Glaser's been keeping the rumors going as much as anyone. He must think he's died and gone to heaven."

"You should have more respect than that, Lewis. He respects you."

Wilder swore under his breath.

"Now, see, that's what I mean. Glaser was genuinely surprised when I called him and asked him about you. Said you've never been a serious suspect as far as he's concerned and he'd be thunderstruck and shit blue if you turned out to be a murderer. A little coarse, but colorful and heartfelt, I'm sure."

"He said we're welcome to let him know otherwise, though," Fisher said, behind his paper again.

"Well, there, see? And he was nice enough to send a guy to help Fisher waltz around your place and even suggested he not waste his time going over the museum just yet and instead wait until there's more compelling evidence than some anonymous joker. Very considerate, I call that, don't you?"

"Yeah, swell. Give someone time to plant some compelling evidence."

"Little green men, maybe. You're not into conspiracy theories are you?"

"No, it's just the story of my life, Rodger, bad timing and coincidence."

"A regular Joe Btsfplk. Okay, so, let's start in with the questions again. What's with the note addressed to the Fox?"

"I don't know. I found it propped on the gate at Sherrill's when I left."

"Who do you suppose left it for you?"

"How do you know it was left for me?"

"You took it, didn't you? Besides, somebody out there knows an awful lot about where you go and what you do. For instance, where were you last Sunday night? Remember that question? You were rude when I asked you at the hospital."

Wilder stared at Meade and said nothing.

"See? You're hiding something. You're not acting like an innocent man, Lewis. Okay, let me refresh your memory for you. That was the night the Fox, no, wait, I refuse to call this guy by some cute name. He's a crook, pure and simple. Let's not play games with what's been happening. That was the night this crook robbed the house of a fundamentalist preacher while the family was away at a revival. A witness, albeit anonymous, places you at the scene during the appropriate time frame."

"Has it occurred to you that unless a large group of people has been hiding in the bushes watching my every fascinating move, the anonymous tipper has also been at the right places at the right time and might also have left the note?"

"Bravo. Yes, we have. So let's find out who that person is and maybe we'll have suspect number two. But don't get all complacent. I notice you didn't deny being there, and I mean to find out what you were doing there. And for that matter, what you're doing here. Fisher, put down the horoscope and start taking notes."

Fisher went through his paper-folding routine again then got up and poured himself a fresh cup of coffee. After sitting back down he pulled out his notebook and a pencil.

"Roger, Rodger."

Meade laughed and turned to Wilder.

"I always laugh when he says that because it's his only joke and it makes him feel good. Okay. How many people are we talking about that knew where you were October 1 and that you were meeting Sherrill and that you were popping in at Katherine's for your once-a-decade visit?"

"No one."

"Lewis."

"No, there's no one who would know about all three. One person maybe heard me talking to Sherrill. Another heard me say something about coming to Stonewall but didn't know why or who I was coming to see. One person knew where I was last Sunday night. And I only told one person I was going to Aunt Katherine's. Well, make that two. None of them would have anything to do with this."

"Someone knows more than you think. Has someone been following you?"

"Don't you think I'd've noticed?"

"You're kidding, right?"

"Well, it would be pretty obvious in Nolichucky, Rodger."

"Not obvious enough. Someone knew where you were on at least two occasions."

"I got a bunch of anonymous phone calls."

"What, obscene?"

"No, just silence."

"Night? Like maybe on nights this guy made a hit?"

"Varied. Day, night. Never in the middle of the night."

"Report 'em to anyone?"

"Glaser."

"Hm. Okay, who has it in for you?"

"You're not too fond of me right about now, so how about you? Otherwise you can take your pick."

"I'm serious, Lewis."

"Well, you got me," Wilder shrugged, "I always thought I was a quiet kind of guy that not much happened to."

"Kind of shakes up your perspective, doesn't it? Let's concentrate on the night at Sherrill's. You got there about what time?"

"Seven-twenty."

"Tipper said seven-twenty-five," Fisher interrupted.

"My watch said seven-twenty. I left at eight-ten."

"Tipper said eight-fifteen."

Wilder shrugged one shoulder in an irritated comment.

"Boys, boys," said Meade. "Did you knock? Ring the bell? What'd you do?"

"Yeah. He didn't answer. I thought maybe I was early or he had to go out or he was in the shower. I waited."

"Did you hear anything while you waited?"

"Nothing unusual."

"What did you hear? You were there, for what, almost an hour, you must have heard a lot of noises."

"A screech owl and a few cars or pickups on the road. The wind was blowing the trees."

"Why'd you wait?"

"I told you. In case he showed up."

"You're awfully patient. Did it look as though anyone was home?"

"There were lights on inside."

"What did you do while you waited?"

"I stood around wondering where the hell he was."

"You didn't like him?"

"No."

"I didn't either."

"Did you kill him?"

"Lewis, I'm hurt. You walked around, didn't you." It wasn't a question.

Wilder hesitated. "Yeah. I walked up and down in front."

"And behind the bushes and looked in the windows," added Fisher with a smirk.

"Yeah."

"Mmhmm. But not around back?"

"No. He was already back there dead, wasn't he?"

"We were hoping you could tell us that."

"Oh, God. Look, Rodger, stopping at Sherrill's was a spur-of-the-moment thing."

"Some murders are like that, too."

"He was supposed to be in Nolichucky for the weekend and didn't make it. He called and said he'd bring the information another time, and when I decided to come see Aunt Katherine, I called him back and said I'd pick it up. He might have told someone I was coming. I don't know who he'd tell. His wife, maybe, but she was in Nolichucky."

"And who'd you tell you were dropping by Katherine's on a whim after your eight-year hiatus?"

"Two people. I don't know who they might have said something to."

"Well, let's not be cagey about this. What are the names of all these two or three people you confide in?"

Wilder pushed egg around on the plate.

"Names."

"Marilyn Wooten and George Palmer."

"Marilyn Wooten?" Meade looked in-credulous.

"It's a fairly common name in that area."

"Which one, Marilyn or Wooten?"

"You're a real asshole, Rodger."

"No, I just have a sense of humor. Do you remember what one of those is? Now, who is Ms. Wooten when she's at home?"

"She runs a bookstore in Nolichucky," Fisher said. "I ran into her when I was up there."

"Fisher, I'm amazed. You stopped in a bookstore?"

"No," Fisher smirked at Wilder. "She let herself into his place when the deputy and I were searching it. She's Sheriff Glaser's niece."

Meade looked at Wilder with a new light in his eye. "Oh. I see. Then she is no doubt aware of our young friend's plight. And I see one of your problems, Lewis. You're bonking the sheriff's niece and he doesn't like it. How's that for a conspiracy theory?"

"Shut up, Rodger."

"What about George Palmer?"

"He's a friend. He's one of the museum's board of directors."

"He's an Episcopal clergyman," Fisher added, pleased with his new role as interpreter of Wilder's social life. "Rector of St. Michael's in Nolichucky."

"Ah, so, you bare one thing to Ms. Wooten and another to St. George. You must have built up a tremendous amount of guilt over these long silent years. All right, let's back up a bit. Which one of those two knew you were going to see Sherrill? No, wait, don't tell me. Let's see if I can guess. I'm rootin' for Ms. Wooten."

Wilder muttered something.

"Sorry, I didn't catch that, Lewis."

"Yes, you stupid prick," Wilder enunciated. "How's that?"

"Fine. Now, who knew where you were last Sunday?"

"Dr. Ramsey," said Wilder. Out of the corner of his eye he saw Fisher smirking again and just opening his mouth. "Edward Ramsey," Wilder rushed to supply ahead of him. "He's a GP in town, chairman of the museum's board of directors."

"He was in Chicago that week," Fisher murmured.

"Just call him, Rodger," Wilder said. "He can tell you what I was doing there. Though I'm not sure he thinks that's all I was doing." Wilder scrubbed his hand through his hair and across his face in frustration.

"Right, we'll talk to him. Now, how'd you manage to pre-mangle your arm so Fisher could finish it for you? You're not going to tell me it was a solo effort, are you?"

Wilder swigged more coffee. "I'd found the note and put it in my pocket. Then I went to pull out my car keys and snagged the note back out and the wind caught it. It blew back through the gate. I reached for it, through the hinge opening. The gate slammed. I thought the wind had blown it shut but the wind was coming from the other direction. The gate swung open again. I grabbed the note and got out of there."

"You didn't see or hear anything?"

Wilder stared at Meade. "No." Then he gave a bit of a shrug and shook his head. "I heard a car start up and take off. I don't know if it had anything to do with it. I sort of looked around but, no, I didn't see or hear anything and didn't really feel like sticking around."

Meade for once didn't smile. "I don't blame you. Lewis, eat your breakfast and take your pill. That's gotta be killing you."

Wilder gave in and ate his, by now, cold eggs and toast. They were surprisingly good. He swallowed the pill with the dregs of his coffee.

"Well, if someone slammed the gate, whoever it was must have had something else in mind other than pinning me like a bug because he let me go and then called you."

"Not right away, though. Remember, we didn't get the call until the next morning."

They looked at each other.

"Well. We'll have to add Katherine to the list."

"And David."

CHAPTER 21

"I see a smile creeping across your face like a fox across a barnyard, Lewis. What exactly about this shit heap you're in is amusing you?"

"David on the list."

Meade grinned wide. "Once an asshole, always an asshole. Words I live by."

"I can tell." Wilder returned the grin. Then he pushed his chair back and slouched, frustrated again. "But look, Aunt Katherine and David only knew I was there at the farm. I never said anything to them about stopping at Sherrill's first. How's this list going to help? What are you going to do, interrogate all of them and hope there really is a conspiracy? That's nuts. And I know Marilyn hasn't got anything to do with it. She didn't have any idea where I was last Sunday night."

"How do you know?"

"I was supposed to have supper with her

and her mother. I forgot. She was pretty pissed."

"Believably pissed?"

"Yeah. She knew I wasn't at home or at the museum working late."

"And you didn't tell her what you'd been up to?"

"No."

"Why don't you tell me?"

"No."

"Ramsey wouldn't have told anyone else?"

"No."

"Not even George Palmer?"

"No."

"Well, you're going monosyllabic again."

Wilder made a sour face and studied the toast crumbs on his plate for a count of ten or twenty, then made an effort and asked, "Where's Linda?"

"Hands off, Lewis."

"Jesus, Rodger."

"Just joking. She teaches kindergarten. Charlie's in a preschool class at her school. They took off before you staggered out of bed. Want some more coffee?"

"Let me unload this one first."

"Fisher, take him to the bathroom. You don't need to go in with him. Just lurk outside."

"You're a laugh a minute, Rodger."

"Not joking, Lewis."

Fisher got up and headed down the hall.

"Jesus."

Meade smiled after them and reached behind him for the coffeepot. He poured more all around and then got up and cleared the breakfast dishes into the dishwasher. He lit a cigarette and waited.

The phone rang just as Wilder reappeared, shadowed by Fisher who was still doing up his own fly.

"Good boy, Fisher. Did you wash your hands? And you, Lewis, did you wash your hand? Hang on while I blow off this salesman." Meade picked up the phone and blew out a stream of smoke. "Meade, wha'd'ya need?" His face lost its bored look and he straightened up. "No kidding. And you're here? I'm glad you could do that. I know Katherine appreciates it. He's more or less in one piece but I can understand your concern. I've got a better idea. You can talk to him in person. No, that's okay, I'll save you the drive and bring him over there. It'll be a pleasure to meet you. Thank you." Meade hung up but stood at the phone with a considering look on his face.

Wilder coughed. Meade turned to him with a smile.

"Phone was for you, Lewis," he said.

"What the hell, Rodger?" Wilder exploded. "I can't take phone calls? I can't take a leak by myself? You don't seriously think I killed Sherrill, do you? You'd have me in jail or arraigned in front of a judge by now if you did."

"All right, no. I don't think you killed Sherrill. But in case you hadn't noticed, the picture here is a little murky. You remember that bit from English class about tangled webs? Well, I'd say I'm looking at one of the master weavers of Upper East Tennessee right about now. For some reason you're in the middle of all this. And now I've got hold of you, you slippery son of a bitch, I'm not letting go until I've either untangled this fucking mess you're in or wrapped it around your goddamned throat and strangled you with it."

Wilder sat down, drank some coffee and watched as Meade made an effort to calm his breathing and get himself back under control.

"Feeling better?" Wilder asked.

Meade finished his cigarette and ground it out in the ashtray. "Yeah. Thanks."

"He always was excitable," Wilder said in an aside to Fisher. "So, Rodger, you want to tell me who was on the phone?"

"That, son, was St. George, your father

confessor. He's at Katherine's. Where you and I soon will be. Fisher, dear, I believe you have enough now to get started on, so go get started and call me later."

"Where?"

"Use your clairvoyance."

Fisher bent down to Wilder's left ear and whispered "Boo," making Wilder jump and slosh his coffee. Then he turned and glided out.

"Spooky guy," said Meade smiling after him. "But I think he likes you."

"I thought he was counting on me being guilty."

"He is. But he's not picky about his friends."

"Swell." Wilder mopped up the spill with his napkin. "So, George is at Aunt Katherine's?"

"Yes, he is. Which brings up an interesting point. How did he know to mount his trusty steed and come to your rescue? No doubt because in a little town like Nolichucky people talk. But you know all about that, don't you? Probably one of the reasons you're so damned closemouthed these days. Matter of self-preservation. So maybe word of your distress got around to old George. Or that's what he'd like us to think.

"But this brings up another interesting

point. How do you know one of these friends you're so staunchly standing by hasn't let some little thing slip to just one other person, who then told only their closest friends in strictest confidence, etc., etc., and first thing you know you might as well have been giving press conferences on Main Street detailing your highly suspicious movements?" Meade lit another cigarette and sucked in a lungful of smoke. "Hmm? You look like you've thought of something."

Wilder shook his head. "I don't know. Something you said reminded me of something."

"Well, what?"

"I don't know. Sorry, I've lost it."

"Let's just hope you haven't lost it in more ways than one. Sit tight, I'll be right back, gotta get something from upstairs." Meade jumped up and headed off on his errand. He stopped, though, and poked his head back around the door. "See there, Lewis? I'm learning to trust you." His head disappeared again.

Wilder listened until he heard Meade bounding up the stairs, then he padded back down the hall to the family room and got his shoes. When Meade popped back into the kitchen he found Wilder tipped back in his chair with his feet on the table.

He stopped in the doorway.

"Well, come on, let's go."

Wilder smiled and re-crossed his ankles.

"What are you looking so smug about?" Meade asked.

"Tell Jeff his friend Benny can eat his heart out," Wilder said. Meade looked confused for a minute then gave a bark of laughter. "Come on, Hot Shot. Time to find out if you really are a one-armed bandit."

Meade grabbed his coffee cup and swallowed what was left, then shepherded Wilder to the car.

They pulled out of Meade's driveway and Wilder looked around him, realizing he hadn't paid any attention to where he'd ended up last night.

"Nice neighborhood, Rodger."

"Are you kidding? These things are monstrosities. Constant plumbing problems, leaky roofs, rotten wiring. Some night all the houses will short out at the same time and we'll roast weenies and marshmallows."

"They're just old."

"They're solid, that's for sure. I tried blowing ours up last year working on the furnace. No such luck. Solid as a rock. But, yeah, we like the neighborhood a lot. I never thought I'd be a city boy. But it's a great place for the kids. They can walk to school, ride their bikes. Write graffiti on the sidewalk. Fall out of the trees."

They turned from the side street onto a busier street and from there onto a four-lane. Wilder was interested to see how much had changed in Stonewall, which hills had been cut away and paved for more parking and shopping, which small businesses had managed to hold on, and how much of the town now looked like every other one he'd been in.

"Aunt Katherine knew I was living in Nolichucky."

Meade looked at him out of the corner of his eye and made another turn. "Cagey old broad. Runs in the family. So have you two been in touch for awhile or what?"

"No."

"How'd you know, then? And how'd she know? And how long has either of you known?"

"She must've known pretty much as soon as I moved there. But I didn't know she knew until yesterday morning. We were sort of talking and she said someone told her I was there."

"Sort of talking? Yeah, I can picture the two of you sort of talking. So who told her?"

"I don't know. I asked her and then the

phone rang. We got sidetracked onto other things. Then you showed up."

"Oh yeah, that was fun. Okay, so we have the elusive Someone again. So I wonder how that fits in with anything. Would she have told David where you were?"

"I don't know. I doubt it."

"Why?"

"Because of what she was doing."

"Yeah? Which was?"

"Maybe you ought to ask her."

"I'm asking you and I'm getting tired of having to work so hard at it."

"She's been sending anonymous donations to the museum."

"Money?"

"Yeah. She thought I'd found out the money was coming from her and that I'd come down to yell at her for interfering in my life again."

"Well, what did you expect? You did it before."

"Yeah, Rodger, I did. I'm a regular bastard. And by now that's real old news. Get over it." Wilder stared out the side window.

"So if not to yell at her, why did you come back?"

"I came to tell her about the rumors. I had this nice idea of letting her know what was going on so she wouldn't be shocked if she heard it secondhand."

"Oh, that was a good plan. Look where that got you. What a sap. You should've just stayed gone."

"I'm beginning to wish I had."

"I bet. That's your style."

"What's with you?"

"Wha'd'you mean?"

"Why are you so angry? Who cares if I haven't kept in touch? How many people from high school have you kept up with?"

Meade lit a cigarette and blew smoke out the window. "It was like you'd died," he said. He suddenly put on his turn signal and zipped around a corner into a parking lot.

"Come on," he growled and jumped out of the car.

"What are we doing at Kroger, Rodger? Is this a cop thing? Need a donut fix or something?"

"Nope. Come on. We're buying flowers."

Wilder followed Meade as he stalked into the grocery and headed for the produce department. Meade went to a refrigerated case and peered in at the bouquets.

"Well, they look half-assed, but how about this one?" He opened the door and pulled one out.

"Yeah, that one's stunning. What're they

for? You trying to make up to Linda for springing me on her?"

"No, they're for you to give to Katherine. I bet all you dragged into that house after eight years and a questionable evening at Sherrill's was your sorry ass and your broken wing. Show some class for a change."

"And white carnations died blue around the edges is your idea of class? Let's at least do it right. Where's a real florist?"

Meade looked at the bunch of flowers he was choking in his hand. "Yeah, you're right." He tossed the bouquet back in the case. Wilder jogged after him as he stalked back to the car.

Meade backtracked through town. He pulled into the curb in front of an old red-brick building in a block of mixed modern and turn-of-the-century storefronts. The large front windows of Anna Marie's Florist were full of green plants and bright flowers. A sign on the shop next door advertised Ledford's Vac and Gun. Wilder stepped over to admire a mannequin in a frilly apron pushing a Hoover near a display of Remington shotguns. Meade put a finger in Wilder's collar and gave a tug. They turned and pushed through the front door of Anna Marie's to the sound of a jingling bell.

Wilder made his way through the displays of ferns, potted palms, and piped-in classical music to the counter. A woman working on a floral wreath behind the counter looked up. Wilder asked if it were possible to get a bouquet of fall flowers that looked more like wildflowers than something out of the deep freeze at Kroger. The florist said she knew exactly what he meant and went to put a loose arrangement together.

Meade stood, humming accompaniment to Pavarotti, staring out the windows. From the counter, Wilder studied him. Meade had always had a restless energy about him. When they were children, Wilder imagined Meade's hair was flaming red because the energy percolated out of the top of his head. Now he smiled to think that was what curled Meade's beard.

The florist returned. Wilder thanked her and paid.

"This," he said, turning to Meade, "is showing some class."

"Hot damn," said Meade in wonder. He wasn't looking at the flowers.

Chapter 22

"Captain Meade, were you looking for me?"

Wilder looked up from admiring his bouquet and wished he'd paid for something larger so he could hide behind it. Barb Sherrill was standing in the open door. An older couple stood behind her, the three of them blocking the exit. Stalemate, Wilder thought. No chance of sidling out unseen.

"Mrs. Sherrill," Meade said, "no, ma'am. I'm here merely by coincidence. I hope you don't feel we've been harassing you."

"No. You'll have to excuse me. This has been such a shock." She put her hand to her hair, to her mouth, her heart, closed her eyes. She opened them again and stepped away from the door. "I think I'm operating on autopilot more or less. Captain Meade, these are my parents, Joe and Betty Grundy."

"Mr. and Mrs. Grundy, I'm sorry for your loss."

They nodded and everyone turned to look at Wilder. He got the feeling his bouquet wasn't meshing well with the occasion or Barb Sherrill's drawn look.

"Lewis, I'm surprised to see you in Stonewall," Barb said. "I see you've hurt your arm. I hope that won't keep you from your dancing."

He knew he would stutter something inane if he opened his mouth so he took his cue from her parents and nodded to her.

"We're all surprised to see Lewis back in Stonewall, Mrs. Sherrill," said Meade, stepping into the silence, making it more uncomfortable by winking at her. "He's taking flowers to his aunt whom he has neglected lo these many years. He had a bit of trouble when we met up yesterday so I'm acting as designated driver." He made a show of taking the flowers from Wilder and then taking his elbow.

"I should let you know, Captain Meade, that after tying up a few loose ends here today I'm going back to Nolichucky. I don't feel comfortable in the house after . . ."

"Completely understandable. Thanks for letting me know. If we have any questions or if we have any information we'll get in touch with you there." Meade tipped an imaginary hat to her and steered Wilder toward the door.

"Your officer, Captain Meade . . ."

Meade stopped and swiveled around to her again, still holding Wilder by the elbow.

"Your officer was asking questions yesterday that made me wonder."

"About what, Mrs. Sherrill?"

"Arguments my husband had."

"And what did you answer, Mrs. Sherrill?"

"I'm sure you know, and I hope you're being wise."

Meade nodded. "In fact, I do know, Mrs. Sherrill. And thank you for your cooperation." He gripped Wilder's elbow harder. "You can rest assured I have everything in hand."

She gave a thin smile at his play on words and turned toward the counter.

Wilder restrained himself until they were back in the car with the doors closed. Then he turned to Meade and started to open his mouth.

"Shut up," hissed Meade as he checked for traffic and pulled out of the parking space. "She's watching."

Wilder stole a glance over his shoulder and caught Barb Sherrill looking after them.

When they'd turned the corner Meade gave him an incredulous look. "Dancing?" he asked. "You're known for your dancing?

296

She hopes your arm won't hinder your dancing?" He looked at Wilder again and shook his head. "No, forget it, I don't even want to know."

"Good."

"On the other hand, what did you think of that performance?"

"Whose? Yours?" Wilder asked.

"The Widow Sherrill's, you moron. Your presence definitely rattled her."

"Probably because Fisher's less-than-subtle questions led her to believe I killed her husband. What kind of reaction did you expect? And your performance sure as hell didn't help."

"Oh, no, even though she brought them up, I don't think it was Fisher's questions that were bothering her. He's the soul of discretion. A regular ballerina tiptoeing around when it comes to questions." Meade was quiet and looked confused for a minute. "What kind of dancing? No, don't tell me.

"No, I'll tell you what I think it is. She's adding other things up. So what does she know about that you haven't told me, hmm? Or what does she know that someone else told her? There's that Someone again. You know, I don't think I like that guy. I hope he isn't Someone I know." Meade wiggled his eyebrows at Wilder.

"Are you going to be an asshole at Aunt Katherine's?"

"It's part of my job description, Lewis," Meade said. "I didn't get where I am today by not being an asshole."

"Swell. Can you at least let me in on what you're planning? I'm sick of surprises. What have you told Aunt Katherine? And while you're at it, what are you going to tell George, what are you going to ask them, why are you still acting like you're about to throw me in the slammer, shouldn't you be out looking for the real bad guy, and don't you ever go into an office somewhere and do paperwork?"

"Okay, since you ask. We've been over some of this before, but maybe that blow to your head impaired your short-term memory. And that painkiller ought to be leaving you a little loopy by now, too. You've complicated the story, as we know it so far, Lewis. I don't think you killed Sherrill but I'm not so sure you don't know something about what's going on or what has gone on with this Fox. The places you go and the things you do fascinate idle tongues in your town and someone else who's not so idle and looks like being more dangerous. Someone Paul Glaser and I'd like to talk to.

"Now, I'm not returning you to Katherine

in the same condition in which I borrowed you, which she was bound to notice. So I've told her about your accident. And," he said, returning Wilder's glare, "my part in making it worse. After singing you to sleep last night I gave her a call. She's probably guessed you're a suspect for something, though it's anyone's guess what at this point."

Wilder groaned.

"But she trusts me to do my job, Lewis. As for St. George, I'll tell him as much as I've told Katherine. And I'm going to ask them, and you, any damned thing I need to. Fisher's handling the murder investigation and he's a damned good detective. And my paperwork habits are none of your damned business. Does that about cover it?"

"David?"

"Damned right, David. Thanks for reminding me. It'll be a goddamned pleasure to question David. So," he asked, smiling around at Wilder, "are you looking forward to once more being engulfed in the bosom of your family?"

"Like a lobotomy."

They rode in silence the last mile. Wilder, lost in thoughts of anonymous phone calls and anonymous donations and anonymous gate slammers, watched the once familiar road unwinding toward the farm. Meade drummed his fingers on the steering wheel to some internal tune.

"Well, they're nice flowers you got her, Lewis," Meade said a few minutes later as they walked up the steps to the porch before ringing Katherine Wilder's doorbell. "She'll appreciate the gesture."

"You really think these are going to make everything all better after eight years?"

"No, but they'll go a long way toward making up for not brushing your hair this morning or shaving or putting on a clean shirt," he said, looking askance at Wilder and making a face.

Wilder was still swearing when his aunt opened the door.

Katherine Wilder's formidable eyes were the only part of her face to register her nephew's inappropriate words of greeting. These she closed as if in pain. Then, accepting the flowers he held out to her, she kissed his whiskery cheek and ushered the two men inside.

"I'll just go put these in some water. They're in the parlor if you want to go on in," she said over her shoulder. She disappeared down the hall toward the kitchen.

"Who's they, Rodger?" Wilder asked,

300

grabbing Meade's arm.

"I don't know. Let's go find out, shall we?"

Meade led the way. Wilder took several steadying breaths and followed.

Sitting in the parlor, drinking tea, were George Palmer and Marilyn Wooten. Meade exclaimed his delight and shook hands. He introduced himself, explaining he was as an old friend of Wilder's, at the same time putting things on an official footing by letting them know he was with the Stonewall police.

Wilder, feeling that most of his waking hours were now being spent in a surreal daze, flapped a hand in greeting to Palmer and wandered over to be hugged by Marilyn. She pulled him down beside her on the love seat and captured his free hand, holding it in both of hers. He looked up to see Meade enjoying the scene.

Katherine came in with two more teacups, left, and returned with the flowers in a vase. Meade poured tea, handed Wilder a cup, and waited for Katherine to sit down before taking a seat himself.

Of the five people now sitting in the parlor, four sat looking at Wilder. He looked back at them, trying to gauge their reactions. He ticked off the high points as he followed their assessing eyes. His face, hollow-eyed, unshaven, hair uncombed. His forehead, patched with gauze. His left arm, plastered and strapped across his chest in a sling. The bloodstains on his shirt. He thought he was carrying the whole look off pretty well, though he noticed he was beginning to list to one side, probably under the influence of the painkiller he'd swallowed at Meade's. Three of the faces regarded him over their teacups with what looked like a mixture of mild curiosity and concerned smiles. Meade just plain regarded him.

Wilder turned his lips up on one side into something not quite a smile, adding a rakish air to his general dishevelment. "Well. This is jolly. You two miss me?" he asked, nodding to Palmer and Marilyn. "I've only been gone a day and a half."

"And look what you managed to accomplish," Palmer said.

"That's funny, you know, George, because I was marveling at that myself just this morning. And I was thinking I should call you and thank you for suggesting I take this little trip to Stonewall."

"Lewis, you never told me this was Father Palmer's idea," Meade said, giving Wilder a look that let him know they now had an appointment to discuss this lapse later when they were alone.

"Oh, it was my idea all along," Palmer said, leaning forward and clasping his hands between his knees. "I've been encouraging Lewis for months to come see Katherine. I've been quite a pest about it, in fact. But I can't take credit for the timing. I kept telling him to make up his mind to do it and Saturday afternoon he just finally did."

"A snap decision," said Meade.

"Oh, I'd say so."

"He certainly left me holding the bag," Marilyn said. "Literally. We were on our way out the door for a picnic supper when he turned around, packed his toothbrush, and took off." She let go Wilder's hand and planted her own hands on her hips, turning to him. "Then, yesterday, what happens, but there's Shorty and some guy I've never seen before searching your place when I went over to feed your newts."

Meade raised his eyebrows.

"Shorty. That would be Susan's neighbor Deborah's cousin," Wilder said to no one in particular, at which they all raised their eyebrows.

"The other guy said they were looking around because there'd been a possible break-in, which sounded like a bunch of baloney, to me."

"That would be my friend Fisher," said

Meade. "He was trying not to alarm you, I'm sure."

"Didn't work. I called Uncle Paul to see if he knew what was going on but couldn't reach him. So I called George and he'd just heard that Don Sherrill was murdered. So then George thought it would be a good idea to call you here, Lewis."

"Which I did," Palmer said. "And Katherine said you'd walked down to the barn with a friend and hadn't come back. Not that your not coming back is anything new to her. But she said there wasn't anything to worry about because your friend is a policeman."

"A large policeman," Wilder said, spilling a bit of his tea.

"I called George back last night after talking to you, Rodger," said Katherine. "I'm afraid I didn't explain much of anything very well, being somewhat in the dark myself, as usual," she said, looking at Wilder. "And I asked George to come down. I thought that might be best."

Meade smiled his approval.

"And I came along for the ride," said Marilyn. She looked Wilder up and down. "Your aunt said you'd had an accident. Twice. What's going on?"

Wilder was caught up in admiring the high

pink color in her agitated cheeks. He blinked and gave his head a shake to clear it when he realized she was waiting for him to say something. He wasn't sure what and he decided he wasn't taking any more of Meade's pain pills. Then something else occurred to him. "Who's minding the bookstore?" he asked.

"Oh, for God's sake," Marilyn muttered.

"He's annoying, isn't he?" said Meade. "Lewis, why don't you take a hike? Go run a dog brush through your hair or something. Katherine, if you wouldn't mind, he might need," he made vague gestures toward Wilder's arm and shirt, "help or something."

"Would you like help, Lewis?" Katherine asked, sounding surprised at the notion.

"Who knows?" said Wilder. "Does it really matter what I think, Rodger?"

"Not a lot."

"I didn't think so. Thank you, then, Aunt Katherine. I'm not sure there is any help for me but I'd be happy to have your company."

"Great," Meade said, waving them out of the room. "I'll fill these folks in."

Wilder glanced back into the parlor as he hauled himself up the stairs. Meade was now sitting next to Marilyn on the love seat. Wilder caught his words on a gust of her soft laughter. "Like riding a bicycle. I can still follow his meandering thought patterns. I'll give you lessons, if you want."

Upstairs, Wilder headed down the hall and turned into the first bedroom on the right. He stopped short when he realized his mistake. This had been his room. Now it was David's.

"It's nice to know some habits die hard," said Katherine from the hallway. He could tell she was smiling.

He looked out the window at the ancient oak tree that had framed his childhood view. The massive branches still reached for him, pulling at his imagination. He pulled his gaze back into the room and looked around at David's belongings comfortably en-trenched, erasing all trace of the boy who had closed the door on it so long ago. An iffy sort of watercolor hung where his NASA posters had been. There was a stack of newspapers where a trail of comic books once slithered under the bed. A box of cigars crowded the bedside table where he'd kept his flashlight and odds and ends from his pockets. No Hardy Boys on the book-shelves. Sherlock Holmes and Isaac Asimov must have decamped. No more aquarium on the desk, no model planes suspended from the ceiling. He sighed.

"I put your things in the attic."

Wilder turned around and looked at her. He felt himself being drawn into her deep eyes. He went to her and gathered her to him with his right arm and hugged her. "I love you," he said behind her ear. They stayed that way until Katherine patted him on the back and coughed.

"Rodger was right about your shirt, dear."

"Yeah, he's a regular peach," he said, releasing her and heading to the spare room. "The trouble is I might not be able to do anything about it." He dumped the contents of his overnight bag on the bed. "I didn't come prepared for mayhem."

"Borrow one of David's shirts. He won't mind and they're large enough to negotiate the cast." She caught the look on Wilder's face. "Oh, don't be so juvenile. Just because he's never outgrown the urge to tease . . ."

". . . Bully. And it's more than an urge."

"You should have grown up by now," Katherine said.

"Sorry. I'm just tired and dopey."

"You should be." Wilder wondered which she meant, he should be sorry or he should be tired and dopey. He shoved his things aside and lay down on the bed, right hand under his head. He let his eyes wander along the thread-like cracks in the plaster ceiling.

"Why don't you see if you can sleep for a bit, Lewis?" Katherine crossed to a rocking chair near the window. "I'll just sit here."

"Why?" he asked, switching his gaze to her.

"I don't think Rodger wants me in the parlor right now. He would make a good sheep dog," she mused.

Wilder muttered something under his breath.

"I also think he doesn't want you left alone."

"I don't need a nursemaid. And I'm not going to run off."

Katherine didn't respond, just rocked, looking out the window.

"You're awfully matter-of-fact about all this," Wilder said.

"Lewis, when you get to be my age you'll realize that there is only so much energy you can afford to waste on the luxury of being emotional before you just use it all up. I spent my quota as far as you're concerned eight years ago. I lost you once. If Rodger wants to save me going through that again I will let him get on with his job and thank him for his kind thoughtfulness."

On that note of rebuke Wilder closed his eyes and hoped he could fall asleep.

"I didn't know you were so interested in

history," Katherine said.

He opened his eyes again.

"Neither did I."

"You weren't, you know. Your pockets and the drawers in your bureau were always full of rocks or bugs. Piles of cicada shells all over the place. You ladled more scum out of that pond for your experiments. You spent whole days staring into your microscope. You got a degree in Biology, for heaven's sake. What changed?"

"Nothing." Wilder had closed his eyes again but opened one now to peer at his aunt. Her eyes were boring into him. He closed his eye again. "Nothing changed, Aunt Katherine," he said. "I realized I like the idea that there is nothing new under the sun. That whatever is happening now, will happen again, and it has all happened before."

"And does this sense of recurrence absolve you from any responsibility for your own life? Your future?"

"No."

"Does it give you a sense of fatality? Do you just accept what happens?"

"No, of course not. Look, Aunt Katherine, I just realized one day that the common thread running through everything that interests me is the question 'how come?'

And it occurred to me that history has something to say about that."

"Well, that sounds very nice, Lewis. Does it give you all the answers you're looking for, then?"

"No. You taught me that well enough. 'How come' doesn't always have an answer, even if you desperately need one."

"You were a very dear little boy and I couldn't give you what you needed," she said. "And apparently you didn't want what I could give you."

"That's not true and you know it," he spat.

"And how would I know it?"

"Christ," he exploded, sitting up and glaring at her. Her face was flushed and unsmiling. She rocked back and forth in quick jerks and starts, as though she were a cat switching her tail, ready to spring. Wilder rubbed his hand over his face, staring at her. He looked down at the floor and out the window, then met her eyes again. "You wouldn't."

He let himself fall back on the bed, an involuntary groan escaping as he jounced his arm. "Look, I owe you . . . everything. And all I've repaid you with is thoughtless, selfish indifference. I'm sorry. If you ask me why, I can only say it's one of those questions that has no answer. But I'm sorry."

The room was quiet, Katherine's rocking gradually slowing, Wilder with his hand over his eyes.

"Tell me about some of the places you've been, Lewis," she whispered.

"I went to Texas," he said almost as quietly.

"And what did you do there?"

"I followed a girl there and I fell madly out of love. So I took the bus to the next dusty West Texas town and got a job. I spent a year working with emotionally disturbed children in an alternative school and another two teaching basic skills in a sheltered workshop. I could have gotten a job in a lab somewhere, drawing blood or doing research or something. But those kids seemed more real to me. I felt raw by the time I left."

"And where did you go?"

Wilder didn't answer.

"Where did you go after your dusty West Texas town?"

"Ohio. Cincinnati." Where he'd lived with his parents.

"Oh. Did you find what you were looking for?" There were no uncomfortable undercurrents in the question this time.

"It's where I went back to school."

"History?"

"Mmhmm. A master's degree in American History. I did my thesis on settlement patterns in the Southern Appalachians."

"And the museum in Nolichucky?"

"That's just part of the old Wilder luck. The job sort of fell into my lap and it seemed like a good idea. At the time. Aunt Katherine, how did you know I was in Nolichucky?"

"George told me."

"Palmer?"

"We've known each other for years, dear. Through the diocesan committee."

"Well, hell."

"The world grows smaller the older you get, Lewis. And time evaporates. I'm not going to waste any more of it with recriminations. So, you sleep for a bit and then go borrow one of David's shirts. I'll sneak down the back stairs to the kitchen."

"What about the sheep dog in the parlor?"

"I'm more concerned about what to feed all these people if they decide to stay through lunch. Besides, I don't always listen to Rodger. It's not good for him." She patted his ankle in passing and pulled the door shut on her way out.

He listened to her diminishing footsteps as she went down the backstairs, then opened the door again and went down the hall to his cousin's room.

CHAPTER 23

Wilder went first to the closet. It pleased him to find that his cousin was as anal in private life as he was an outright asshole in public. Everything in the closet was hung up according to color. The spectrum started at one end with a surprising assortment of yellows and pinks. They blended into the predominant browns and greens and Wilder's hand skipped over these to find something blue.

He pulled out a work shirt he was sure had never seen physical labor. He held the shirt up and made an uncomplimentary remark about long arms he wouldn't have made if Katherine had been there. He managed to change into it out of his own shirt and resettle his arm in its sling, taking time out once to swear and wipe the sweat off his forehead. He didn't bother to tuck in the tails. Then he turned to Collins' desk.

An appealing vision of Collins as the

traveling salesman of raunchy legend and song, with a woman in every port and a burglarous heart, swam through his muddled thoughts. He stopped to wonder if burglarous was a word and decided the pain pills were expanding his vocabulary. But maybe good old Cousin David was the Fox and he'd been there at the preacher's house and seen him there, too. And maybe he'd gotten carried away and knocked off Sherrill along with his house. Not a bad scenario, Wilder thought. Except that it gave him an uncomfortable feeling down his spine.

And it involved too many coincidences. Still, it sounded better to him than thinking George or Marilyn could have had anything to do with it. So why not help out good old Rodger by snooping around. Rodger could be Holmes and he would be his Watson.

There wasn't anything interesting on top of the desk. Collins had his pencils all sharpened and standing upright with his pens in a holder set two inches from the edge of the desk and another two from the stapler which in its turn sat two more from the Scotch tape dispenser. Wilder returned the ruler he'd used to check these irritating measurements to its own location, then turned it several degrees out of line and smiled at a petty job well done. The blotter was pristine. No scribbled phone numbers. No hasty list of houses broken into. Unfortunate.

He pulled open one drawer and slammed it shut again, shuddering. A photograph of Aunt Doris had smiled out at him. In the next drawer he found monogrammed stationery. He pushed the pages and envelopes aside, thinking how much he'd never liked monograms. And then his hand stopped almost before his eye caught what he was looking at. Plain white folded paper with matching envelopes. The kind any number of people had lying around. But he slipped them out of the drawer and put them on the blotter and stared. A slow fire began burning somewhere in the pit of his stomach. He looked through the other drawers but found nothing else interesting.

He sat tapping one of Collins' pencils against his teeth, looking out the window, past the branches of the oak, trying to think. It wasn't easy. Was this paper the same as that of the Fox note, or just similar? If it was the same, what about fingerprints? Had Meade or Fisher checked for fingerprints? If there were no fingerprints, other than his own, could a lab determine if the paper came from the same batch? If it was the same, and David had written the note, how had he known where to find Wilder? Or had he been trying to catch someone else? Did he slam the gate? Did he, David, now want him, Lewis, to smash his teeth down his throat for him? He tapped the pencil against his teeth and pondered.

The wastepaper basket. It sat in the corner made by the end of the desk and a floor lamp. Wilder pulled it to him and looked inside. He stirred the contents with the pencil and stopped. With care and shallow breath, he extracted a crumpled piece of white paper from its nest of spent Kleenex. He unfolded it. A rough draft of the Fox note stared up at him. He sat, hunched over it, staring, until he heard a noise behind him. He looked over his shoulder and saw Collins rigid in the doorway.

"What're you doing in here in general and in my shirt in particular?"

Wilder stood, tipping the chair over as he lurched toward Collins. He was too angry to speak. Collins came into the room and Wilder met him with a fist to his stomach.

"Hey, what the hell?" Collins appeared more surprised than hurt. Wilder hit him again, making him back up.

"You maniac." Collins tried to grab Wilder. Wilder sidestepped, then jabbed him again, following him out into the hall. Collins stepped into the next punch and landed one of his own on Wilder's nose. Wilder found his voice, then, and launched himself at Collins. "You bastard. You son of a bitch."

Feet pounded up the stairs. Wilder felt hands yanking him off Collins and tossing him aside. And then he heard the satisfying sound of a solid fist connecting with another nose. He untangled himself and rolled over to see Meade on top of Collins, one hand twisted in the front of his shirt to hold him steady, the other cocked back for another punch.

"What's all that noise?" they heard Katherine calling from the bottom of the back stairs. "Lewis? David? What's going on up there?" They heard her starting up the steps.

"It's all right, Katherine," Meade answered. "It's nothing." He let go of Collins and got to his feet, standing over him, daring him to say otherwise.

"Is that you, Rodger? Well, that's fine then. Lunch will be ready soon." Katherine's voice retreated back toward the kitchen.

"In there. Now," Meade said to Collins, jerking a thumb toward the room behind him. Collins rose, returning Meade's unwavering glare. He made a show of dusting his pants and holding a Kleenex to his bloody nose. They circled each other like tomcats ready to spring as Collins eased past Meade into his room.

Wilder let Meade pull him to his feet. He blotted his own nose on his borrowed shirtsleeve. Meade guided him after Collins and dropped him on the bed.

"All right, boys," he said after closing the door and settling himself in front of it. "Dave, take a seat."

"You can't keep me in here," Collins said.

"Humor me. Take a seat." Collins backed up and perched on the edge of the desk. Meade looked the two men over, shaking his head and muttering under his breath. "I cannot believe I forgot about those goddamned back stairs," he said. "And Katherine's just as shifty as you, you shifty son of a bitch," he turned on Wilder. "Jesus, I'm a moron. I should've locked you up."

"I knew it," Collins leapt back to his feet. "What the hell were you thinking, Meade, letting this maniac loose? I'm bringing the biggest damned lawsuit this city's ever seen. And I'm suing you, personally, for assault. Except you're first, buddy boy," he said, stabbing a finger at Wilder. "What the hell were you doing in here?" He turned again to Meade. "I want him searched."

Wilder stood up, ready to go another round with Collins, but Meade shoved him back down on the bed in passing.

"That's enough out of you, Slick," he said. He advanced on Collins who backed off but remained standing, face flushed and breathing hard with his mouth open. "Take it easy, Dave," Meade said. He reached out to put a hand on Collins' shoulder. "Have a seat."

Collins jerked away. "Keep your hands off me, Meade."

"Fine. I'll sit down, then. You guys make me tired." He righted the desk chair and sat down, sighing. He wiped the back of one hand across his forehead and looked at Wilder. "You look a little green, how's the arm?" Wilder gave a brief nod. "Good. Because next time, I ain't sitting at the hospital all afternoon with you." He stretched his legs out and appeared to contemplate the toes of his shoes. "So," he said, raising his eyes to Wilder again. "Davy Crockett, here, has a point. What were you doing in here?"

"Stealing my shirt, to begin with," Collins started in.

"Shut up, Dave," said Meade. "Lewis?"

In answer, Wilder pulled the paper he'd found from its crumpled safekeeping in his sling and tossed it to Meade.

"Oh, thanks, the fresh blood's a nice touch, Lewis. Now, what have we got here?"

Meade straightened out the paper. He whistled, looking up at Collins, a smile crossing his face for the first time since connecting his fist with Collins' nose.

"Why isn't he under arrest yet?" Collins hissed. "He's that ass who calls himself the Fox. How much more proof do you want? For God's sake, he killed that man Saturday night."

"You're right, Dave," Meade said nodding. "This is serious. How'd you figure it all out, anyway?"

"Face it, Meade, everything you've ever done is second rate."

"Well, Dave, I thought that was a first rate punch on your schnozzola."

"And that's about your limit, isn't it?" Collins sneered. "You've always resorted to muscle in a crisis. You and your fellow officers couldn't detect your asses if you were sitting on them. Which is what you obviously spend most of your time doing. Well, I didn't. There are professionals out there, Meade, real detectives . . ."

"Chuck Nelson," Wilder said to himself in wonder.

Collins crossed his arms over his chest and looked smug.

"What?" Meade asked, turning in surprise to Wilder.

"Chuck Nelson," he repeated, staring at Collins. "You sneaky son of a bitch." But before he could jump on Collins, Meade was between them again.

"Come on, Schwarzenegger, be sensible for a change." He pushed Wilder back toward the bed. "Who's Chuck Nelson?"

"Ask him," Wilder said.

Meade turned to Collins.

"He's a private detective," Collins said. "A licensed professional."

"Who pretended to be a travel journalist writing about Upper East Tennessee," Wilder said. "Who talked to half the people in Nolichucky, but never managed to visit any of the other towns in the area. Who, along with everyone else on Main Street, happened to be there when I had my one and only argument with Don Sherrill."

"And you didn't think you were being followed," tutted Meade. "Well, Davy, I think we need a phone number right about now, and an address, and a whole lot of answers."

"Like hell."

"That's obstruction, son."

"But I thought it was that nice boy of Maude Fisher's who broke Lewis' arm," Katherine said as she poured more iced tea for Meade. "And you say David has gone back to work. Well, I just don't know." She sat shaking her head. "Help yourselves to more soup, George, Marilyn." She took a spoonful herself and then looked at Meade again. "You should have been clearer, Rodger. If I'd known you wanted me to be some sort of deterrent, that you wanted me to guard Lewis, I would have."

"Katherine, I'm sorry about all this," said Meade. "I should have been smarter." He rolled his tea glass between his hands. "We knew someone was convinced enough of Lewis' guilt to try serving him up to us on a silver gurney. But we didn't know who that was. There are just too many 'someone's waltzing around in this. I had an idea whoever it was might try again when we didn't run right out and arrest Lewis." He shrugged and took a swallow of tea. "And I wish I'd remembered the back stairs. When Dave came home for lunch and headed for the kitchen I didn't even think. Except that I thought I could keep an eye on Hot Shot here without keeping him under lock and key."

"There's your mistake," Katherine snorted. "Though for that matter I don't know why you didn't think I might go after him. I've certainly felt like it any number of times."

"He does bring that out in a person, doesn't he?" Meade agreed, looking more cheerful.

Katherine turned a scowl on Wilder. "And now you've gotten blood all over that shirt, too. It's becoming a habit with you. Tcha."

"But David didn't have anything to do with the murder, did he?" asked Palmer, reaching for a roll.

"No. He's not that accomplished a villain. And he's not the Fox, either. So that clears up one rat nest of questions. But, as I say, the threads of this entertainment run anything but true. And the complicating factor is slurping his soup right next to you."

Wilder raised his soup spoon in salute.

"But what was David doing following Lewis?" asked Marilyn. She looked at Wilder and clucked. "You look more disreputable every time I see you."

"Thanks."

"Actually, that's what Dave was trying to find," said Meade. "Lewis the Disreputable. He hired Nelson to find Lewis and dig up some dirt on him. And then, surprise, surprise, here's Lewis living not very far away after all and conveniently wallowing in rumor and suspicion."

"Actually, to begin with, he was hoping I was dead," Wilder said.

324

"Lewis," snapped Katherine.

"And that would have saved us all a lot of bother," Meade said, nodding. "But Nelson found him and reported all the latest juicy gossip from Nolichucky. And the bad jokes about the Fox. And for Dave that ended up being more satisfying than finding Lewis dead. So he paid Nelson off and started following Lewis himself."

"Why?" Katherine asked.

"Nelson's expensive and Dave's a cheapskate."

"That's not what I meant, and you know it. Why was he doing this?"

Meade looked at her, his lips a thin uncomfortable line.

"Why?" she demanded.

"Because he's always been jealous, Katherine," he said.

"Of Lewis?"

"Yeah, he's always wanted to be a short, disreputable orphan, Aunt Katherine," Wilder said.

"Stop it, Lewis. You're not funny."

"Jesus, you two. If you'd ever stop sniping at each other, you'd see what's so obvious to anyone else, but especially a sad sack like Dave."

"And just what are you talking about, Rodger Meade?" Katherine pulled herself up straighter in her chair as though she could now tower over him.

"Forget it, Katherine," he said, his eyes meeting her piercing glare. "You'll have to figure it out yourself. But I'll tell you something a little easier to grasp. Dave told me he hired Nelson about a month ago. About the time you updated your will."

Katherine thought for a minute, then asked, "What's that got to do with anything? I've never shown David my will or discussed it with him."

"But you had your cleaning girl witness it."

"She only signed it. She didn't read the thing."

"Well, enough of the high points, anyway."

"Why would she do that and why would she tell David?"

"He has, I think we could call it, seductive charm."

An angry red flush crept into Katherine's cheeks and her eyes sparked. "He didn't. He wouldn't. Why, she's half his age." She stood abruptly and took the not-yet-empty iced-tea pitcher to the kitchen.

"Every Wednesday at noon," Meade said, nodding in happy confirmation.

Palmer rose from his place. "Yes, well, I'll just go see if Katherine needs any help."

And he followed her to the kitchen.

Marilyn was choking quietly into her soup. "He told you all that?" she said, wiping her eyes with her napkin.

"Rodger's a persuasive guy," said Wilder.

"And your cousin must be persistent to have followed you around. Not to mention having a high threshold for boredom. Why did he slam the gate, though? How could he do that?" Marilyn shuddered.

"He said to clinch the evidence. To provide some literally physical evidence that Lewis had been there. Though that wouldn't be any real proof. Lewis could just as easily have been clumsy and slammed his arm in his car door. No, I think it was a fit of pique. Very childish. I wonder how long that made him feel good?"

"He was pretty cool when I showed up here on the doorstep afterwards, Saturday night."

"Yeah, well he's always been a sneaky chicken shit."

"Turns out he was the one making all those phone calls, Marilyn. Just another way to show he cared." Wilder stirred his soup. "You know, you probably didn't need to break his nose."

"What, you're all of a sudden feeling sentimental? There's no probably about it. I wanted to break his nose. Probably, hell. I liked breaking his nose." Meade drank the rest of his tea in one long swallow and thumped the glass down on the table. "And I still feel good about it and will for a very long time."

Marilyn looked from one to the other of the men. "Well, so, this lets Lewis off the hook, right?"

"We're getting there," Meade said.

"Rodger, for Christ's sake."

"Well, Sport, there are a few smallish details left and I've yet to hear from Fisher the Wonder Boy."

At his words, the phone rang. Palmer stuck his head back around the corner. "Katherine says it's for you, Rodger."

Meade wiggled his eyebrows at Marilyn and Wilder and went to the kitchen.

"I like your friend, Lewis. And your Aunt Katherine," Marilyn said.

"Thank you."

"So I guess you do look just like your father because you sure look like her."

"Except I'm taller by three inches and that makes all the difference."

"Have people always thought she's your mother?"

"Mmhmm."

"And you don't like that."

He didn't answer.

"Well." Marilyn rearranged her bowl and tea glass on her tablemat.

"I didn't like it when I was a kid. I wanted my own mother." He shrugged. "It's not a problem now."

"You should tell her that."

"I probably should."

"So, what're the details Rodger was talking about? George and I thought one of us could drive your car back for you. Preferably with you in it."

"Thanks for coming down."

"What details, Lewis?"

"Oh, little things like did I kill Don Sherrill or am I exactly what David and your uncle would love to think I am?" Wilder gave her half a smile. "Don't worry. It's all just an endless quagmire of dumb coincidences. They haven't got anything on me."

Meade stepped back into the room and stopped at the end of the table. He looked at Wilder without saying anything, then gave his head a shake. "Fisher," he said, indicating the phone with a jerk of his head toward the kitchen. "Barbara Sherrill has revised her statement. It seems she found something missing after all." He stopped and stared out the window. He looked tired.

Wilder and Marilyn exchanged looks.

Wilder turned back to Meade.

"What?" he asked.

Meade pulled something from his pocket and put it down on the table. "This." The bird pipe sat mutely regarding the crumbs on Katherine's plate. "I found it with your stuff upstairs. Care to explain it, Lewis?"

CHAPTER 24

"I have a loan agreement, Rodger. I told you, it's like a receipt."

"But not with you."

They were sitting in Katherine's small study across the hall from the parlor. Meade had finally stopped pacing from the door to the desk and back. He sat in a window seat now, back braced against one side, one long leg bent and braced against the other side. The effort it was costing him to sit still was evident in every line of his body. Wilder slumped in a straight-backed chair feeling exhausted.

They'd left Marilyn stuttering out this latest development to Katherine and George, Meade growling to Wilder when he got him behind the closed door that he hadn't wanted to lose control and beat him to a bloody pulp in front of his aunt and these poor people who seemed to like him.

"And you didn't show the pipe to anyone

at all. And even though you told George that Sherrill made a donation to the museum, you didn't tell him what it was. In fact you wouldn't tell him when he asked you."

"And I told you why. And I told you where the loan agreement is. And I told you that Sherrill had a copy of it, too. Damn it, I knew that pipe was going to be trouble. Rodger, think about it. There wasn't any evidence of a break-in."

"Oh, didn't you know? S.O.P. for the Fox. He's a sharp guy."

"What about Dr. Ramsey?"

"Yeah, Fisher got hold of him. That was good of you, Lewis. I understand what you were doing there for Ramsey, delivering clandestine medicine so the poobah preacher wouldn't know his wife is hedging their spiritual bets by taking the sick kid to an actual doctor." He shook his head and looked out the window, following the fence line down to the pond. "That's a little too scary for me, you know? Why do people take something so simple as faith and complicate the hell out of their lives with it like that? Poor silly woman. Poor little kid."

He looked back at Lewis. "But you said it yourself. Ramsey doesn't know what you did there on your own time. And he says he asked you, in particular, to leave the medicine for him while he was out of town because he knows you're the cagey type who doesn't go around talking about what you've been up to."

"Christ. Well, what about the dates of the other break-ins?"

"What, you're thinking about an alibi? Don't delude yourself. You're that quiet guy that not much happens to, remember? You don't go anywhere, Lewis. You live alone. And your newts aren't talking."

"I knew I should've bought that parrot."

Meade guffawed. "Oh, hell, Lewis." He rested his forehead on his knee.

"I can't have been doing nothing every one of those nights."

Meade just looked at him.

"Well, I guess I won't bet on it."

A knock came on the door and Marilyn called in to them. "Now that you all have quietened down a bit, may we speak to, or about, the prisoner?"

"She's a good one, Lewis," Meade said. "Yeah, come on in," he called.

Wilder got up and crossed over to the bookshelves filling the wall opposite Meade's window seat. He leaned against the shelves and watched the door, his face blank but his right index finger tapping a muffled staccato on his cast. Marilyn pushed the door open and peered around the edge.

"Oh, no more blood. That's a good sign." She stepped in followed by Katherine and Palmer with his hand on Katherine's elbow lending comfort. They ranged themselves just inside the door, looking tentative and uncomfortable.

"Neither of you two has seen the pipe before, and neither of you has seen the loan agreement Lewis says he left on his desk, am I right?" Meade asked without preamble, nodding to Marilyn and George. He remained braced in his window seat.

"No. Why don't you call Uncle Paul and ask him to go look for it?" Marilyn suggested.

"That's the next step. But first let me ask you something. I haven't asked any of you three what you think of Barbara Sherrill."

"I don't know her," Katherine stated. "I've never met her."

"Okay. Father Palmer?"

Wilder watched Palmer's face as he tried to frame an answer.

"Off the top of your head. What you think of her, how long you've known her."

Palmer hesitated. Then he sighed and came further into the room. "May I?" He indicated one of the leather wing chairs facing Meade's window seat.

"Sorry, of course. Katherine, Ms. Wooten, please, sit down."

Katherine appeared reluctant but joined Palmer, sitting in the twin of his chair. Marilyn glanced over at Wilder. He just stared back, feeling empty and unable to dredge up any sort of reaction to her at this point. She took the chair he'd been sitting in earlier, moving it so that she could see everyone's faces.

"I have been aware of Barbara Sherrill for several years," Palmer said.

"How many?"

"Oh, quite a few, perhaps fifteen or twenty years. The Sherrills have been summering in Nolichucky at least that long."

"You said you've been 'aware' of her. That's as opposed to knowing her?"

Palmer gave a quick smile. "Barb Sherrill is the type of woman one is easily aware of long before making her acquaintance. She has tremendous presence. I was better acquainted with her husband, though, through Rotary. In a town the size of Nolichucky we were bound to cross paths often, but in general we don't, didn't," he shook his head, "don't, I guess, travel in the same circles."

"From what you do know of her, what do

you think of her?"

"In terms of what?"

"Do you think she would lie about a break-in?"

"I think it more likely," Palmer said, "that a mistake was made. Don't you think Don gave the pipe to Lewis and just forgot to mention it to Barb?"

"Is that a personal assessment or a professional assessment as coming from a good Christian man of the cloth?"

"I don't think the two are entirely separable."

Meade regarded Palmer. "And I don't know you well enough to know if in your case that statement is, in fact, true," he said and Palmer again gave his quick smile.

"Rodger, I'm very uncomfortable with the direction this conversation is taking," Katherine said. "I don't care to hear a dissection of Mrs. Sherrill's character and I don't think it's appropriate that I do. And I certainly do not want to sit here and hear you doubting the character of a very good friend of mine. I want to know what's going to happen. Are you going to arrest Lewis?"

"Katherine, Captain Meade was only making an honest statement," Palmer said.

"Nevertheless. Rodger, answer my question."

"I don't want to arrest him, Katherine. But I will do my job."

Katherine stood, shaking Palmer's hand off her arm. "I'll be in the kitchen," she said.

"Shall I go after her?" Palmer asked.

"No. I'll talk to her. I need to go call Sheriff Glaser, anyway. And Fisher. Might as well do it from the kitchen," said Meade. He made no move to get up.

"Oh, bother, and I should call Hart," Marilyn said.

"Why?" Wilder asked. The others started at hearing him, as though forgetting he might have a speaking part.

"He's helping my mother at the store today. I told him I'd be back by now."

"Jesus."

"Lewis, what is it with you?"

"Who's Hart?" asked Meade, interested in this charged interchange.

"Didn't he have to be back teaching all the little mathophobes this morning?" Wilder asked, ignoring Meade.

"Fall break," Marilyn replied.

"Who's Hart?" Meade asked again, louder.

"Hart Warren," supplied Palmer. "Teaches math in Charlotte or someplace near there. Came back this weekend for the Pickers' Picnic. Wonderful guitar player. He grew up in Nolichucky."

"He's a friend of mine," said Marilyn.

"He's a jerk," said Wilder.

"He's not looking at a prison term." Marilyn drew her breath in, as though she could pull her words back before they flew across the room to slap Wilder in the face. "Lewis, I didn't mean it like that."

"Like what?" Wilder turned to Meade. "Rodger, Hart saw the bird on my desk."

"When?"

"He came in the office Saturday afternoon and he must have seen it."

"How do you know?"

"It was sitting in the middle of the desk. I was, Christ, I was reading a damned poem George left for me, out loud to the bird. Warren slunk up the stairs so quietly I didn't hear him. He was standing in the door. He can tell you I had it Saturday before I came to Stonewall."

"You're sure he saw it?"

"He must have. Ask him. And he overheard me saying something about coming to Stonewall."

"Well." Meade sat stroking his mustache, eyeing Wilder. "I'll go call Glaser and Fisher."

Wilder stayed motionless, leaning against the bookcase, until Meade had left the room. Then he crossed to the door. He stopped with his hand on the knob.

"George, Aunt Katherine says you two have known each other for years."

"Yes."

Wilder pulled the door open.

"Lewis, stay," Marilyn said.

"Lewis, I think it would be better if you did stay here," Palmer added.

"Why?" Not waiting for an answer and without a glance at either of them, he walked out.

"You didn't run far this time."

Wilder was sitting on the front porch steps, looking down the gravel driveway toward the road beyond. Meade had come around the corner of the house, inhaling a cigarette as though he couldn't suck quite enough smoke into his lungs. He stopped in front of Wilder and blew out a blue stream.

"I didn't run."

"You just didn't come back for a long time."

"Rodger, if you want to kick the shit out of me, just do it and get it over with. David and your friend Fisher had their turns so you might as well stop enjoying it vicariously and take your turn, too. Then drop it. I'm sick of it."

Meade ground the butt out on the sole of his shoe and flipped it into the bushes. He leaned down and gathered the front of Wilder's shirt in his fist. He pulled Wilder to his feet and backed him up the stairs and across the porch until Wilder's back hit the wall of the house and he was breathing down into his face.

"Don't think I won't enjoy it."

"Then go ahead."

Wilder's eyes held steady with Meade's. The grip at his throat didn't slacken but he became aware of a shift somewhere in Meade. The fire in his eyes died and the growl at the back of his teeth ended in a deep sigh.

"Shit. I'm sick of it, too." He let Wilder go and dropped down on the steps. Wilder joined him.

"It's good to have you back, Lewis. I just wish to hell I knew if it's for real or for very long."

"I didn't do anything, Rodger."

"Story of your life. Sin of omission."

"Don't start."

"Sorry. Sin of commission."

"You been talking to George? Jesus, talk about a sin of omission. He's known Aunt Katherine for years. Never let on."

"He's not such a bad guy, Lewis."

"Yeah, well, neither am I."

They sat for awhile not speaking. Wilder listened to the birds obliviously whistling away in the oaks and maples as a pessimistic cricket somewhere warned of hard weather to come. There was more traffic noise out on the road than he remembered there being. It probably wasn't safe for small boys to race their bikes on the blacktop anymore.

"So how long are you and I going to be joined at the hip?"

"I called Glaser. I think he's feeling like a wallflower at this party."

"Oh yeah, that's all I need, you two fighting over which one gets to bust me."

"Settle down, Lewis," Meade murmured. "He said he'd be happy to go look for the loan document but he wondered if maybe Fisher and I wanted to come up for an intelligence powwow. Very thoughty of him. Of course we could do it over the phone but I was thinking you and I could drive up there now, take your car. Fisher can come up later tonight after he's looked for Sherrill's copy of the loan form. Or in the morning."

"I could just go back with George and Marilyn, save you a trip."

"No, you couldn't."

Wilder picked up a stray piece of gravel and shied it out into the driveway. "Well, it was worth a shot. But you didn't really answer my question. Are we taking my car because you're going to cut me loose up there or what?"

"We'll see, Lewis. We'll see."

"All right. I'll get my things." He started back across the porch.

"And say goodbye to Katherine this time."

Wilder looked back over his shoulder at Meade.

"Well, you never know. If things don't go well, you won't be making another stop here for awhile."

Wilder went into the house. He couldn't even muster the interest to swear under his breath at that thought. Meade's barbs were all too likely to prove prophetic.

At the bottom of the stairs he hesitated, wondering if he should find Aunt Katherine first or wait until he'd repacked the little he'd brought with him. He heard Marilyn and George making leave-taking noises somewhere near the kitchen and ducked up the stairs deciding he would rather avoid them for now.

As boy and teenager he'd bounded up these stairs two or three at a time with a two-fold purpose. The first was to annoy his aunt who objected to the galumphing. The second was in the fervent hope that stretching his legs at every opportunity might lengthen them. With everything that had happened in the past two days and with the morning's painkiller long worn off, he felt lucky now not to be crawling up them.

As he passed Collins' room he thought of nipping in and borrowing another shirt. He decided it wasn't worth the effort or the aggravation. He continued down the hall into the guest room, wondering if Collins would be in residence much longer. Or if Aunt Katherine would be looking for someone new to help with the cleaning. Or if the current, now infamous, cleaning girl would soon have a new roommate.

He had just made a decision against refolding everything and was jamming it all en masse into his overnight bag when he heard Katherine come up the back stairs.

"You've become a negligent packer, I see."

He tossed his shaving kit in on top of his rumpled clothes and looked up at her. "Only under trying circumstances, Aunt Katherine. Ordinarily I pack with real bloody panache. I'm a member of the packing elite. A packing god. You'd find yourself weeping over the organization and the crisp folds. But today I'm feeling like a dog and packing like a rat."

"Why do I put up with you?" she asked,

shaking her head to hide her smile.

"Well, I gave you a break for a few years, didn't I?" he asked softly.

"It was too long, Lewis. Promise me you'll come back soon."

"I do promise, Aunt Katherine, and I'll try to keep it. But all of a sudden my life that I thought I had so nicely under control has come just a bit unglued."

Katherine stepped over to him and took his chin in her hand. "Young man," she said, "if you make a promise I expect you to keep it, with no excuses."

"Yes ma'am."

"Good. Now help me change the sheets on the bed. George has decided to stay the night. Apparently he thinks I need a shoulder to lean on."

"Silly George."

"That's what I told him. Although, frankly, I don't look forward to facing David alone. If he comes home."

"Aunt Katherine, about your will . . ."

"I'm not discussing my will with you or anyone else."

"Why are you such a stubborn old woman?"

"That's my privilege. And since when am I old? And for that matter why are you so mule-headed?"

"Because you raised me up well."

Katherine snorted and smoothed the fresh sheets on the bed. "George asked me about my grandmother's fern stand. Do you remember that dreadful thing? I hadn't thought of it in years. I asked you to carry it to the attic when you were nine or ten and the door blew closed behind you and you couldn't get out and I'd gone out to the garden and no one could hear you up there or knew where you were for hours. Gave us both nightmares. Do you remember that?"

"That must be why I shudder every time I see a fern."

"Oh don't be silly."

Wilder made an attempt to flip the blanket onto the bed one-handed but only managed to tangle it around his shoulders.

"Lewis. Here, I'll do it. Tcha."

"No, I can get it."

"Famous last words. Get going, now. You're just delaying the inevitable."

"And here I am, Mr. Inevitable himself." Meade appeared in the doorway. "Come on, Hot Shot, Marilyn's waiting. She's riding back with us. Where's your bag?" He snatched it up then gave Wilder a push toward Katherine. "Give your aunt a hug and a smooch like a good nephew and tell her you love her and you're sorry she has to put up with such a sorry piece of . . ."

"Rodger Meade."

Wilder folded Katherine into his one-armed embrace. "Goodbye, Aunt Katherine. I love you. I'm sorry you've had to put up with Rodger, he's such a sorry piece of . . ."

"Lewis. Honestly, the two of you."

Wilder kissed her and they left her muttering and fussing and fiercely jamming the pillow into its case.

CHAPTER 25

"I'll sit in back," Marilyn said, as the three of them approached Wilder's car.

"No, take the front."

"Yeah, Marilyn, sit up front," said Meade. "Lewis has decided not to take any more pain pills and I don't want to be sitting next to him when he starts moaning and making ghastly faces."

"I'll be sure to sit so you can see me in the rearview mirror."

"How is it you both ended up driving Rabbits?" Marilyn asked, looking from Wilder's more worn car to Meade's bright shiny vehicle.

Meade gave her a prissy look as he held the door for her. "Please, mine is a Golf."

"Like there's a difference?"

"That makes mine obviously newer. They changed the name years ago. As to how we ended up with virtually the same kind of vehicle, simple answer."

"We're twins, Marilyn. Practically identical."

"Identical smart-asses."

"Well, at least you two are talking to each other again," said Meade as he pulled out onto the highway. "You had me worried. I need to keep this boy attached to someone, Maid Marilyn, so he doesn't come mooning after my wife."

"Jesus, Rodger."

"Shut up, Lewis, I'm going to interrogate Marilyn. And she can give me directions when I need them. You just pass out back there or do whatever it is you do best."

"That seems to be open for debate."

"You got that right, now hush."

He hushed and let the feeling of heading back to Nolichucky wash over him. Some of the strain of the past few days began to slip away as they left the strip malls and multi-lanes behind. Wilder imagined he could feel even the air becoming lighter as Stonewall receded and the foothills of the mountains rose ahead to meet them.

It was true what he'd told Marilyn's mother about his friend from West Texas being claustrophobic in the mountains. Wilder smiled to himself at the memory of the poor guy climbing the walls, practically suffocating when surrounded by sixty- and eighty-foot trees, wide-eyed and sweating when he couldn't see the horizon for 360 degrees.

Wilder felt embraced by the mountains. His claustrophobia only came writhing and twining out of the crannies of his mind when his thoughts strayed to memories of his problematic childhood. But now the seventy-five miles between Stonewall and Nolichucky looked like being a good, maybe even sane distance, not too far and just near enough. And now Nolichucky, nestled in its mountains, felt like going home. Unless instead he was going to prison.

"Hey, Lewis, come up for air."

"Let him sleep, he's had a rough time," Marilyn was saying.

"No, it'll only get rougher if this thing isn't solved in some way that doesn't involve his head on the block. Fisher's heard talk about Barb Sherrill having an affair with a younger man."

"Where did he hear that?" Marilyn asked.

"The ways of Fisher are rare and wonderful and don't bear delving into. It sounded reasonably on target to him, though, and I respect his hunches along those lines. What do you think?"

"Rodger," Wilder said groggily, "I haven't got very warm or fuzzy feelings toward rumors." He straightened up in his seat, coming more into focus. "Now you mention it, though, it wouldn't surprise me. She made a pass at me at a street dance."

"There's that dancing again," Meade said. "Marilyn, have you ever seen this boy dance?"

"He doesn't strike you as the dancing type, does he? But yeah, now you mention it, I saw the two of them doing the two-step at the street dance. This was back before he and I became what might almost be called an item. But I did have my eye on him. Anyway, it looked to me like she saved his life. There were some teenage girls blowing hot all over him when she swooped down and scooped him up."

"More like out of the frying pan and into the fire," muttered Wilder.

"You never told me she made a pass at you," Marilyn tsked. "Maybe Lewis is the younger man they've been talking about."

"It was a younger man, Marilyn, not a shorter one," Meade corrected.

"Why should that stop her?" asked Marilyn. "He's very attractive."

"Well, yes, he is. I know I have trouble keeping my hands off him."

"Thanks, Rodger, I've felt like strangling you a few times, too. Did you know she's a big-game hunter? Maybe she's been on the prowl for another kind of game."

"Ooh, Lewis, your head could be on the wall next to the majestic moose."

"Or the wily fox," murmured Meade. "But you haven't heard that rumor making the rounds in Nolichucky?"

"No," Marilyn said. "That could just mean it's not someone in Nolichucky, though. But what difference does it make to Lewis if she is having an affair?"

"Trite though it may sound, a spouse is still the best bet in a case like this, for various reasons, including the good old triangle. Of course, Lewis could fit nicely into that scenario, too. You didn't like Sherrill and I didn't like him, so who's to say that Barb's taste hasn't improved and she decided to cut her losses, only Sherrill wouldn't give her a divorce. Lover to the rescue. That's you, Lewis. You brain him, and after a suitable period of mourning, the two of you ride off into the sunset together in a new Lincoln. That sounds good to me. You've got to admit, she was rattled to see you in Stonewall this morning. Maybe she was expecting you to lie low."

"I hope you're joking," Wilder said in a strained voice. He was suddenly having trouble breathing.

"Jesus, you could've even made it look like a botched Fox job. And we would have been none the wiser about your part except for good old Dave. I don't know, Lewis, I just keep digging you in deeper."

Meade didn't seem to notice that both his passengers looked sick. Marilyn reached her right hand back between the car door and her seat. Wilder took it and held it in his own.

"So if she and I are in this together why did she revise her statement about the break-in?"

"She's going to let you take the fall because she doesn't stand by her men."

"Rodger, I guarantee, if Lewis and Barb Sherrill were having an affair, word would be out in Nolichucky. Wilder-watching is an Olympic sport in some circles. The entire third grade class knew the first time we ate lunch together before we'd even taken a bite."

"You don't think that out of good taste or manners or sympathy or whatever that you might be the last person this rumor would get around to?"

"There are people in town who would delight in making sure I was the first."

"See, now, Lewis?" Meade said in the calming tones he probably used when his children had nightmares. "Rumors have their good points, too. So we'll have our little meet with Sheriff Glaser and check out the loan papers. Then we'll see what's what."

Darkness fell. Meade punched a cassette into the player and they heard what sounded like a bagpipe and saxophone blues number.

"Hey, Rodger, don't you think this music is just a bit off kilter?" Wilder asked.

"Hey, Lewis, I sure hope it doesn't turn out that you kilt him."

"Me too." He kept hold of Marilyn's hand and her arm fell asleep but she didn't seem to mind.

They rolled into Nolichucky a short time later.

"Rotten to the core, sure enough," Glaser said. "But that didn't bother me. I took my hatchet and went after . . ."

"Are you two going to be much longer exchanging tree conversion techniques," Wilder interrupted, "because if you are I'm heading up to the museum and finding that loan form myself."

Glaser and Meade turned from discussing Glaser's tree trunk cupboard and looked at Wilder. He'd been pacing the office since they arrived, but stopped, uncomfortable now he had their attention.

"What?" he asked.

"Where's Marilyn?"

"I don't know. Bathroom, maybe."

"Sit down, Lewis," Meade said.

"No, he's right." Glaser closed the cupboard and brushed off his hands. "Let's get this thing over." He picked his jacket off a coat tree and tugged it on. "So, Lewis, this loan form, this is one of those professional innovations you've implemented at the museum, huh?"

"Yeah."

"Useful."

"Well this isn't exactly the situation I'd pictured needing it for."

"Still, good thing you're so clever."

"Paul, could we just go get it?"

"And I take it you plan to accompany us?" Glaser said this to Marilyn who now stood in the doorway.

"Yes I do."

Glaser sighed and rolled his eyes and rubbed his stomach as though he'd eaten chili at Willie's Café for dinner. "All right, but I want you three stooges, oh no offense meant there, Meade, I want you three staying out of the office while I look. That clear?"

"Yes sir," Meade and Marilyn said together. Wilder muttered something and when he caught Glaser's eyes on him stretched his lips into a false smile that did nothing to improve either of their moods.

Glaser took his own vehicle, the others following in Wilder's. Meade drove again with Marilyn beside him in the front. Wilder watched as Nolichucky slipped past the window he leaned against. He felt as though he'd been gone for weeks. Everything looked tidier and smaller. They passed Lillian's and he couldn't picture ever having seen Glaser embracing his bass. Although he had seen with his own eyes the tree trunk wet bar, alive and well, in the corner of his office. There had to be hope in that somewhere.

"Welcome to the Nolichucky Jack History Museum," Glaser said, plucking Wilder's keys from Meade's hand when they were all on the porch. He opened the door and ushered them in. "We're mighty proud of our little museum. And some people are even fond of the curator." He shot a look at Marilyn who had just pleased Wilder by linking arms with him. "Well, let's go see what we can do about keeping him around." Wilder caught the alarm and they headed up the stairs to the office.

"Lewis, where will I find your get-out-of-jail-free card?"

"Pretty sure I left it on the desk."

"Pretty sure." Glaser unlocked the office door, flipped on the light and went in.

Meade stood in the open door. "Jesus. Good thing you don't want company in there. Just between you and me we'd use up all the available oxygen. See it?"

"Not off hand."

Wilder jabbed Meade in the ribs with the elbow of his cast. "Move over." Glaser was moving things around on the desk. "In the middle of the desk, Paul."

"Not there, Lewis."

"Well, check the top drawer. Maybe I left it in there."

"Not there, Lewis."

"Well, then let me look."

Meade grabbed him by the collar and pulled him back. "Paul, let me have the desk chair. Thanks." He put it next to the wooden chair near the door. "Okay, here, Marilyn, sit down. Lewis, sit down. I'll help Paul. You two sit tight and don't touch anything." Wilder watched in growing unease as the two sifted through all the papers on the desk and in the drawers, coming up with nothing but a folder with blank copies of the form.

"Where else, Lewis? Did you take it home with you? You had the bird with you."

"No."

"Where else, then? You got a file of these things filled in somewhere?"

"Top drawer of the filing cabinet. Sorry, I must have filed it without thinking about it. Key's in the desk drawer." Glaser found the key and turned around to eye Wilder, one eyebrow cocked. Wilder clamped his right hand in his left armpit to stop its sudden shaking.

After opening the drawer Glaser stood for awhile with his back to them. Then he pulled a file out and handed it over his shoulder to Meade.

"Here. Take a look through there and see if you find it."

Wilder didn't watch as Meade flipped through the papers, his eyes were on Glaser who still stood looking in the drawer. He didn't strike Wilder as someone who would stand that long just admiring the neatly labeled files. Glaser's right hand was kneading his left shoulder. It wasn't a confidence-inspiring scene.

"Not in the folder, Lewis."

"I've got something here," Glaser said.

Marilyn looked back and forth between Meade and Glaser as though she were at a tennis match. "Oh, thank goodness," she said, turning and putting her forehead on Wilder's shoulder. "This has been too

357

much. Lewis, promise me you'll never file anything away again. Just staple anything that important to the middle of your forehead."

Wilder didn't respond. He, Glaser, and Meade were too busy staring at each other and at the silver gravy boat swinging back and forth on the pencil Glaser held through its handle.

"From that last haul at the preacher's," Glaser said. "Now would be a good time to read him his rights, I think, Captain Meade. I'll leave the issue of handcuffs to your discretion."

CHAPTER 26

"Who all has keys to the museum?" Meade asked. Wilder hadn't moved or said anything since Glaser pulled the gravy boat out of the filing cabinet. Meade punched him on the shoulder now. "Hey, c'mon. Glaser'll find it any minute out there at Sherrill's. Who has keys?"

Meade had been able to stall Glaser long enough to get through to Fisher on his cell phone. But Fisher hadn't found Sherrill's copy of the loan agreement in Stonewall and was already on his way to join them in Nolichucky. Glaser placed Wilder under arrest, then, and at that point Wilder shut down. He heard Marilyn arguing with her uncle but if the words they exchanged held any meaning for him it passed him by.

She'd attached herself to Glaser's arm and hadn't let go, telling him to get in touch with Hart Warren, who had left town but not yet arrived home in Charlotte. Telling him he should dust the gravy boat for fingerprints. He should go check the Sherrills' Nolichucky house for the loan form, because who said Sherrill ever took it to Stonewall in the first place?

Maybe Glaser had agreed with her because he was gone now and Meade was saying something about finding the form any minute. And keys.

"Who has keys, Lewis? Jesus, we'd get more sense out of his newts."

"Marcie and Pam, the two receptionists, Jim Honeycutt, he's a sort of handyman, Dr. Ramsey. That's it as far as I know. And me."

"Well, hell, he walks, he talks, he crawls on his belly like a reptile."

"Newts are amphibians, Rodger."

"Marlin Perkins is restored to us."

"Let's hope it's for good," said Marilyn. "Rodger, can't we go help Uncle Paul? Can't you go help Uncle Paul? Why don't we all go and you can handcuff Lewis to the car while you and I go in?"

"You're brimming with good ideas, Marilyn. You probably have a career in law enforcement ahead of you. Or you can take over for this guy if we throw him in the slammer." He looked Wilder over. "Lewis, if

I were to cuff you to, say, the door handle of your car, back seat, you know, where you might feel comfortable, who knows, have a few happy memories, while I go lend a hand in the search for your shaky salvation, are you gonna go catatonic again?"

"Would that matter?" asked Marilyn.

"Marilyn."

She shrugged. "Well, it's all in a good cause, Lewis."

Meade prodded the two of them the rest of the way to Wilder's car, tut-tutting as they bickered back and forth.

They made a quick stop at the bookstore where Marilyn ran in to get the Sherrills' address because they'd forgotten to look it up before they left the museum. Wilder waved to Martha Wooten who came to the door smiling. He thought about her and Palmer as they'd laughed and listened to the pickers together and he let his head fall back, closing his eyes, wondering if he and Marilyn would be laughing together at next year's picnic.

"What are your theories, now, Rodger?" Marilyn asked. "How did that gravy boat get there and where's the loan form?"

"Well, let's see. First thing that comes to mind is that there never was a loan form. Lewis is either lying or he's delusional."

Wilder didn't feel like rising to the bait and said nothing. He decided he couldn't even be sure at this point that Meade was trying to bait him.

"Or," Meade continued, "the form is just somewhere else in the museum or at Lewis' place. That seems unlikely, though, because he turns out to be a well-organized guy. So, someone might have removed the loan form from the office. And the gravy boat, well, it could have been planted. Or he could have known it was there all along and just be putting on a good show. What was he supposed to do, after all, plead with us to look anywhere but the filing cabinet?"

"I don't think he lies all that well, does he?"

"I don't know. Mostly he just leaves important information out of a conversation, which isn't exactly the same thing."

Meade stopped the car to check the number on a mailbox, then went on slowly. The lots were wooded and the street wasn't well lit. He looked at the next mailbox and the next then pulled into a driveway and rolled to a stop next to Glaser's car.

"But I don't know and that is why, dear friends," he said, getting out and opening the back door next to Wilder, "I'm going to do this." He snapped a handcuff on Wilder's wrist, attaching the other end to the door handle.

"I thought you were joking," Wilder said in disbelief.

"No joking now, Lewis. It's gone too far for that. Marilyn, you keep him company."

"I'd like to come with you."

"I think we'd better keep this official from here on in. Stay with Lewis, okay?" He looked back at Wilder. "Bet you can't tie your shoes, now, Hot Shot. Bye."

They watched as Meade went up the steps and crossed the porch to ring the doorbell. They couldn't see if anyone came to the door but Meade opened it and went in.

"Well, this is the most unusual date we've had so far," Wilder said.

"Do you think we'll get the chance to have many more?"

"I'm not making any plans if that tells you anything."

"Lewis, who would have taken the form and left that gravy boat? Who could have?"

"Paul?"

"Oh my God," she said. "No. Oh my God, Lewis. It couldn't be. But it could, too." Wilder thought she looked suitably stunned.

"It all adds up when you think about it," he said. "Right from the beginning with the rumors and him egging it all on. Questioning me every time there was a break-in. Making jokes about it. And it's all played right into his hands this weekend. He offered to search the office. Who's to say he didn't make a trip here earlier this evening, after Rodger's phone call?"

"No, Lewis, I don't want to believe that. You don't think he killed Don Sherrill, do you?"

"I don't know. I think he's the Fox, though."

"But now that he's arrested you he'd have to stop being the Fox. Why would he do that?"

"Maybe that's just part of the game. And now it's over. Or maybe he's run out of houses to knock over, I don't know. But I think he's the Fox."

"Well, if he is and he finds that form in there you can kiss it goodbye. Lewis, I'm going to find Rodger."

"Wait, I'll come with you." Wilder opened his door and came around to her side.

"How did you do that?" she asked, her mouth hanging open.

And even that didn't look unattractive on her, he thought. He held up his wrist. The door handle dangled at the other end of the handcuffs. "That handle falls off," he said and opened her door for her.

"An advantage to owning an older car I would never have guessed."

Together they climbed the steps and crossed the porch as Meade had done. Wilder tried the door. It wasn't locked. He started to pull it open. Marilyn stopped him and gave him a lingering kiss. With a glint in his eye and a new fire in his belly he stepped inside the Sherrills' summer house.

And immediately pulled Marilyn around a corner and flattened himself against the wall.

"Lewis," she started to say and he put his hand over her mouth.

"Shh. Something's wrong." Marilyn shook his hand off and was opening her mouth to say something else. But he held his hand up, cautioning her to wait, as he listened for whatever it was he'd heard in the other room. And then they heard Meade's calm voice.

"He's not dead. Let me call 911."

"Who's not dead?" Marilyn whispered. "We should go help."

"Marilyn, no," Wilder whispered back. "Rodger wouldn't be asking anyone to let him call 911, he'd just do it." But she pushed past him and ran around the corner.

Wilder shrank back against the wall again. Damn, now what? He looked around the

365

room he was in and realized he was being watched by a dozen or so dead, stuffed, and mounted animal heads. Then he heard Marilyn cry out and he swore at the nearest pair of glazed eyes. He didn't know what was going on but he couldn't let her tackle it alone.

He looked around the room again and saw Sherrill's gun cabinet. He crossed to it and tried the doors. Jesus, they weren't locked. The guy should be arrested for arming wandering jailbirds. He grabbed a shotgun and crept to the corner Marilyn had gone around. He stopped short when he heard a familiar voice.

"Well, well, if Captain Meade is here and the bookstore maiden is here, can Lewis Wilder be far behind?" It was Barb Sherrill, sounding like a convivial hostess.

"What happened?" he heard Marilyn ask. "Why haven't you called an ambulance? How long has he been like this?"

Then Meade's voice. "We'll get him help, Marilyn. Do you know CPR?"

"Back away, Marilyn," Barbara snapped. "Now answer my question, where's Lewis?"

"Locked up," Meade said.

"I don't think I believe you."

"We've got enough circumstantial evidence. We're just tying up loose ends,"

Meade said.

"That's not the way I heard it," said another voice. Hart Warren.

"Hart." Marilyn again. "What the hell is going on?"

"Hello, darlin'," Warren drawled. "Thanks for clueing me in to the disputed loan document. I guess ya'll didn't find it there at the museum, though, did you?"

"Did you know there's another copy here?" Marilyn asked. Wilder almost dropped the shotgun. Marilyn? Then he heard her swearing at herself and he came close to laughing with relief.

"That's all right, sweetheart," Warren said. "Too bad we didn't know about that sooner, though, or we could have avoided this confrontation with your old fart of an uncle. I think he maybe has a heart condition and you might ought to get that checked out later, if he's still alive. Now, answer Barb's question, where's your little wild friend?"

"Glaser arrested him when he found the gravy boat in the filing cabinet," Meade said.

"Now that was a nice touch, wasn't it? Poor little fella. Whatever will happen to him now? And what do you want to do with these two, Barb my love?"

"Drop the gun, Barb." Wilder eased around the corner, the shotgun aimed at

367

her heart. Three heads whipped around at his voice. Barbara was holding a gun on Meade standing in the middle of the room. Marilyn crouched near her uncle who was lying on the floor in front of a desk. Even from where he stood, Wilder could see that Glaser's skin was gray and his breathing shallow. Warren was leaning against the far wall enjoying the scene. He was the first to recover.

"Don't listen to him, Barb," he sneered. "He can't shoot that thing one-handed. Hell, it's probably not even loaded."

"Want to find out?" Wilder asked, his finger tensing on the trigger. "Drop it, Barb. Me and my friend here are both loaded and very capable. I've had a lousy couple of days and I'm doped up to the eyeballs. You want to see how really wild I can get?"

Barb hesitated then she smiled and put the gun on the floor. She pushed it toward Marilyn with her foot. Marilyn scooped it up and held it on Warren.

"Well, shit," he said and slid down the wall to sit on the floor.

Meade looked at Wilder, then the floor, shaking his head. Wilder wondered why he didn't do something more useful, like call for backup or whatever cops were supposed to do in a situation like this. Call an ambulance. Handcuff the bad guys. Well, that was a problem. Then Meade shrugged and looked down the hall past him.

"Cuffs?" he said. He held up his hand and a pair of cuffs sailed over Wilder's head. Meade caught them and went to snap them on Barb Sherrill and Hart Warren.

Marilyn put Barb's gun down and took her uncle's head in her lap. Wilder lowered the shotgun. He looked over his shoulder. Fisher was there holstering his gun.

"You were standing behind me there the whole time?" Wilder asked.

"Yeah, but I haven't got your style. Ambulance is on its way, Rodger."

CHAPTER 27

"Paul's stable. They'll keep him in cardiac ICU for awhile, but he'll make it." Ed Ramsey climbed the steps to Wilder's porch and lowered himself into one of the rockers.

Wilder sat with his back to one of the porch columns, head leaning against it, eyes closed. "How're Marilyn and her mother?"

"They're fine. They'll stay the night."

"Mmm."

"You're looking slightly wretched. How bad is the arm?"

"It's fine."

Ramsey looked at him skeptically and started to say something when he caught movement out of the corner of his eye. Meade came toward them out of the shadows at the end of the porch. He pulled the vial of painkillers out of his shirt pocket and tossed it to Wilder.

"Here you go, Houdini. Just in case. Dr. Ramsey? I'm Rodger Meade." They shook hands and Meade sank into the other rocking chair. "I'm glad Sheriff Glaser will be all right."

"Oh, I think it'll take something more than that to drop that old water buffalo." Ramsey looked Meade over, taking stock of what he saw. "I hear you've been a little hard on our boy, here."

"All in a day's work. Nothing he couldn't handle."

"I don't doubt that, I don't doubt that." He rocked and nodded, agreeing with his own assessment. He pulled out his cigarette case and extracted a thin brown cigar. "Mind?"

"Not at all."

"Will you join me?"

"Thank you." Meade reached over and lit Ramsey's before taking one for himself.

"Lewis?" Ramsey started to offer the case to Wilder. "Well, perhaps not, been a long day, I expect. So, Captain Meade, you made an arrest?"

"Officially some of Glaser's men did. We'll have to work out jurisdiction and extradition. Fisher, from my department, is over there now."

"Barb Sherrill and Hart Warren. I swan." Ramsey rocked, blowing smoke rings and musing. "Now, I heard a rumor awhile back that she was seeing a younger man and I thought it might be Lewis, here."

Wilder turned and looked at him in disbelief.

"Well, you two cut quite a rug there at that street dance. And there was that argument you had with Don. I didn't hear the details of that, but it made me wonder. But Hart Warren. Huh." He rocked awhile and blew a smoke ring that floated over Wilder's head. "I remember when Hart was a child, two or three years old, I suggested to his mother she attach him to the end of a short leash. Now, if the skin on my ears wasn't almost as thick as my very thick skull, well, they would be blistered still.

"Hart had to be first up every tree and higher, usually the first to fall out, too. First into the deepest water. Diving in where he couldn't see. Reckless child. He was driving his daddy's car before he had a license. Drove faster than any of them. Had more girls than the other boys. I took more fish hooks out of that boy's hide. Put more stitches in. Smart as a whip, wild as sin, and handsome as the devil. Always looking for something. Never satisfied. Couldn't wait to grow up and get shut of Nolichucky.

"And then there he was teaching math like a lamb all those years. Will wonders never cease, I thought. Well, I guess they did." He sighed and coughed and took another pull on his cigar. "His music kept him traveling around on weekends, I take it, and that's how they met up? He and Barb cook the whole thing up between them?"

"They're in some disagreement over the details," Meade said and Ramsey snorted.

"Which one killed Sherrill?" Wilder asked.

"Barb."

"Big Bad Barb. How, if she was here?"

"It's one of those cases where enough people remember seeing someone at one time or another throughout the day that it seemed as though she was here the whole time. She must have left here shortly before you did, Lewis, and come back right after she killed him.

"Warren was on stage from six to seven. Then he was part of a pick up band from seven-thirty to eight-thirty. He's very slick. When Fisher was up here asking around, Warren told him he saw Barb in the audience. Said he didn't know her but made it obvious that he would like to. Fisher said he made it sound as though he was shocked to remember seeing her there, happy and swaying to the music, all the while her husband was being murdered back home."

"And together they were the Fox."

"For kicks," said Meade. "Warren clerked summers in his cousin's antiques store in high school and college. He developed an eye for a pretty thing."

"And a talent for opening doors."

"That too. And Barb has a taste for adventure."

"Well, hell," said Wilder. "And poor Don the boor didn't have a chance against that."

"Nope. Divorce wasn't an option for one reason or another. If you believe Barb he wouldn't give her one and Hart convinced her to kill him. If you believe Hart she just enjoyed the sport of hunting and took it one rather major leap further."

"They make quite a pair," said Ramsey. "I'm glad he was never quite able to get Marilyn wrapped around his little finger. She's got her head on her shoulders but sometimes I wonder about the men she's attracted to." He gave Wilder a brief sideways glance. "Where is George, by the way? I expected to see him at the hospital propping up Martha."

"He stayed in Stonewall to lend my aunt moral support in the face of reprehensible nephews," Wilder said.

"Necessary support, I'm sure. Well, he's a good man." Ramsey hoisted himself upright. "I'll say good night now. Lewis, it's good to

374

have you home. Glad you're not going to prison." He waved a hand in farewell and stumped down the stairs. They heard him still talking as he melted into the darkness, the glowing end of his cigar a small beacon. "I hate search committees."

Wilder stifled a yawn and stood up slowly, stiffly.

"Calling it a night?" asked Meade.

"Calling Aunt Katherine. Let her know everything's okay." At seeing Meade's expression Wilder stopped. "What? Everything is okay, isn't it? No nasty surprises like you're arresting me as a third wheel in Barb and Hart's affair or you've decided the bird pipe was rustled illegally and I'm now a receiver of stolen goods?"

"No, Lewis."

"Then what's the look for?"

"Just glad, Lewis. I'm glad you're calling Katherine. Glad everything is okay. Happy I don't have to lock you up, happy to have all the complications of your little trip home over with and out of my hair. Glad to have you back in my life. Glad I didn't go with my first gut feeling and strangle you on the spot. Glad you've found someone like Marilyn. Happy for you that they like you so much here in Nolichucky. Very, very happy that it's Fisher's car up here and he'll be the one driving back. Got any beer?"

"Fridge, help yourself."

Meade pulled out two cans. He popped the top of one and handed it to Wilder at the phone. He opened his own and went through to the living room. He looked around at the room first through his policeman's eyes and saw nothing extraordinary. Then he walked around it, looking at it as a friend, and he could see what was familiar and much that was new to him and he saw the comfort of an old acquaintance. He sat on the floor next to the coffee table watching the newts.

Wilder wandered in and dropped into the old blue chair.

"I'm bonding with your newts."

"Mmm."

"Quick call."

"Oh, just your basic reassurance. Not much chit chat."

"And? You look like you're suffering from shell shock."

"She's coming to visit next weekend," Wilder said.

"Well, that's nice, Lewis," Meade said, grinning. "Here's to renewed ties." He raised his beer.

"The ties that bind," Wilder muttered, "and sometimes chafe. That reminds me.

You still have my Swiss Army knife."

Meade finished his beer and crushed the can. He stood up, fished the knife out of his pocket, and tossed it to Wilder.

"Thanks, you never know when I might need to cut loose again."

ABOUT THE AUTHOR

Molly MacRae spent twenty years in the foothills of the Blue Ridge Mountains of Upper East Tennessee. She was the curator of the history museum in Jonesborough, Tennessee's oldest town, and later managed The Book Place, an independent bookstore; may it rest in peace. Her stories have appeared in *Alfred Hitchcock's Mystery Magazine* and she is a winner of the Sherwood Anderson Award for Short Fiction. These days, MacRae lives with her family in Champaign, Illinois, where she pushes books on children at the public library.

The employees of Thorndike Press hope you have enjoyed this Large Print book. All our Thorndike and Wheeler Large Print titles are designed for easy reading, and all our books are made to last. Other Thorndike Press Large Print books are available at your library, through selected bookstores, or directly from us.

For information about titles, please call:
   (800) 223-1244

or visit our Web site at:
   www.gale.com/thorndike
   www.gale.com/wheeler

To share your comments, please write:
   Publisher
   Thorndike Press
   295 Kennedy Memorial Drive
   Waterville, ME 04901